Phillipa Bowers spent her childhood in the suburbs of London and attended Notting Hill and Ealing High School for Girls. She was employed in a variety of ways, including as a stewardess with both BEA and BOAC, before marrying and raising two sons.

Her childhood dream of becoming an artist was eventually realised when, after attending West Surrey College of Art and Design as a mature student, she earned her living making ceramic sculpture and painting in watercolours.

While residing in Wookey Hole in Somerset she heard the local legend of the wicked witch who had lived in the nearby caves and believed it to be based on a true story. Then, after moving with her partner Terry Walsh to the North Coast of Cornwall, she began writing novels – including a series about the descendants of the wise women of a small village in Somerset.

G000277627

The Wise Woman's Tale

Phillipa Bowers

PIATKUS

PIATKUS

First published in Great Britain in 2006 by Piatkus Books
This paperback edition published in 2008 by Piatkus Books

A CIP catalogue record for this book
is available from the British Library

ISBN 978-0-7499-3839-0

Papers used by Piatkus are natural, recyclable products made from
wood grown in sustainable forests and certified in accordance with
the rules of the Forest Stewardship Council

Typeset in Times by
Action Publishing Technology Ltd, Gloucester
Printed and bound by
Mackays of Chatham, Chatham, Kent

Piatkus Books
An imprint of
Little, Brown Book Group
100 Victoria Embankment
London EC4Y 0DY

An Hachette Livre UK Company

www.piatkus.co.uk

For Sarah Walsh and all the friends and family who believed in the dream; for Judith Murdoch who made it possible, for Gillian Green who made it come true and, above all, for Terry Walsh who believed in me.

Author's Note

For many generations the inhabitants of Wookey Hole in Somerset have handed down the legend of how they were saved from the curse of a wicked witch by a monk from Glastonbury Abbey who went into the cave in which she lived and sprinkled her with holy water, thereby turning her to stone.

I believe it is possible that during a time when midwives, herbalists and healers were being persecuted, burned and hanged all over Europe, a local wise woman could be blamed for any misfortune befalling the community. The sickness of people and animals caused by pollution of the water supply by the lead mines on the hills above the village for example, would be understood today, but might have been seen as the work of the devil in less enlightened times.

A stalagmite ball, human bones and the remains of a knife found during excavations in a cave may have belonged to one who, in company with many other victims of witch-hunts, deserved better than the evil reputation for which she is still remembered.

This story is about the twentieth-century descendants of a woman living in a small village with a similar legend.

Chapter One

'Catch her!'

Kate paused to listen and, hearing only the swish of a breeze, grabbed a low branch and pulled herself upwards, then, seeing a nearby bud already swollen in waiting for spring, groaned aloud – she'd be in smelly mucky London when it burst open. How could God let this happen?

Suddenly the wind increased, hustling and bustling the tree, filling the air with menacing whispers and a stifling stench of rancid sweat and piss.

Something held her back. She glanced down, heart thumping and lungs pierced with icy shards of fear until, seeing the hem of her petticoat caught on a twig, she wrenched it free ripping the fabric into a jagged tear.

'Catch her. Catch her.'

Looking up she could see no chinks of sunlight. Only dense, deep grey sky was visible beyond the thrashing boughs. Suddenly unseen hands pulled her down and down backwards with arms flailing into the darkness, on and on until the sky lightened into a leaden grey and she was sliding down a muddy slope towards the river.

A man crashed through a spinney nearby, staggered, almost fell and, holding onto the sapling bending under his weight, shouted, 'There she be!'

For an instant she thought it was the shepherd, but as hands reached out and pulled her to the ground, she saw instead the farrier's livid face with glittering eyes ablaze and parted lips shining with drool.

1

The first slap jerked her head sideways and the second sent a myriad of stars hurtling through the darkness behind her eyes. Burning pain seared through her body in countless waves until she escaped into oblivion.

Awakening sometime later, she peered through one eye at the large looming shapes around her and knew from the smell of cider and sweat and piss that they were men, and as they spoke, she knew which men.

'Here's the rope!'

The strident tone surprised her. She had thought the cider-maker to be an amiable fellow, with cheeks as rosy as the apples he pressed.

The carter shouted, 'Let it be done!'

Why so? He swore eternal gratitude when his wife was safely delivered Michaelmas last.

'String her up and put an end to our bad luck.'

'She killed my babe.'

'And mine, and mine.'

'Tie it tight, Jan, tie the knot tight.'

She had called him brother and now he was putting a rope around her neck.

'String her up and put an end to her evil ways.'

Oh no! Not him! How could he speak so, knowing they were lovers all those years?

A sudden heavy blow left her in a deep impenetrable blackness in which she could see nothing of the men who were shouting all around her. Warm tears trickled down her cheeks and ran into her mouth. The taste was of blood, not tears. Yes, it was blood. Let death come soon.

'Please wake up, little girl, *please, please* I beg of you, wake up.'

The voice was anxious and kindly, and, in place of the sickening stench, were the blended scents of damp tweeds and sweat and shaving soap. She tried opening her eyes. How extraordinary! The thick, velvety darkness was gone, and, silhouetted against the light, was the head of a stranger.

'Thank God!' He sounded close to tears. 'What a fright you gave me, young lady.'

Focussing on the man kneeling beside her, she watched water trickle down from his dripping brown hair into one eye as he

2

attempted to fan her with a sodden trilby hat. Then, looking at the gently rustling branches above her, she put a trembling hand to her throat; no, there was no harm done to her neck, and yet, why did she think there might be? Looking into the man's anxious blue eyes, she asked tremulously, 'Where are they?'

'Who? Were you with someone? Are you lost?'

'No, sir, not lost.' She raised her head slightly to peer around for movements in the bushes or behind trees.

'I don't know how badly hurt you might be. D'you think you can move?'

'I don't know, sir.' She cautiously eased herself up onto one elbow. Yes, she could move. Gazing at the damp grass around her, then up into the tranquil oak in bewilderment, she said, 'I thought there was a storm.'

One side of the man's mouth rose and then the other until it had spread into a broad, uneven grin. 'I'd have called it a March bluster myself, a sort of sudden windy shower. We do get dramatic storms here sometimes, when the thunder reverberates through the hills. I didn't see any flashes of lightning or hear any rumbles, did you?'

She shook her head, remembering only the lashing wind and tormenting voices.

'I think you fell out of that—' he looked up at the beautiful oak '—and banged your head.' Then, smiling gently at her, he added reassuringly, 'I'm sure it's nothing to worry about. I remember my old nanny kept me walking around for hours when I fell off a wall. I think we should try and get you moving, when you're ready to try.' He threw the brown felt hat on the ground and took a large white handkerchief from his pocket. 'In the meantime, take this, you've bitten your lip.'

'Thank you, sir.' She dabbed her mouth. 'How odd! It tastes like ink.'

'I'll remember that.' He shrugged. 'If I have time to taste it!'

'My granny will be needing me to help with tea.'

He held both her hands, saying, 'Come along then, gently does it.'

Having pulled herself upright, Kate stood looking glumly down at the grubby triangle of torn petticoat hanging below her muddy skirt and badly stained pinafore.

The man grinned. 'Girls will be boys, eh?'

3

She nodded. 'My mum will say a girl of my age should know better.'

'And how old is that?'

'I'll be fourteen in July, sir.' She raked her fingers through the long tangle of dark hair whilst adding, 'She'll be ever so cross when she sees the state of me.'

'I'll come and explain what happened. Where do you live?'

'Old Myrtles, sir.'

'Then we're neighbours—' he offered his right hand '—I'm Charles Wallace, commonly known as Charlie. How d'you do?'

'I'm Katharine Jane Barnes—' she grasped the long fingers '—commonly known as Kate.'

'Here, Kate, take my arm and we'll walk back together.'

On reaching the edge of the copse, she stopped and looked back up the grassy slope at the majestic tree. It had done her no harm. Perhaps it tried to protect her from the bad dream? Yes, it was still her friend. Bobbing her head, she whispered, 'Goodbye, My Lady Oak.'

Charles Wallace waited until she turned back to join him. 'Is that your special tree?' he asked with a smile.

'Yes, sir, and this is my special place.'

'Hankeys Land?'

'Yes, sir. But I do like everywhere else here too. I like up top, and the dell, I like the old mill and the river. I like the village and the school and—' her swelling lip hurt as she struggled to stop crying '—and I have to leave, 'cos my Dad's back from the front.'

'I see—' he frowned '—but you're pleased he's home from the War, aren't you?'

'Yes, yes, I'm glad he's safe and I'm sorry he's badly wounded in his knee.'

'He's survived, that's the main thing, and he can stay in England with his family.'

'Yes, sir. I am glad, truly I am.' Fighting to stop the rising tears, she stammered, 'It's j-just, I d-don't – I don't want to go back to London. I want to stay here with Gran and Uncle Albert, and my friend Alice and—' she wiped her eyes on the silk hand-kerchief '—and . . . and I'd like to see the tree in summer.'

'My Lady Oak in all her finery?'

'Yes, sir.'

'When are you due to leave?'

'Tomorrow. This is my last day.'

'I like everywhere here too. I like the hills up top and Hankeys Land, and the river and my home. I don't want to face any more filth and degradation. I'd like to stay here with my dear baby son and my beautiful wife, but I too must leave tomorrow and return to ...' He paused and gave a slight shake of his head, then, lightly placing his hands on her shoulders, he looked into her eyes and added, 'We're soulmates you and I, we can't do as we want, but we can put on a brave face for other people, can't we?'

'Yes, sir. I know I can be brave for Mum, and for Gran, but my poor Uncle Albert will be so sad when I leave. We do dote on each other, you see.'

'Is he the Albert who tends the hedges and the graveyard?'

'D'you know him?'

'Oh yes. He often salutes me when I drive past.'

Realising this must be the gentleman with the motor car from the big house, she said shyly, 'Uncle Albert doesn't talk much; hardly ever in fact, 'cos he's a bit different, well, my brother Eric says he's simple, but I've heard him say he likes your motor car. Mr Nelson, the gardener, lets him help polish it.' Had she said too much? She added anxiously, 'I hope you don't mind, I wouldn't want to get him into trouble.'

Mr Wallace smiled and lowered his hands. 'Nelson's a good fellow and I'm pleased he has help in my absence. Those brass headlamps need cleaning, whether I'm here to drive the car or not.'

As they walked down the narrow winding path through the undergrowth and brambles to the copse, she looked back apprehensively from time to time – could there be anyone lurking in the bushes and might they follow her home? The kind gentleman wasn't worried; he'd hear them wouldn't he? Yes, of course he would. There was no one there. It was a dream, a very strange and frightening dream.

On arrival at the edge of the sheer cliff overlooking the back of the cottage, she said, 'I'll be all right now, sir.'

'No, I'd like to see you home, Miss Barnes. I don't want to hear tomorrow that my neighbour's granddaughter came to an untimely end on my land.'

'Your ...!' Oh no! He *owned* Hankeys Land and the tree.

He nodded solemnly. 'Now I know you trespass here. I'll instruct the gamekeeper to remove the mantraps.'

5

'What! Traps! I didn't know—' seeing the laughter in his deep-blue eyes, she blushed '—I'm truly sorry, sir, I'd no idea. Soon I'll be gone to London and I won't be walking here, ever again.'

'Miss Katharine Jane Barnes, commonly known as Kate, I was teasing you. There's an ancient commoner's right of way through Hankeys Land and on up all the way to Pridden.'

'Was your dad called Mister Hankey?'

'No, I've never really thought about the name before. It's a strange one isn't it?'

She nodded. 'I've asked lots of people and nobody knows why it's called that, not even Miss Gregory my schoolteacher. Eric says a witch put a curse on it when she lost her handkerchief here, but he just wants to annoy me 'cos he knows it's my favourite place.'

Charles Wallace chuckled. 'That's an imaginative addition to the old legend. I thought she just put a curse on the village for the hell of it.' He looked thoughtful for a moment before adding, 'I suspect it's more likely there was a man called Hankey long ago and I must say I think having a piece of land named after one is rather a nice way to be remembered.'

She led the way down steep steps in the rock and into the garden close to the washing line, and, seeing her mother taking down some shirts, called, 'I'm back, Mum.'

'This is wetter than when I put it . . . Oh my lor!' Polly gave a small scream of shock on seeing the man.

'It's all right. This kind gentleman's seen me home. He lives at The Grange and is going back to the War soon.'

Charles Wallace smiled. 'Your daughter does you credit, madam.'

'Thank you, sir, thank you.' Polly blushed and bobbed in a half curtsey.

'She's had a little fall . . .'

'A fall! Kate, what've you been up to?'

'I'm sure she's not suffering from concussion, but I thought it wise to see her home.'

'Oh my lor! You naughty girl, you've been climbing trees again, haven't you? How many times must I tell you not to be so un-ladylike?'

'I'm sorry, Mum.' There was no point in arguing, she'd fallen from a tree and couldn't deny it.

'Haven't I told you not to behave like a village boy?'

'Yes, Mum, I'm sorry.'

She heard Eric shouting, 'Bang bang you're dead, you filthy swine.' Followed by Eddie's childish piping cry of, 'Take that you dirty Hun!' Thank goodness they were in the dell at the end of the garden! They'd snigger and be *utterly stupid* if they saw the gentleman with her and she'd be *so* ashamed.

Polly blushed as she said, 'I was a maid at the Grange years ago when you was a boy, sir.'

'Of course, Polly, you married a groom, did you not?'

'Yes, sir. Jack brought two special horses from Northumberland for old Mr Wallace.' She looked at the ground and gave a small smile. 'He never went back home on account of me.'

Charles Wallace nodded. 'I remember my father thought him an excellent horseman and was loath to part with him.'

'He had his heart set on London, sir.'

'I'm sorry to hear he's been wounded.'

Polly bit her lip. 'Yes, sir. He'll not ride horses again.'

'I wish you a happy reunion.'

Polly thanked him and bobbed again, then scurried away to the back door.

They walked along the path towards the lane, and, reaching the overgrown front door, Charles stopped and bent to sniff the jonquils growing at the foot of an old rambler rose. 'Damn!' he exclaimed on catching his sleeve in some large thorns. Then, having extricated the brown tweed from their tenacious grip, asked, 'What colour are the roses when they bloom?'

'White, sir, it's my granny's favourite. There's a pink one on the other side of the porch that my mum likes best.'

'And you, Kate, which do you prefer?'

She wanted to say any old rose would do if she could stay here to see them flowering from June until Christmas as usual, but instead she mumbled shyly, 'I don't know, I like 'em both.'

He smiled. 'Let's hope we'll both return to see them when they're in bloom.' Then, having walked to the small gate and opened it, he added, 'I wish I could say au revoir, but I doubt if we'll meet again. Goodbye, Miss green-eyes Barnes.' He lifted his right arm in a salute.

She reached in her pocket and pulled out the handkerchief he had given her under the oak tree and, while offering it to him, froze with horror. For a flash of time, less than a second, in place of his

7

raised hand was a hideously scarred stump.

'Goodbye and good luck!' Turning abruptly, he walked away up the lane towards The Grange.

'Wait, Mr Wallace I've got your hand ...' She stood for a few moments looking after him. What a strange gentleman and so very kind, he'd even understood how much she loved the tree! Turning back she walked into the glory hole and, while standing beside the line of overcoats and mackintoshes hanging there, heard her grandmother's voice above the clatter of crockery in the scullery. ''Twill break Albert's heart when Kate goes, Polly. He do dote on that child.'

Oh no! Poor Uncle Albert! Why couldn't Dad come *here*? They shouldn't have to leave Oakey Vale and go back to living with rats running about in the roof and the stink of their droppings in the shed behind the washhouse. She kicked her uncle's Wellington boots. Damn and blast! It was *so unfair*!

An hour later, when her mother was washing the boys in the tin bath in the scullery, she went outside and walked down the garden looking for her grandmother. On finding the old woman sitting on the rock seat leaning her back against the ivy covered cliff, she sat down and told her about the strange experience on Hankeys Land.

'I'm glad you told me, my lover. I been hoping you'd have the gift, though why I should want it for you I don't know. 'Tis a great burden at times and I sometimes think your mother, my dear Polly, be lucky for not having it like me and my lovely Jane. You'm at the age when it started for me, when I became a woman. And Jane, my firstborn, was the same—' she reached out to touch Kate's head '—her hair was long and black like yourn. I mind the time we had with her, mirrors fell off the wall and furniture moved from one side of the room to t'other.' Her mouth worked as she wiped her eyes. Then she added quietly, as though talking to herself, 'Such a time we had!'

'It was very frightening, Gran. I'd feel scared of going to the tree now, in case they're waiting to get me.'

'Don't you fret about that—' the old woman clasped both Kate's hands in hers '—'tis in the past. They can't hurt you now, they'm all long gone.'

'D'you know who they were?'

'No, but I can guess who *you* was, my lover.'

'Whatever d'you mean?'

'I knows you was one of *us*. You know the fireweed?'

'The tall pink flowers Miss Gregory calls rosebay willowherb?'

'Aye. D'you know why we calls it that?'

She shook her head.

''Cos 'tis the first to grow again after a fire. That's what we'm like—' she nodded '—we keeps coming back, no matter what befalls.' Turning Kate's hands over she studied her palms and smiled before saying, 'Aye, I thought as much. 'Tis a pity it's happened just as you'm going, but 'tis just as well I found out before you left.' She picked up a white enamel jug from the ground beside her, saying, 'Come with me, I want to show you summat.' Then, reaching under a nearby rock, she pulled out two candles which she lit with matches from her apron pocket and led the way through the ivy hanging down beside them and into a cave.

Kate was looking around her in surprise when her grandmother walked six paces to the rocks facing them, reached forward and moved a slab sideways revealing a black space through which she climbed. Following behind she watched while the old woman lit several more candles and then, seeing a beautiful figure in the rocks looking down on her, gasped with surprise and delight.

'There she be; our secret lady,' the old woman whispered reverently. She pointed at the water emerging between rocky breasts and running down over pink crystals between slender arms into the red pool formed between stony thighs, then, dipping the jug into it, added, 'And her magic water.'

'Magic?'

'Aye, 'tis powerful good and cures many ills. 'Tis what I uses for my special recipes.' She turned to look down at a large slab on the ground beside them and, putting her arm around Kate's shoulder, said, 'Under there be all they women going back into the long ago what's guarded this source both in life and death. My old granny told me as how we've kept watch here ever since foreigners came with their strange gods and goddesses building temples and lord knows what. And, you know the story they tell here about the wicked witch who lived in one of the caves hereabouts?'

'The children at school say she's still in there.'

'Aye, turned to stone by a monk from Glastonbury so the legend goes. Well, my gran didn't hold with that nonsense, her reckoned 'twas all lies to cover up a bad deed done to one of *us.*'

'D'you think it's this cave they're talking about, Gran?'

'Maybe, I dunno.' The old woman gently hugged her. 'I wants you to promise you'll put me in there when I dies.'

'But I'm going to London tomorrow, Gran.'

'You'll be back, my lover.'

'Did you see that in my hand?'

'Aye.'

'Anything else?'

'Everything you wants be right here, that's all I'm saying, so don't go asking no more questions.'

They walked up to the house together and once inside the kitchen, the old woman went to the chimney and pulled out a dirty linen bag. 'Here—' she withdrew a rag doll with long black woollen hair '—here be your poppy-doll, be sure and take good care of her and bring her back when you comes home.'

Reaching towards the bag and trying to see inside it, Kate asked, 'Have you got dolls for all of us?'

'Aye, 'tis my way of caring for you all.' The old woman pulled out a doll similar to Kate's and cradled it. 'I'm only giving yours to ee 'cos I knows you'll bring it back.'

'Mother!' Polly stood in the doorway to the scullery with hands on hips. 'I thought you'd given up such superstitious nonsense.'

Fearing it might be taken from her, she hugged the doll close as she sidled out of the door into the hallway and then ran upstairs. When safely in her room, she wrapped the doll in the handkerchief the kind man had given her and, remembering the ugly stump held up in salute, she shuddered and buried her face in the soft white silk. Was seeing such a hideous thing part of the gift? If so, Gran was right to think Mum lucky not to have it.

That night, lying staring into the darkness listening to her brothers giggling and the floorboards creaking, she longed for sleep in order to escape from the pain of anticipating departure; but the image of the cave with pink and white stalactites hanging over the tomb and the beautiful figure formed from the rocks beside it appeared behind her eyes whenever she closed them, and she was instantly wide awake.

After a while she heard Uncle Albert sit heavily on his squeaky bed, then her grandmother sigh with relief as she climbed into hers. A long time later, seeing candlelight flicker under the door, she knew her mother was tiptoeing across the landing in order to slide quietly in beside the old lady.

Eventually, as the sky began to lighten in the east, her eyes grew heavy and she dreamed she was in the old oak tree looking down at a group of men staggering around under the tree shouting at each other and waving their arms about.

'Wake up! Get dressed, hurry up!'

What a relief! The air was no longer filled with the stench of drunken men. She breathed in and savoured the scents of soap and lavender water.

'Kate, for goodness sake, get up!'

'Sorry, Mum, I was dreaming and it seemed so real.'

'Never mind that, silly girl. We've got a train to catch.'

An hour later, after climbing onto the rickety cart outside the cottage, Eddie looked down at the small man who was pulling agitatedly at one side of his dark hair and called, 'Bye, Uncle Albert.'

'Will it really kill him, Mum?' she asked, wiping her eyes on the handkerchief wrapped around the doll.

'What, love?'

'Granny said that me leaving him would break his heart. Does that mean he'll die?'

'He'll be very upset, love, but I doubt it will kill him.'

The carter clicked his tongue and the mare flared her nostrils before beginning a gentle, rhythmic trot down the lane towards the village.

She looked back and waved to the two figures standing by the gate; and despite her inability to see them through her tears, whispered, 'Goodbye Old Myrtles.'

Hearing her, Eric shouted, 'Goodbye, dell.' Adding, 'And goodbye, wicked witch.'

'Yeah,' Eddie yelled, 'Goodbye, old witch,' then, as they crossed the river, the two boys shouted in unison, 'Goodbye, bridge!'

As they passed the graveyard she remembered walking there with Uncle Albert and reading out the names to him. How would he know who was buried in which plot without her by his side?

11

Eddie waved and called out, 'Goodbye, church.'

'Goodbye, school,' she said mournfully.

Eric grimaced and screeched, 'Goodbye to bad rubbish!'

Polly looked anxiously around the village, saying angrily, 'That's enough noise. Whatever will people think?'

The two boys made faces at each other and waved silently at the baker standing in his doorway.

Looking back as they passed the Methodist chapel Kate blew a kiss.

'Who's that for?' Eric asked.

'Oakey Vale.'

'For the whole village?'

'Yes.' She sniffed and sat staring ahead.

Eric nudged his younger brother. 'She's just kissed all the boys, *especially* Teddy Nelson.'

Polly wagged her forefinger at the giggling boys. 'Leave your sister alone.'

Kate turned her head and looked determinedly away over the brown hedgerows lightly hazed with green and watched a boy walking along behind two enormous horses dragging a plough trailed by flocks of gulls gleaming starkly white against the rich red earth.

When the cart reached a rise in the road she could see the cathedral below them and Glastonbury Tor rising from the strangely flat landscape to their right, and looking back to the hills and the village now hidden behind the trees, she said, 'I do love it so. Do you think we'll ever come back to live here, Mum?'

Chapter Two

Nettles are a good spring tonic and regularly drinking tea made from the dried leaves will ease rheumatism and arthritis. Harvest in May before flowering.

Having arrived at the station in good time for the train, Kate stood dejectedly beside their bags and baskets, staring miserably at the platform, whilst her mother chatted to a couple seeing their son off to join the Army. When the boys played the fool, pushing each other sideways and pretending to almost fall onto the track, she turned her back on them to show she was too grown up for such childish nonsense. How could they be so stupid at such a time?

'Good morning, Miss Barnes, what a nice surprise!'

Seeing the kindly gentleman from Hankeys Land now dressed in khaki uniform, she greeted him and looked around her, asking, 'Is your baby son here?'

He shook his head. 'Sadly, no. My wife can't bear partings in public. And you, Kate—' he placed his hand on her shoulder, '— are you finding *goodbye* a difficult word to say today?'

'Oh yes, my poor Uncle Albert's broken hearted because I'm leaving. My mum says he won't die of it, but I'm very worried about him. Sometimes he doesn't speak for days and he pulls his hair out too, and, and I do love him so.' She brushed away a tear from each eye.

'My dear Miss Katherine Jane Barnes, commonly known as Kate. Your uncle is a very lucky man. I wish I had a niece like you, but sadly my brother's not yet married and my sister has no children. Ahgg!—' he rubbed at his eye with his left hand '— there's always so much filth in the air at a station.'

13

She reached in her pocket and pulled out the handkerchief he had given her under the oak tree. Oh no! She gasped as he raised his other arm and, expecting to see the hideous stump, closed her eyes momentarily: then, on opening them and seeing the long fingers held to his face, exhaled with relief.

'I have something in my eye. Goodbye, Kate, and good luck!'

'Wait, Mr Wallace, your hand, wait.'

'I must go, I have something, a smut, I don't know.' He walked away to the end of the platform where he stood wiping his eyes.

The train steamed into the station and Polly appeared beside her, exclaiming, 'Fancy you talking to gentry bold as brass in front of everyone like that! My friend said Mrs Wallace is a beauty and rich too, from somewhere up north. Come along, we must get the bags on.'

Looking along the platform she saw Mr Wallace wave to her, and, finding she was still clasping his handkerchief, fluttered it towards him quickly before helping her mother load their belongings onto the train.

The boys laughed and chatted happily for the whole journey, oblivious of their silent mother and sister.

Kate sat remembering the two blissful years in the cottage. Staring out of the window, she thought of Alice and the fun they had mixing potions and casting spells to find their true loves. They'd whiled away the hours so happily together, giggling helplessly one minute and reading to one another the next. Would she ever find such a boon companion again? Would anyone ever love her as her uncle did, or be so generous with praise as her grandmother? Would the teacher at her new school be impressed with the letter from Miss Gregory who had encouraged her to think of becoming a teacher like herself?

Looking around the carriage at the other travellers she thought the soldier sitting opposite her seemed very young, probably only a few years older than she was. His uniform was made of rougher cloth than Mr Wallace's and his lower legs were bound with fabric strips above short black boots instead of brown leather riding boots reaching the knees. Next to him was an elderly lady with no teeth and beside her was a pretty young woman in a grey uniform hat and coat with a red shoulder cape. Kate wondered if being a nurse might be preferable to a teacher? No, no, she wanted to have a little cottage in a village with a school nearby and lots of children admiring her and calling her Miss Barnes.

The soldier opposite looked even younger when he fell asleep. Some of the boys at school boasted they would lie about their age and enlist as soon as they could. Might this man have done that? What could he possibly know of fighting? He couldn't be allowed to go to France, could he? What was war? Mr Wallace made it sound horrible, but when Miss Gregory brought a book about it to school she proudly showed them a page headed 'Roll of honour' and all the children looked in awe at photographs of heroic young officers who had died for their country. There had also been drawings and paintings showing soldiers bravely going to fight the foe and one of the injured men being cared for by beautiful ladies dressed in white. Words like 'gallant' and 'courageous' featured on every page, not 'filth and degradation' as Mr Wallace had said and now he was on his way to the front whilst she was going to London. What had he said they were? Two soulmates who might never meet again.

The soldier snored. Oh no! His face was a red mess and he was covered in mud. There was an indescribable stink, worse, much worse, than when Uncle Albert dug out the privy. Horrified, she stared down at her lap feeling the clickety-clack, clickety-clack, clickety-clack rhythm of the train reverberating through her head; was this what Granny called a 'sight'? First she'd seen Mr Wallace looking strange and now this man. Why was such a horrible experience called the 'gift'? Surely a gift was a nice thing to receive for a birthday or ...

'Excuse me, miss, excuse me, you've dropped this.'

She forced her head up and peered at the soldier who was awake and offering her the large white handkerchief with the blue embroidered initials CW in the corner. She looked at his hairless pink face and then directly into the rounded clear-grey eyes. 'Thank you.' The words came out in a sigh of relief.

Pulling the little doll out of her pocket she tidied its long black woollen hair and wrapped the silk handkerchief around it, then, feeling her eyelids drooping, she leaned back and drifted into sleep for the remainder of the journey.

Jack Barnes was waiting on the platform when the train steamed into the station and beamed with pleasure on seeing them.

Although seeming smaller than Kate remembered, her father looked very dashing in his black uniform jacket and breeches with

15

leather boots to his knees. Seeing his delight as he hugged the two boys and put his arm around her mother, she felt a surge of love for her family and joined in enthusiastically with the reunion.

Eric gasped when he saw how Jack limped and pointed at his stiff leg.

Polly grabbed her son by the back of his neck with one hand and slapped his fingers down with the other. 'Your dad's a very important man now, children, he doesn't mess with horses anymore, he's a chauffeur!'

'Where's the motor car?' The two boys looked excitedly around them.

'No, it's not here, lads,' Jack Barnes said, leading them to a wooden handcart. 'Two wheels for the bags and Shanks's pony will have to do for us.'

They walked along narrow streets lined with grimy houses and littered with horse droppings, past grubby children and the occasional beggar. Then on and on they traipsed for what seemed a very long time, with Eddie trailing farther and farther behind. When they reached a wide carriageway with tall buildings on either side, Kate waited for her youngest brother and crossed over with him. The sight of several motor cars and a large omnibus revived his spirits and she was coaxing him along with the suggestion there might be another such road to traverse when she saw her parents stop at the end of a long terrace.

'Here we are,' Jack said proudly.

'This one?' Polly asked incredulously, pointing to the small, red brick house.

Her husband grinned. 'Aye, bonny lass, built only twenty-five year ago, not like that old place of yer mother's. Nothing but the best will do for my family.'

'The rent must be high. Can we afford it?'

'*I can afford it,* bonny lass, *I provide* for my family.' He unlocked the front door and limped into the narrow hall where he hung his black peaked cap on the newel post at the bottom of the stairs. 'Here we are, home at last!' He led them past a door on their left and the stairs to their right along a passageway into the kitchen. Taking his wife's arm he pointed to a small range set into the chimney breast, saying, 'When you've lit that and set the place to rights, yer won't know yer born!' He gestured towards the assortment of wooden orange boxes beside the plain pine table.

16

'We'll have to manage with the basics for a while—' his jaw tightened '—seein' as we've ter start out again fresh, like.' He sniffed. 'It's not been easy coming back ter nothing and nobody.'

Polly smiled reassuringly at him. 'This is perfect, Jack, just perfect. We'll all be very happy with this—' she looked at Kate '—won't we, love?'

'Yes, Mum. I'll look for the coal hole and the water.' In the scullery she found a square, brown ceramic sink with a handpump in one corner and the copper boiler facing it in another. It was all very familiar, just like her grandmother's and much better than the dilapidated washhouse they'd shared with neighbours in the previous London home. She tested the pump which was stiff but easier to use than a well in the garden like Mrs Smith had in the village and the mangle turned easily but squeaked loudly. Several spiders scurried from under the sink when she pulled out the dirty wooden washboard and she wrinkled her nose; she'd have to give it a good clean before scrubbing Dad's collars and cuffs on it next Monday. Unless she'd already started at the school here, then maybe she could escape wash day?

She walked out through the back door and looked into the empty coalhole, then, opening the door next to it, shouted to her brothers, 'Eric, Eddie, come and see this!'

The two boys who had been exploring upstairs came running and whooped with delight as she ceremoniously pulled the chain. 'Hurray, a water closet, hurray!'

She left them waiting for the cistern to fill up and wandered into the yard where a broken wooden fence to her right marked the boundary with the neighbours, while on the other two sides was an alleyway giving access to the narrow passage along the back of all the yards in the row. Having opened the gate, she nodded with approval. The coal man wouldn't need to carry the dirty black sacks through the house; he'd be able to leave his horse and cart at the front and walk along the alley, through the yard and into the coalhole. Mum would be very pleased with that arrangement!

Returning to the house, she went up the stairs and into a small bedroom at the back of the house where, peering through the grimy window, she saw row upon row of roofs and yearned for the wooded slopes up above her grandmother's cottage and the garden beside it bounded on one side by the high hedge and the ivy covered cliff on the other.

'Kate, Kate, come and help yer mother!'

Hearing her father's voice, she ran downstairs to where Polly was unpacking the basket of provisions Gran had given them.

Whilst they ate a meal of bread and cheese, Jack explained their future to them. He'd been very fortunate, he assured them, Mrs Burns-Leon for whom he had worked as a groom before the War, had decided to replace her carriage with a motor car. 'I'm that lucky, bonny lass,' he said, with his arm around Polly. 'She's been so good to us and she's even pulled a few strings for our Kate.'

All eyes turned to her as he explained, 'There's this big drapers called Harvey's Emporium. D'you know it?'

Shaking her head, she swallowed a piece of cheese with difficulty.

'Well, you're a lucky lass, because Mrs Harvey's a friend of my employer Mrs Burns-Leon.'

She stared in horrified silence at her father, and then, beseechingly, at her mother who avoided her gaze and looked down at the floor.

Jack Barnes went on oblivious of any adverse reaction, 'I drives the ladies on their rounds, yer know, doing their good deeds for the poor.' He grinned. 'Mrs Harvey's a real toffee-nose, though what she's got ter be snobby about I don't know since they're trades-people no matter how rich they are—' he pursed his lips '—not like Mrs Burns-Leon, *she's a real* lady.'

He rubbed his wounded leg. 'Sometimes it puts me in mind of my old Ma and how she used to tell the la-di-da charity ladies she was so poor she had ter bath the baby in the frying pan, what a joke!' He bent to pick up a piece of bread, his face screwed up as if in pain, then continued, 'That Mr Harvey done well for himself, of course, marrying the daughter of a draper and then taking over his shop.' He sighed exaggeratedly. 'That's where I went wrong, I should've married someone with a bit of money, then my sons could go to one of them posh schools and my daughter could marry a nice rich lord.'

Polly's laugh was nervously shrill. 'I'm afraid I didn't bring much in the way of shops in my dowry.' Her eyes met Kate's momentarily before she looked down again. After taking a deep breath she said hesitantly, 'Er, Jack, love, Kate's been doing very well at school. Miss Gregory thinks she could be a teacher. She's set her heart ...'

'I said it's all arranged, bonny lass—' his tone brooked no argument '—I canna change it now, not after all Mrs Burn-Leon's done for us.' He turned to Eric. 'As for you, lad, there's an apprenticeship with a cabinetmaker as soon as you can leave school.'

Eric shouted with joy, 'Hooray, hooray, hooray!' He shook his father's hand, pumping up and down while repeating, 'Thank you, Dad, thank you, Dad, thank you, Dad.'

Kate stood up. This wasn't fair! She'd listened to the conversation in silence as she'd been taught to do, but her heart's desire was being dismissed without any thought for her feelings. 'Miss Gregory's written a letter to my new school.'

'You heard what I said, Katharine.'

'But, Dad, I could've stayed with Gran and been a teacher. Can I go back and stay with her, please? Oh, please, Dad, if I went there . . .'

Jack Barnes was red in the face as he rose to his feet. 'You seem to have forgotten your manners, Katherine Jane Barnes. I'll not have a daughter of mine argue the point with me.'

'But, Dad, if I went back to the village, I could . . .'

His hand landed across her face, thwack!

She fell backwards, crashing against the wall. Holding her hand up to protect herself from the next blow, she screamed, 'I hate you, I hate Lond . . .'

Another slap only caught her ear as Jack swiped wildly towards her, shouting, 'Get out of my sight, you ungrateful little wretch!'

She crawled to the door and, keeping her arms up to guard her face against any further attack, left the room and ran upstairs. Once inside the tiny bedroom at the back of the house, she took the little doll, still wrapped in the silk handkerchief, and lay on the narrow horsehair mattress, weeping uncontrollably. There was no point in living. Maybe she'd die of a broken heart. Would anyone care if she did?

Later, when the boys had been settled down for the night, her mother came and knelt beside her on the bare wooden floor. 'I'm sorry, love.' She smoothed the heavy blanket and stroked Kate's hair, 'I'm so sorry.'

'I'll be all right, Mum. I'll just have to leave the new school when I'm fourteen.'

Polly shook her head sadly. 'No, love, your dad says you're to help me here until you start work. I'm truly sorry, love—' she bent

19

and kissed her '—your dad's done really well for us. This house is so much better than what we had before, isn't it?'

'Yes, Mum.'

'And the boys are happy.'

'Yes, Mum.'

'And your dad does care for you. It's just he can't abide argument with him. And—' she hesitated '—he don't hold with what your Gran does. He worries she'll lead you astray.'

'But she looks after people. She picks the nettles and dries them for Mrs Smith's arthritis and the comfrey for ...'

'More than that. He don't hold with, you know ...' Polly grimaced and bit her lip whilst reaching out and holding Kate's arm.

'With the seeing you mean?' She winced as her mother's fingers dug into her flesh.

'Don't you never speak of that to him. He thinks 'tis the Devil's work. You promise me?'

'Never—' she nodded and ran her forefinger across her throat '—cut my throat and hope to die.'

Polly released her grip. 'So, could you try and be a good girl, love?'

'But I want to go to school.'

'I know you do, love, I know how much you want it, but we can't always have what we want and girls have to accept they're going to be wives and mothers one day, so they don't need the schooling so much as boys.'

She'd been top of the class. It wasn't fair! Screwing up her eyes, she raged inside her head.

'It's a big drapers and you're so good with a needle; it'll be just right for you really.'

She could have taught the girls to sew if she'd been a teacher. How could her mother be so stupid?

'So can you be a good girl and not argue with him any more?'

She responded with a low moan.

Polly kissed her again. 'There's my girl. I knew I could rely on you.' She walked to the doorway and added, 'You'll be the best shop assistant Harvey's ever had and I'll be so proud of you.' Then blew a kiss and left the room.

She held the poppy-doll close. Dad was mean and horrible and hateful. Could she run away? Where would she go? Not to Oakey

20

Vale, Dad would fetch her and hit her again. Uncle Albert would pull his hair out and Gran would cry.

Closing her eyes she imagined being on the bank beside the river at Oakey Vale and soon drifted into a dream.

It was so peaceful with only the sound of birds and the whisper of willow fronds rustling in the breeze. Looking into the gently flowing stream she peered down in the swirling green weed watching the small fishes emerge from it from time to time. Turning round she saw the blur of iridescent blue and green as a dragon-fly hovered at the edge of the water, then gasped in surprise on seeing the bare legs of a woman with a skirt tied up around her waist as she waded to the bank carrying a round cage made of willow stalks in one hand and a large brown fish in the other. Looking up into the woman's face, she saw the love in her mother's eyes and smiled. Leaning back against a tree trunk a few moments later she thought how very clean and pink her feet looked after being in the water so long. Feeling her eyelids droop, she yawned and fought to keep them from closing. Helping her mother take the fish from the withy traps had been tiring, but she would never admit to such weakness for they must make the most of this abundance before the days grew short and cold.

On seeing her grandmother coming along the path carrying a sack on her back, she stood up and went to greet her. The old woman gave a small cry of pleasure and walked with her to the river bank where she put down her burden and placed one hand on her back and arched it as though in pain.

Her mother clambered out of the water carrying the brown fishes and waited while the old woman lifted the sack, then the three of them walked in single file along the narrow track through the woods.

The air was cooler and the red sun seemed to hang between the trees as they trudged wearily along. A bird flew alongside her and landed on a branch nearby squawking loudly ...

With a sudden shock shuddering through her, she opened her eyes and found she was lying in the small bedroom of her new home clasping the poppy-doll and the shrill noise was not the call of a bird, but the sound of her brothers shrieking with laughter on the other side of the wall.

She lay with her eyes closed for a long time trying to return to

21

the dream, but no matter how hard she screwed up her eyes or struggled to visualise the spot on river bank, it was lost to her.

When the sky was lightening into a pale grey tinged with lilac, she remembered the old woman looking at her hand and sighed. Was Gran right? Would she really return there one day? If only she could believe that!

Chapter Three

A tea made with Horehound is good for bronchitis and when used externally helps wounds to heal.

January 1919

New green shoots on the willows meant winter was over, soon there would be warmth in the sunshine and the days would be long. She saw her mother smiling whilst setting a trap for fish and also when looking towards the path to Wells from whence her grandmother would soon return.

Small flowers were blooming all around. She picked some with bright shiny yellow petals and made three circlets. Then, seeing a duck swim into view, she stood absolutely still until, in a blur of movement, it was caught in her mother's net. She ran to see the dead bird and hugged her mother around the waist in delight at the prospect of a feast.

Looking up she saw a small figure in the distance and, although longing to go and meet her grandmother, knew she must stay and wait within the safety of the woods. She had never yet crossed the river, for, although she had walked many miles through the forest and up along the hills, that side of the valley was as yet forbidden to her.

The old woman's face was haggard as she approached until, on reaching them, a smile transformed it. She could not, however, disguise the limp in her gait as they slowly made their way to the dwelling. Once there, despite her exhaustion, she moved a turf on the fire a little and set it to blaze more freely. Taking something

*from her bundle, she sat down, saying, 'Come, child, come see
what I have brought thee.'*

*In that delicious moment of anticipation she thought it might be
some new wooden pattens to keep her feet out of the mud in wet
weather.*

'There, my little lover, this be for thee.'

*She stared at the piece of metal uncomprehendingly, wondering
why the two women were looking so excited.*

*Her mother said, 'I made a handle, just like mine—' she held up
a newly carved piece of wood '—when I've made it fit, then thee'll
be able cut withies for me.'*

*A knife! It was her own knife! She held the rough end with one
hand and ran her finger along the flat side of the blade. 'And skin
a goat and, anything, I can do anything now!' She laid the blade
down then went and took the handle from her mother's hands.
'Beautiful, so beautiful and just like yourn and Grandma's,' she
murmured, gazing at the figures of a man and woman intertwined.*

The old woman said, 'Let us go prepare the bird.'

*Although loath to put down the carving, she did so and went
outside with her and helped to pluck and gut the duck. When she
returned inside carrying the meat for roasting, she gasped with
delight, for there, lying beside her sleeping shelf, was her knife
with its handle fixed and a leather sheath beside it. Her heart was
filled with joy.*

*'Come, we'll sharpen it together,' her grandmother said, and,
picking it, up led the way out through the leather flap in the wall
and began rubbing the blade against the rock outside. Forward and
back, first one side then the other, she scraped the metal.*

Kate awoke. No, that wasn't the sound of a knife being sharpened,
it was the mangle being turned in the scullery below. This was a
cold dark Monday in January and her mother had been up before
dawn to light the fire under the copper.

Looking at the ice inside the windows, she snuggled down into
the bed and wriggled her toes in the thick woollen bedsocks her
grandmother had sent at Christmas. Maybe she could drift off to
sleep again? The temptation to revisit the peaceful place she often
dreamed of in which she was a young girl living with her mother
and grandmother was very strong. It seemed like Oakey Vale and
yet was different. Instead of the cottage there was a shelter of rocks

24

built up against the cliff topped with thatch of willow and grass, and there was no lane leading down to the village one way and up to Pridden the other, only a narrow path through the woods. That life was hard in winter with none of the comforts of the present day, there were no lights within the dwelling at night, not even oil lamps like Gran had in Old Myrtles and no coal fires or range to cook the food, but it was quiet and peaceful and ... No, it was no use; she couldn't lie in bed knowing her mother was down there working so hard. Poor Mum had been so frail since having Betty two years ago; she needed help.

She eased herself out of the warmth and squeezed carefully through the narrow gap between her bed and the wooden cot in which her little sister lay asleep, then pulled a skirt over her nightgown and wrapped a shawl around her shivering shoulders. She then crept past the room where her brothers were sleeping and the one where her father was snoring rhythmically, before descending the stairs and going through the kitchen and into the scullery.

The red bricks of the floor were already slippery with soapy water overflowing from the bucket under the mangle. Steam from the copper had created a fog of vapour that converted back to water as it hit the cold windowpanes. Rivulets running down the glass were forming puddles on the whitewashed window ledge underneath, which would eventually run over the edge and down the wall to collect in yet more puddles on the uneven floor. Wash day was the worst day of the week. It was bad enough in normal circumstances, but especially difficult when her mother looked so ill.

'Can I help you, Mum?'

Polly pushed strands of greying hair back into a bun at the nape of her neck. 'Bless you, dear girl, could you mangle a while for me?'

Poor Mum. She looked drawn and weary, but then, she was an old woman, getting on for forty, well, thirty-seven at least.

'Don't get too wet, you have to go to work soon.'

'I'll dress before I go,' she replied, sliding her feet into a pair of old galoshes by the door. Then, guiding her father's Sunday shirt between the rollers with one hand, she began turning the mangle.

Polly gave a small smile. 'So grown up, so à la mode in those outfits you make. What a young lady you are, love! I was in service at the big house when I was sixteen, no fashionable clothes for me. How different things are now, I never thought I'd be living in London with a daughter going out to work in Harvey's looking like gentry. Oh, I must sit down awhile.' She sank onto a stool and, with elbows on knees, rocked back and forth holding her head.

Kate continued wringing the clothes, then rinsing them in the bucket of cold water, and wringing again, until she had a large basket piled high with clothes ready for hanging out. 'I'll take these to the line,' she said, bending towards it, then froze on seeing her mother stand up, take a step, and fall in a crumpled heap on the wet floor. 'Mum, Mum,' she shrieked and ran across to kneel beside her. 'No, no, you can't be ill—' she cradled her in her arms '—oh no, no, no.' Where was Dad? He might still be in bed, asleep. She shouted to him, then, having placed a linen sheet under Polly's head, ran along the corridor and up the stairs.

Her father, who was standing by the bed in his combinations, asked anxiously, 'Whatever's going on, bonny lass?'

'It's Mum, she's fainted. Oh, Dad, it's not going to be another baby, is it?'

'Oh, my God! Another bairn—' he grabbed his trousers off the chair beside him '—I've had my suspicions, but you ladies don't tell us about these things. Go back down, I'll be right there.'

Betty was standing up in her cot, calling, 'Mummy? Mummy?' Tears glistened in her large blue eyes and her full pink lips quivered as she demanded, 'Mummy? Where gone my mummy?' She held up her plump arms. 'Carry!'

Picking her up, Kate said, 'She's not well at present, I want you to be a big girl for me and stay in bed for a little while.'

Betty wriggled free and landed on the hard wooden floor with a loud thump, then screamed, 'Mummy, Mummy, Mummy!'

'Oh very well, I'll take you with me.' Bending and scooping her up she carried her down the narrow staircase and along to the scullery to where their mother was lying on the floor and asked, 'Mum, are you all right?'

Polly leaned on one elbow. 'I think I'm a bit off-colour, love.' Then, when Betty tried to pull her up, added, 'Thank you, darling, you're such a good girl to help me.'

Jack arrived, asking, 'Is it another bairn, bonny lass?'

'Yes, it is, but that's not it. Such a headache! So bad, so bad. I ache all over, all over.'

26

'Here, lassie, we'll get you upstairs.' He pulled her up and helped her to their bedroom. 'She's burning with fever,' he said as Kate followed him carrying Betty and stood by the bed. 'I'll have to get ready for work. You can take care of her, keep her warm.'

'Could you tell them at Harvey's why I'm not coming to work, Dad?'

'I don't go anywhere near there, bonny lass.'

'Please, please,' she beseeched him, 'I don't want to lose my position there, please, Dad, *please*. It was you that got me the post. Dad, *please* tell the manager why I'm not there.'

'All right, all right, I'll have to leave a few minutes early to do that. You tend to your ma and the bairns, there's a good lass.'

The two boys were still curled up under the blankets when she went into their room and called their names. There was no response. Having tried cajoling and pleading without any success, she shouted, 'Boys! Just get up and get ready. Mum's not well. Get up, now!'

Jack heard her and stomped in. Pulling back the blankets, he shouted, 'Get up, yer lazy little good fer nothings, yer mum's ill, now try and help yer sister. Get up!' He clattered down the stairs and, on reaching the range, shouted, 'The kettle's not on, I need hot water to shave. Kate!'

She ran down and fetched the water from the scullery where the fire under the copper was cooling down, but dared not stop to deal with it. Having put the kettle on the range to heat, she began to make the porridge. When at last the water was hot enough, Jack Barnes shaved his face whilst looking in the mirror beside the warm stove and she ran upstairs to hurry her brothers along.

After the boys had left the house Betty kept vigil by her mother, and, taking her thumb out of her mouth from time to time, prodded the inert figure in the bed, saying, 'Mummy, diddup. Mummy, diddup.'

Kate returned to the washing and was on her third journey carrying a basket to the back garden when the next-door neighbour, who was doing the same, called out, 'Is yer mum ill, dearie?'

Kate answered, 'I'm really worried, Mrs Dooley, she looks so bad. I don't know what to do.'

'She ain't got that influenza has she, ducky? There's a lot of it about. I'd get the doctor, if I was you.' Picking up the empty basket, the neighbour added, 'Yer'd think we'd 'ad enough

27

troubles, what with the War an' that.' She shook her head sadly then walked away towards the back door of her house.

Whilst struggling with the wet laundry, pegging it onto the rope tied between the house and a hook in the wall across the yard, she admitted Mrs Dooley was right. Mum had had enough to bear since coming back to London. First Betty arrived in March of 1917 and now here was another on the way. She blew on her cold fingers and grimaced at the wet sheets; work at the emporium was preferable to tedious household chores like this, especially now she had progressed from being the lowliest employee in the shop to a sales assistant. She paused to count how long they had been in this house; almost three years had passed since the heartbreaking day when all her dreams had been destroyed.

She had made the best of things since then and life was really not too bad, although her longing for Oakey Vale, and, above all, her grandmother, never diminished. The old lady was the only person who would understand how she had known her mother's baby would be a girl, and would have been sympathetic about some other more worrying experiences too. 'I knowed you had the gift, just like me and my Jane,' she would have said on hearing about the time in the shop when the horrible arrogant woman was being so rude to the paid companion who traipsed along behind her carrying the parcels. What an extraordinary sight! Suddenly the long-suffering, shy little woman was laughing happily in a portly gentleman's arms. And then there was the time when Mr Harvey was inspecting the shop: that really was so distressing. For an instant, a blink of an eye, she watched in horror as his huge body shrank and his face became cadaverously thin. On that occasion, when Tilda asked if she was ill, she had blamed a headache and then had to take the aspirin her friend fetched for her.

Gran's letters were full of village gossip like who had given birth and what plant was in bloom. They made Oakey Vale seem close, as if she could get on a tram or an omnibus and be there in a few minutes. If only that were true and the river was nearby and the mill and Hankeys Land. Oh, to sit by the tree! To walk out of the house and climb the steps, then follow the path through the copse and see the huge oak awaiting her return. That would be such bliss!

When she had all the clothes either hanging on the line or rolled up ready for ironing, she went upstairs. Betty had climbed under the covers and fallen asleep beside Polly whose pale face was shiny with sweat as she lay curled up and moaning quietly. Kneeling by the bed, she listened fearfully to the strange rattling sound as her mother took in each shallow breath. A short time later, on hearing the front door bang, she ran down to find Eddie standing in the hall, saying he had been sent home by the teacher who thought he had the influenza.

Eric came back at six and immediately went to bed refusing any food. Only Jack, who returned later in the evening, ate the stew and dumplings she had made.

'Should I write and tell Granny, Dad?' she asked as he laid down his knife and fork on the empty plate.

'That old witch? I don't want her poking her nose in where it's not wanted. She'll be all for potions and spells to cure them. No, I don't want her knowing all our affairs.' He took out a pipe and filled it with tobacco, then went on, 'She's done enough damage to our family. She'd no right to make you all leave London when I was away at the War. No right at all! Meddling old meadow lady!'

'The people in the village all go to her ...' she began, then, remembering her promise to her mother, fell silent.

'More fool them.' He lit the pipe from a taper and sucked on it in several short bursts, before blowing a stream of smoke into the room. Then, narrowing his eyes, he said, 'I'll not have that interfering woman in my house, bonny lass. D'you understand?'

'Yes, Dad. Yes, I understand you don't want her here, but she'll be expecting a letter from Mum, she'll wonder why she hasn't written.'

'She's only been took bad today.'

'I know, but it's over a week since the letter came from her and ...'

'Show it to me, bonny lass.'

She went to the drawer where her mother kept all the writing requisites and took out the most recent of her grandmother's letters.

Seeing her hesitate, Jack said impatiently, 'Give it me.' Taking it from her, he sighed in exasperation as a few dried flowers fell onto the floor, then read aloud, 'Dear Polly, I am sorry to hear you have had your old problem again. Dandelions are the best cure. Eat the leaves or make a tea of them and that will help.

'Mr Wallace has come home at last, I hear he was wounded

29

bad poor man. His brother died and his brother-in-law also. One of the Nelson twins died in France and there's the Roaches at Pridden lost both boys. I don't know how they do bear such a thing. We must be thankful the war is over and no more young men will be killed.

'The snowdrops are blooming in the churchyard. Tell Kate I picked some and took them to our special grave. Tell her also the fireweed is shooting underground, even though it cannot be seen, it will flower later, she will understand. From your loving mother—' he looked angrily at Kate '—fireweed! What on earth's that?'

'Rosebay Willowherb, is what some folk call it.'

'Rubbish!' He screwed the letter into a ball and threw it towards the range. 'Bloody rubbish that is! Now you see why I wanted to get you back in London as soon as I could. If you'd stayed much longer with her, you'd be filled with the same stuff and nonsense.' He sat puffing on the pipe as he stared angrily at the wall.

Kate sank to the floor and picked up the scattered flowers. Her heart was thumping and her hands shook as she fought to control her anger. Whilst rising to her feet, she found the room spinning around her in a green blur for a few seconds, and then, when her vision cleared, she saw a road curving around a steeply sloping and densely forested hillside. A sudden loud screeching sound was followed by a thump and a figure was silhouetted against the sky before falling down into a valley filled with trees. Feeling dizzy with shock, she subsided into a chair and sat in silence until her father went outside to the water closet, then, instantly alert, she leaped up, retrieved the letter and quickly hid it under a pile of shirts before returning to her seat.

Walking back into the room, he said, 'I'm looking for the rubbish I threw here.'

'It's gone, Dad, I burned it.'

'Well done, bonny lass, I'll not have nonsense like that in my house and as soon as yer ma's fit and well again, I'll see she understands that. I'll away now and sit with her for a bit.'

The moment his footsteps sounded on the bedroom floor above, she took all the old woman's letters from the drawer and clasped them to her chest. Where could she hide them? The mending basket: he'd never look in there. Pulling back the torn shirts, worn socks and unravelling pullovers, she dug deep under some balls of

30

wool and, sighing with relief, placed the bundle of paper beneath them. The precious hoard would be safe until her mother was well again and the family was back to normal.

Chapter Four

An old way to ease the pain of gout was to apply the squashed berries of Lords and Ladies mixed with hot ox-dung. The plant was also a remedy for the plague.

Eddie wouldn't wake up. He was so cold. He needed warmth. He'd always been pale, never had much colour even when they lived in Oakey Vale. He'd been ill now for three days. Naturally he'd be cold. Of course he needed her to hold him and warm him. Of course he needed her to sing to him. Dad didn't understand little boys. She'd sung nursery rhymes to her brother when he was little. 'Ba ba black sheep, have you any wool? Yes sir, yes sir, three bags full.'

Dad was talking nonsense. Eddie couldn't be dead. 'Mary, Mary, quite contrary, how does your garden grow?'

Suddenly Mrs Dooley was singing with her, 'Rock a by baby on the tree top. When the wind blows the cradle will rock—' they were swaying to and fro '—down will come baby, cradle and all.'

'Yer dad's gone to fetch the doctor,' Mrs Dooley said, leading Kate downstairs, 'I heard you carryin' on so I come in to help for a bit.'

Everything seemed far away and small as though cut out of paper like the little theatre she had made for Christmas three years ago. Only Betty seemed the right size and felt warm snuggling into her arms. Could Eddie really be dead?

When the doctor arrived, pale and yawning, he looked cursorily at the little corpse and then at Polly and Eric. 'A bad business,' he said sadly.

'Why should my lads and my wife be so ill and ... and I ...?' Jack faltered and looked away.

'The weakest are dying—' the young man opened his hands in a gesture of helplessness '—all over the country, in every city and every town, the influenza is killing us.' He attempted to stifle a yawn and departed.

Kate cleaned, washed and baked in a daze, as though living in a nightmare without end. Whilst knowing she longed for her grand-mother's loving presence, she was too exhausted and befuddled to think how she could send for the old woman without upsetting her father.

When Mrs Dooley, who had brought many bowls of broth and much advice, offered to help lay out her brother in the parlour, she gladly accepted. Raw pain broke through the fog as they washed his body. Seeing the ribs jutting up through the thin white flesh, she felt searing pain in her lungs whilst holding her breath to suppress wild screams of furious anger. How could this be? How could a loving God allow such things to happen? This cold remnant of a body had been a warm, healthy boy only a short time ago. Could a God of mercy and love allow this?

Somehow she carried on until her little brother lay in the small coffin and she could escape from the horror of mortality revealed by Mrs Dooley's instruction. She tried to persuade Eric to see his brother ready for burial, but he refused. He had been jealous of Eddie from the day he was born and had fought and teased him unmercifully ever since. He had persuaded him to eat earthworms in the garden, had led him into many pranks and much mischief, had tormented and terrified him in all manner of ways, but now he was distraught with grief and lay in bed facing the wall. When Polly insisted between the painful coughs wracking her body that she wanted to see her younger son before he was taken to the cemetery, Kate tried to dissuade her. Jack however thought she should, and so the descent was made. Wrapped in shawls and leaning heavily on the banister rail, she made a slow, sideways descent, resting for an agonising breath on every step of the stairs until, on eventually reaching the parlour, she sank down beside the coffin on the floor making little keening sounds while stroking Eddie's face and hands.

On Jack's insistence that she must leave her son because the handcart was outside ready for taking him to the graveyard, she tried to stand, but her legs crumpled beneath her and she lay on the floor with Kate holding her whilst two men in black entered the room and banged the lid down before carrying the coffin out of the house.

Mother and daughter stayed huddled together until Mrs Dooley brought a distraught little girl in search of them. 'I couldn't hold her back no longer, not even my Davey could keep her quiet. Oh no! Oh my Lor!' she screeched on seeing Polly, 'Whatever's she doing out of bed?'

Kate started to explain, but the woman ignored her. 'I'll fetch my Davey.' She rushed off and returned with her son, who blushed bright red at the sight of Kate.

With Davey taking most of the weight and Betty pulling at her nightdress, the three of them lifted Polly who was now drifting in and out of consciousness. No one could persuade the little girl to let go as she hung on, ignoring a collision with the glazed display cabinet and the resultant sound of breaking china.

When they reached the bedroom, Betty climbed onto the bed and lay beside her mother as they covered her with blankets and Mrs Dooley, looking down at the pale face on the pillow, sighed. 'She'll not be long in following him,' she said sadly. 'My Davey an' me will always be here for you, Kate. Any time, day or night, you come and call me.' She left the room followed by her son.

Kate knelt beside the bed holding her mother's hand. 'Please don't go,' she whispered. But even as the words had been uttered, she knew it was too late. She saw Polly lying in a coffin with pink roses against her white cheek; it was only a momentary glimpse, but she knew it would be so.

When Jack returned from the cemetery, he kept repeating, 'He said it's the weak ones are dying. I thought she was strong.' From that moment he stayed with his wife for every minute he was not at work.

Sitting beside her mother's bed three days later, Kate struggled to keep her eyes open whilst darning one of Eric's socks. Sometimes she could have a special kind of daydream about her grandmother's house, and she needed one now, anywhere around the cottage would do; a wander through the garden perhaps with butterflies, those small blue ones, alighting on the rosemary. A walk by the river to the ruined mill would be so good; she might see iridescent dragonflies bending their tails while laying eggs along the bank or the flash of a kingfisher swooping along the water. Best of all would be to walk up behind the cottage to the oak tree in Hankeys Land. My Lady Oak would listen to her weary heart and ... Her head nodded drowsily and the wooden mushroom inside the woollen sock slipped from her hands as her eyes closed and she dreamed of the secret cave.

Her heart was joyful as she knelt beside her grandmother and drank water from the red pool. The blood had frightened her at first, but now, knowing it was from this that her child would be formed one day, she felt part of a great and mysterious sisterhood.

The old woman grimaced with pain as she pulled herself upright. Then, with a smile transforming her face, she held her close and said, 'Thee must bear a daughter to carry on. Remember me and be strong. All women are plants that bloom a while, bear fruit, then die, but we are like the fireweed. Like the first plant to shoot through the scorched earth after burning, we cannot be destroyed.'

The light was dim and the shadows around her deep, but she could see the outline of the figure in the rock and the water glistening as it tricked down over the pink crystals.

Suddenly, she was wide awake, brought to her senses by a strange silence. 'Mum!' she exclaimed, slid to her knees, and watched in horror as the colour drained from the dear, gaunt face. 'Mum, oh, Mum, oh, my Mummy!'

After weeping for several minutes, she dried her eyes and fought the rising panic. Eric! How was he going to cope with this? And Betty too, what would become of her? She must be strong for them. Standing up, she looked down at the pale face on the pillow and saw a wisp of white floating above the greying hair. Thinking it was the sunlight catching specks of dust in its beam, she stepped towards the window to close the curtains. No, this side of the house was in shade, the bright March sunshine was nowhere near the room. Turning back and seeing the last, tiny, smoke-like remnant melt into the air: she knew Polly's spirit had left her body.

Betty, who had fallen asleep beside her mother, awoke and started screaming in panic. Kate picked her up and held the furious, frightened little body close to her. 'It's all right, sweetheart, your Kate's here. I'll never leave you.' Whilst cuddling and comforting the little girl, her mind cleared and she knew what must be done. First she'd have to stand up to her father and send for Gran. Then she would have to care for the family. There would be no more happy days at Harvey's, no giggling comparisons of beaux, no more fun. She would cook, clean, sew, mend and make do on too little money. She would take her mother's place and keep what was left of the family together.

Carrying her little sister, she ran to the house next door where Mrs Dooley held them both in her arms and wept.

The rest of the day was spent in practical arrangements and domestic duties carried out in a strangely detached manner, as though it was not she who was living in her body, but another remote self who watched her movements with surprised interest.

That evening, when the dishes had been washed and both Betty and Eric were at last asleep, she fetched the writing materials and placed them on the kitchen table. Sitting as close as possible to the gas light on the wall, she dipped her pen into the inkwell and wrote, *Dear Gran*.

How does one tell a woman her daughter is dead? She chewed the end of the wooden nib holder and looked at her father who was sitting slumped in the old armchair close to the range, staring blankly at the wall. She knew that he disapproved of her grandmother's country ways and gift of seeing, but had not understood the depth of feeling until the scene with the letter on the day Polly was taken ill. She had tried several times to write and tell her of Eddie's death, but a terrible lethargy had made her procrastinate and delude herself Polly would know what to say when she was well again. Now she had no choice, she must send news quickly, but how? What could she say? Remembering the monthly letters describing the weather, what trees were in leaf and which flower in bloom, who had died and who given birth, she understood. Gran wrote as though she was talking to you, yes that was how to do it!

I am so unhappy to write and tell you bad news. Eddie died four days ago and now our mother has died also of the influenza. She was so loving, she never complained even when Eric played the fool, like he used to, or argued with Dad like he did which made her unhappy, he is very quiet and sad now. Betty is only a baby, just two last week and is very upset, I am also. I shall not go back to work because I am needed to care for the family. I often think of the happy time we had when we lived in your house with you and picked the flowers. With love from your Kate.

Looking across the room at her father, she said, 'I've written to Grandma, Dad.'

'I don't want that old witch in my house!'

She bit her lip. 'Do I say she's not welcome for the funeral?'

Jack Barnes sighed. 'No, no, lass, she's Polly's mother, whatever else she is. You'd best send a telegram as well—' he nodded as if affirming his resolve '—I'll have to bear it, but not for long mind!'

Her head ached with tiredness and even going to bed seemed too much effort. Folding the letter, she said, 'Gran may not want to come all this way on the train.'

'She'll come all right, bonny lass, you mark my words—' his eyes narrowed '—it won't take long on her broomstick neither.'

Chapter Five

Chickweed when applied to the skin for several hours will draw out poisons from boils, abscesses, wounds and sores. It can be eaten raw, and a tea of leaves and flowers soothes and cleanses the system.

'I've brought some tonics for Eric,' the old woman said to her unsmiling son-in-law, 'I'll only stay until the burial. You won't be wanting me around you for long, I know.'

'Aye, suit yerself. There's two nights before she's taken to the cemetery.' Jack turned away, staring fixedly at the wall.

The small plump woman went into the parlour where her daughter lay in the plain pine coffin and closed the door behind her.

Kate hovered in the hall from time to time and heard low, grieving moans. Eventually, when Eric had been settled for the night, Betty had finally fallen asleep, and her father had gone to bed, she knocked cautiously at the parlour door. When there was no reply, she went into the room in which several candles were burning and found her grandmother lying on the floor beside the coffin. For one terrible moment she thought the old woman was dead, but on kneeling beside her was relieved to hear the familiar voice say, 'Leave me be, my lover. I'll stay with her tonight.'

She fetched a warm blanket and, while covering the recumbent form, breathed in the heady scent of roses. Sinking to her knees she touched the dried pink petals around her mother's head and, seeing the small poppy-doll tucked under the dead hands, smiled despite the pain.

The next morning, on descending to the kitchen, she found the old woman stirring a pan of porridge on the stove, some dough was proving in a china bowl and the oven was already nearly hot enough to bake it.

Feeling anxious about the lack of mourning clothes, she explained she had made black armbands for her father and Eric but, apart from an old black overcoat of her mother's, she had nothing suitable to wear and there was neither money nor time to make anything.

'Don't you worry, Kate,' the old woman reassured her. 'I don't hold with all that blackness. 'Tis only the custom, that's all. 'Tis what's in your heart that counts—' she kissed her on the cheek '—when my time comes, I wants you to wear green to match your eyes. Black don't become you, my lover, green is what I likes.'

Later, after Jack had gone to work and they sat together in the parlour gazing into the coffin, the old woman said, 'I knew it would be a short life but I didn't know it would be like this. That's why I was so worried about her having too many babies. So many her lost after months of carrying them, so many. Her came to me that time begging for help and I gave her the special mix of plants I know will get rid of a baby if taken early enough. These plants are made by God for the purpose I do believe, but others think different. When your father heard what Polly'd done he swore never to forgive me for doing the Devil's work and forbade her to set foot in Oakey Vale ever again.'

'But we came here while he was away at the War.'

'Aye, I fetched you from that filthy place when she was ill from losing another one. I'd promised her father I'd look after her before he died. What else could I do?'

Memory stirred in Kate. 'I remember when we came to stay with you at the farm. I knew I'd met Granfer. I did, didn't I?'

'Aye, you came for two weeks that first time. He loved you so much, five years old you were, a copy of your Aunt Jane at the same age.' She sat silent for several minutes then sighed and added, 'There's no good in regretting or being sad. Happy times we had on the farm, hard work it was, but I loved it.' Her face looked young and girlish for a moment. 'Courted me from when I were thirteen year old, he did. Wouldn't take no for an answer.'

'Didn't you like him, Gran?'

'I liked him all right, but our family hadn't never married no one before. My old Gran had eight sons and a daughter and boasted as every one were by a different tinker passing through. My mother had but one child and never did tell who fathered me.' She shook her head and gave a wry smile. 'I seen her watch the diddicoys when they camped up top for the horse fair at Pridden, and by her yearning look I reckon 'twas one of they, but I never asked.'

'That's really sad, Gran.'

'Aye, by some folks way of thinking so it is, but they'm travellers and she couldn't leave the village and go off gallivanting around the country. She was sworn to mind the secret cave and that was that.'

'So she thought you should do the same?'

'Aye, and she argued long and hard against me marrying, but I was lucky on account of my man having the farm up top so close and she knew I'd do my duty when my turn came so she gave in. Then, when my dear one died, what with your uncle being the way he is, and no one else in the family wanting to take it on and with my old mother getting feeble so I was forever traipsing up and down, I took on a tenant. Though he be not an easy man, I get's along all right with him and he's always paid come Michaelmas.'

'So you moved down to the village, to Old Myrtles?'

'Aye, my lover. Back to the house where I were born.'

'I loved it, Gran.'

'I know, and 'tis where you belong. You were so happy when you came to me while your father was at the War and you liked the village school too, didn't you?'

'Oh, Gran, I loved everything there, I loved it so much. I cried every night for weeks when we came back.'

'I cried when you left, I don't mind admitting it.' The old woman pulled a white linen handkerchief out from her sleeve and dabbed at her eyes.

'I thought we'd come to live with you for always.'

'Aye, I hoped so too, and you settled into the way of life very quickly. But it wasn't to be, not yet.' She looked down at the corpse, her mouth quivering with pain.

'Do you remember how I used to read stories to Uncle Albert?'

'I remember and so does he—' the old woman gave a tight smile '—my Albert don't talk too much, but when he do 'tis often of you.'

'I remember him sitting in his special chair and carving wood in the evenings.'

40

'He's a bit different, my son, God bless him. Some might call him simple I know, but he has his special gifts, as do we all. He knows everyone in the graveyard, but as to how he do is a mystery for he cannot read.'

Kate grinned. 'I read them out to him. He loved learning all the names and dates; it made him so happy. But I also remember him being very upset when we were coming back to London, he looked so sad.'

'Aye, he didn't speak for a long time after that. He'll be pleased to hear what a fine young lady you are now. I'll tell him you have the green eyes of your mother and the same fine features, and—' she reached out and touched the heavy dark coils over Kate's ears '—the loveliest hair in all the world.'

'The same sharp beak.'

'That's a good nose and with those strong cheekbones you'll be a beautiful woman.'

'Betty's like Dad.' She kissed the little girl on her lap.

'Aye, her has the fair hair of him. He was such a handsome fellow. I could see why my girl fell for him. I remember the day he arrived with the horses for the old master at The Grange; one was a very special mare for breeding from up north somewhere.'

'From near Newcastle, that's where he grew up. He's promised to take me there for a visit one day. He has many brothers and sisters he hasn't seen for years.'

'Me too, me too,' Betty said, pouting.

'Yes, sweetheart, you'll come too,' Kate reassured her.

The old woman gazed down into the coffin. 'Her father begged and pleaded with her to wait a year, but no, she would have him, and then the next thing we knew they were off to London.' She looked around the room at the two new chairs and a sofa upholstered in red plush with embroidered white antimacassars and the red and blue Persian-style rug. 'Seems like he's done his best, I'll grant him that.'

'Mum was very proud of this room—' she grimaced at the display cabinet '—we had an accident with that.'

Her grandmother looked at the cracked pane of glass in the door and the broken china on the three shelves. ''Tis of no consequence, my lover. You'll learn how things don't matter, only people ...' her voice gave way to tears as she bowed her head and wept.

Later, as they sat at the kitchen table drinking tea and eating freshly baked bread, Kate placed her hands on the white linen cloth, saying, 'When you said you knew about Mum, was it like me hearing things on Hankeys Land?'

'In a way, 'tis part of the same gift. What you heard that day by the tree was your first taste of it. You was picking up something, like an echo I suppose, or a memory in that place, of something what happened long ago to one of those who went before.'

'Before?'

'Aye—' the old woman looked steadily at Kate '—was that the only sight you've had?'

'No, Gran. I saw Mr Wallace by the gate of the cottage and his hand—' she shivered at the memory '—was missing. And I saw Mum with the roses too, and some other things, not all of them bad, but I don't want the gift if that's what it's like.'

'I think what you needs is a little trick to help it along, so you can get the sight when you want it and not just any old time it forces itself on you. The really very bad things come on you whether you like it or no, in an uncontrolled way, but you don't want to know only bad things do you?'

She shook her head.

'You'll find your own way in time. You'll see. Give me your hand, my lover.'

She looked at Betty asleep in the armchair then eagerly obeyed.

The old woman examined her palm for several minutes before a broad smile spread across her face and she said, 'You'll be fulfilling your destiny, my dear.'

'What about marriage and children?'

'Well, that's not so easy to say. You'll know love, of that I'm certain.'

Feeling her face flush she looked away.

'There's two children here. Yes, definitely two.'

'And what of my husband?'

'The best I can say is two loves, whether they be husbands or no I cannot say. Two's a generous number. Some never knows love at all.'

Kate suddenly felt dizzy ... *She was running, panic-stricken, overwrought ... A bramble caught in her skirt and she tore it away ... She was sitting on the ground cradling her grandmother. The bright beam of sunlight shone on the white hair of the old woman in her arms. A sound like the frenzy of bees gradually became a*

42

hymn tune and the sun faded until she was surrounded by great purple and black shadows interspersed with soft creamy patches of light. She could smell candle-wax and roses and, above the sound of Uncle Albert humming his favourite hymn, she heard the sound of water trickling over the crystals. Then, seeing the old woman lying on a flat rock, she felt the deep, deep sadness of loss.

She blinked and found her grandmother watching her.

'What did you see, Kate?'

'I was holding you, we were in the garden. Then I was in the cave with the lovely lady with shadows and candles. I saw you with dried rose petals all around.'

'And Albert, was he there?'

'I could hear him nearby. And before that I was running, my skirt was torn on some brambles, it was all so strange. '

'I'll sleep easy now, my lover.'

Betty awoke, slid off the chair and, pulling at her grandmother's sleeve, demanded, 'Me, me, me! My turn! My hands now!'

'You're too young, little one.'

'I want hands!'

'Hush, hush,' the old woman said gently.

'Me too, me too.'

'Here, my little lover, come sit on my knee and we'll have just a tiny peek.' Gazing at the small palms, she said, 'My goodness! What a clever girl you'll be. You'll ... er, you'll be a good girl for your sister.' She looked over the blond curls and winked before beginning to play pat-a-cake, pat-a-cake baker's man, bake me a cake as fast as you can. When the little girl climbed down and picked up her doll, the old woman took Kate's hand and said earnestly, 'You already have the gift. Your special way of doing it will come to you.'

'Will I get just flashes like I do now?'

'Aye, sort of like glimpses of the past and the future too, but enough, you'll see.'

'But how will I know what is my way?'

''Twill be like meeting an old friend. It may be with a set of playing cards, I've known a woman could see all a person's life laid before her in the cards. Or maybe 'twill be by other means, but fear not, my lover, you'll know.'

That night her mind would not rest as she lay sleeplessly remem-

43

bering the conversation with her grandmother. What would be her way and when would she find it? How could she ever find it when living here with her father who disapproved of such things? Tears of grief and self-pity overwhelmed her for a while before she finally slipped into desperately needed sleep.

The tallow was burning low and the cave was swathed in shadows except for circles of light surrounding the lamps placed either side of the red pool, but still she could see the water glistening as it trickled down the pink crystals of the secret lady. Her heart was joyful as she knelt beside her grandmother and scooped a drink of water.

The old woman turned and held her close then said, 'This be a secret never to be shared.'

'Aye, Gran, I knows it.'

'No man must ever find it for they will take it and desecrate it, calling it by the name of some saint what never came here. This water be powerful for healing and though we give it to the people to drink in potions to heal them they cannot be trusted to know from whence it came. Do thee swear never to tell a living soul of this place?'

'Aye, Gran.'

'Then I can rest in peace when my time comes.' She placed her hand on the rock beside the pool and went on, 'It will not be long before thee must put me here, but though thee weeps for my going, remember I shall return and so shall thee.' She stood up and untied the leather pouch hanging at her waist. 'This be yourn now.'

'Mine?' she gasped. 'I cannot take thy scrying ball, grandmother.'

'Thy mother has no need of it, for she prefers to call on the moon to help her and 'tis mine to give. Take it. Use it only for the good of others who have need of thy gift and it will serve thee well.'

Awakening to find Betty had climbed into bed with her and was whimpering in her sleep, she gently reassured her for a few moments. Then, once the child was breathing quietly, she carefully eased herself out of bed and hurriedly dressed before running downstairs.

A short while later the old woman came into the kitchen where she was preparing porridge for Betty and said, 'I may not get the chance to speak again, my lover, as I has to leave after the funeral.

I'll not be wanted by your father, as you know.' She stroked her hair and kissed her, 'Don't forget to bring that poppy-doll back to me. Old Myrtles is where you belong. Promise me you'll come?'

'I don't see how I ever could, but thank you all the same.' The floorboards above them creaked, 'That's Dad getting up, I'd best get his shaving water for him.'

'You won't forget?' The old woman persisted.

Betty could be heard yelling at the top of the stairs, 'Tate, Tate, Tate!'

'Kate,' her father's voice joined in, 'I need a clean shirt for the funeral.'

Eric shouted, 'Kate, where are you?'

'No, Gran—' she sighed '—I won't forget.'

Chapter Six

A tea of Yarrow flowers and leaves is effective for reducing fever and good for colds, influenza, diarrhoea and urinary problems including cystitis. The crushed leaves may be applied to cuts and chewed for toothache.

Mrs Dooley went to Liverpool in May and brought back two small nieces whose parents had died in the influenza epidemic; one was the same age as Betty and the other a year older. These poor orphans touched Kate's heart and they soon became frequent visitors who brightened up a dreary home in mourning. The three little girls played houses under the large kitchen table, dressed up in her old clothes and walked their rag dollies around the garden in the small wooden box on wheels that Davey had made for them.

Kate's life followed a regular pattern in which there was no joy other than the laughter of little girls and much blank cold grief whilst doing household chores from early morning until late at night. Eric was quieter than he had ever been in his life as was their father who rarely spoke except to demand clean clothes, hot shaving water or some other necessity of life.

When Jack Barnes forgot her seventeenth birthday in July, she accepted the disappointment as natural in the circumstances, but felt Polly's absence even more keenly, and that afternoon, having left Betty with Mrs Dooley, she went to the cemetery and knelt beside the grave of her mother and brother. How could God have let those lovely warm beings die?

Watching a woman walk past carrying a bunch of flowers, she felt a sudden shock, understanding she too was visiting the place where a loved one was buried and all around them were hundreds of rectangles marking the place where corpses lay rotting beneath the earth.

She had read out the names to Uncle Albert in the graveyard in Oakey Vale without ever thinking about the skeletons lying six feet away. The old man hummed as they walked from one headstone to another. He did that if he was happy and yet he knew about the dead bodies because he had dug many of the recent graves. He always smiled and stood to attention by his grandmother's plot humming his favourite hymn, 'Eternal father strong to save'. The tune flooded her mind and she felt her heart lighten. Yes, she'd die, of course she would, but not for a long time yet. The sun was shining on her birthday and she was alive!

She walked to the wrought-iron gates leading out onto the wide carriageway and, enjoying the freedom to walk at her own pace without Betty slowing her down, stepped between the cracks of the paving stones singing, 'Oh hear us when we cry to thee for those in peril on the sea.'

'I can't resist a musical lady.'

She knew without looking around it was the deep, well-educated voice of Mr Hugo whose father owned the emporium and felt her face grow hot as she wished him 'Good afternoon.'

He raised his hat and, falling in step with her, asked, 'May I walk along with you, Miss Barnes?'

He remembered her name! 'Yes, yes, of course you may.'

'Where have you been these past months?'

'My mother died and I have to look after the family.'

'I've been spending some time recently in the shop. It's a duller, quieter place for your absence—' he grinned '—the Manager's remarked on the difference more than once.'

She blushed again, aware that her friend Tilda had no one to giggle with now.

'I'll be assistant manager in September,' he went on. 'The old lady wanted me to go to university, but I opted to start in the business straight away, which pleased the old man. I've just left school, thank God—' he rolled his large brown eyes dramatically '—what a relief to get on with life! I was keen to start at the grindstone straight away, but the dear mater insists on being accompanied to the country for a month. God, what a bore! All those ghastly tea parties and croquet on the lawn, that sort of thing. D'you know Surrey?'

'No, I'm afraid I don't. I've only been to Somerset to stay with my grandmother.'

'D'you visit her often?'

'No. I haven't been there for years. I loved it there. She writes telling me about it and I imagine I'm with her collecting the comfrey and the nettles.'

'Nettles!'

'Yes, she dries great bunches of them in her kitchen for making special tea. And she eats them too. They're really good, like spinach.'

'What! Don't they sting your mouth?'

She laughed up at him. 'Not when they're cooked, you silly goose—' realising what she had said, she put her hand up to her mouth in horror '—I do apologise, Mr Hugo.'

He grinned. 'You shouldn't, Miss Kate Barnes.' Then, putting a hand on her arm, he stopped walking and, as they stood under a lime tree beside the railings enclosing a small park, he looked down at her. 'No one with sparkling, dancing eyes like yours should ever apologise for . . .' He blushed, suddenly looking young and unsure of himself. He raised his hat, saying, 'I have to dash, goodbye.' And he strode away back in the direction of where they had met.

She sang all the way home and, looking in the small mirror on the hallstand whilst removing her hat, whispered to her image, 'Sparkling and dancing eyes.'

When Tilda called on her way home from work bringing a small piece of lace for a birthday gift she sat in the kitchen watching Kate stirring the stew on the stove and said, 'That smells good.' Looking sideways at Betty who stood staring up at her she added, 'Aren't you lucky to have a kind sister looking after you?'

Betty poked out her tongue.

'I'd wallop her if I was you.'

Kate tried to sound cross as she told the little girl not to be so naughty, but she was thinking of her encounter that afternoon.

Tilda sighed. 'She'll never learn manners if you're so weak with her.' Turning her back on the child, she continued, 'I wish you'd come and see us more often, it's not so lively without you, in fact it's positively dull. There's hardly any larks or fun at all. Really, really dreary. Oh! I almost forgot; there *is* something exciting

48

about to happen. Young Mr Hugo will be joining us in September. We're all in love with him already; the manager said he'll dismiss the next one to giggle when he walks in.'

'I can't afford to buy anything from Harvey's nowadays and I daren't come to see you without actually buying anything. Old Droopy Drawers would give you the sack if he caught us chattering.'

Tilda laughed. 'Actually, Mr Drew suggested you might like to do some work at home. The woman who does the alterations has too much work to take on the small bits and pieces. She said you were really good at invisible mending, lace repairs, that sort of thing. Would you be interested?'

'Of course I would. Oh, Tilda, thank you. I'll come in tomorrow and thank Droopy ... sorry, Mr Drew. This will make all the difference to me!'

Lying in bed that night she looked back on her birthday and, remembering young Mr Harvey looking into her eyes, smiled into the darkness before falling asleep.

The old woman winced with pain as she raised herself on one elbow and then sat huddled, holding her hands towards the fire. 'My time is almost done, my lover.'

'But already the days are longer ...'

'No matter, I'll not see the windflowers blooming in the woods again. But thee—' she leaned towards her '—shall see them and be glad of it.' She coughed and held her chest as though in pain for a moment before continuing, 'Thy mother—' she smiled at the woman stirring the pot hanging from a metal stake over the flames '—says young men be taking notice of thee.'

Knowing this alluded to the handsome young farrier who smiled at her whenever she passed by the forge, she blushed and said nothing.

'Remember we mun stay apart.'

'Must I never go with a man?'

'Thee mun lay with men, how else may thee get the daughter to carry on? Thee mun lay only with strangers, dear child, never with the local men.'

'But, Grandmother ...'

'Nay, there be no buts about this. No man could keep our secret

49

from they new foreign lords. Already there's talk of the chapel over the river being built anew to suit them and I heard as there's to be a great new church in place of the sanctuary near the holy wells also.' The old woman paused for several moments, raising her shoulders with each intake of breath, then went on, 'Those holy wells was once sacred springs no different from our secret one, my lover. The new lord of this land would take our lady from us and give her to their church. That's why thee must never take a local man to thee. Not even a maying with the other young folk, not ever, ever, do thee swear?'

How had the old woman known she had planned to go into the woods the night before May Day in the hope of meeting the farrier? She sighed and nodded before saying, 'Aye, grandmother, I swear.'

Seeing the Dooley family walking along the pavement towards them the following Sunday, she greeted them cheerfully and explained she was taking Betty to church.

Mrs Dooley looked at her appraisingly. 'My word, but you're *à la mode* today. Such a stylish young lady, ain't she, Davey?'

Her son, who was gazing at the pavement with his mouth slightly open, made no reply.

'I said Kate's a smart young lady.'

He nodded.

'Davey could come with yer—' Mrs Dooley prodded him '—off yer go, lad.'

'I've already been ter mass, Mum.'

'Yer can walk her there, yer don't have ter go inside.'

'No really—' she tried protesting '—there's no need.'

The rest of the Dooley family ignored her and turned homewards while Davey took Betty's free hand and walked along chatting amiably to her until they reached the church.

Standing by the gate Kate thanked him and turned to go in, then, finding him still behind her as she entered the porch, said tartly, 'I'm sure your mother told mine it's a mortal sin for Catholics to go into a Protestant church.'

'I'll take the chance,' Davey replied cheerfully. Smiling down at Betty, he pulled a blue paper package of toffee pieces out of his pocket and slid it back again, saying, 'Will yer help me through it, Betty?'

The little girl looked up adoringly before leading him through the doorway and down the aisle.

The service seemed interminable. Kate made no attempt to follow the vicar's sermon and, on glancing sideways from time to time and always finding Davey's grey eyes upon her, she quickly stared ahead. How was she going to get rid of him?

She'd seen him peeing in the alley every Saturday night whilst his brother made comments that caused his father to laugh and look up at her bedroom window. The family seemed to have made up their minds she'd be walking out with him. No one had thought she might refuse him. He was a good catch by their standards, in a well-paid trade with plenty of work in the offing. He was a very nice young man in some ways; he loved children and was kind and thoughtful to his mother, so she said. He was handsome too, there was no denying it, his beautiful eyes with long dark lashes would charm many a girl she was sure, but not *her*.

Mrs Dooley would be offended if she refused him, in which case she wouldn't be so keen to mind Betty whilst she collected and delivered the mending. Then what would she do? Mr Drew would frown on a small sister being dragged along, especially one who might throw a tantrum in the emporium.

She peered sideways at Betty who was sitting between them looking angelic; could the beastly child know what she was doing?

The vicar drew the sermon to a close. 'And so, dearly beloved, I hope you will all think on these words as you go about your normal, mundane and ordinary lives during the week. Remember even the humblest of tasks can be offered up to the glory of God our father.'

After leaving the church, with Davey and Betty hand in hand alongside her, she walked homewards feeling despondent. How on earth was she going to get rid of this boy? Whilst passing the open park gates Davey saw Eric, and, saying, 'There's your brother by the pond,' walked towards him.

Eric waited for them smiling. He puffed out his chest and gestured to the young girl at his side, saying, 'This here's Daisy. Her and me'll be married one day—' he crooked his arm and pulled her hand through it '—this is the first time her dad's let us walk out together, it's a special occasion. Bye.' He led her away, strutting proudly with his head held high.

Davey offered his arm to Kate, smiling beguilingly at her.

51

'Would yer do me the honour?'

'I really don't think so.'

'Come on now, there's no harm in a walk around the pond.' He took her arm and held it through his own.

Beginning to panic, she pulled away. 'Please, Davey, I really don't want to offend you, but ...'

'May I be of assistance to you, Miss Barnes?' Hugo's voice was loud as he hurried towards them.

Davey said, 'The lady's with me, she doesn't need your help.'

'I think we should allow the lady to speak for herself,' Hugo replied, his eyes narrowing.

'Thank you, Mr Harvey—' she stepped towards him '—you are most kind. I was explaining to this gentleman that I really don't wish to take his arm. He's a neighbour and didn't intend to compromise me I'm sure.'

'I thought we was walking out—' Davey's voice wavered '—that's what my mum told me.'

Hugo looked quizzically at her. 'D'you wish to walk out with this, er, gentleman?'

She was near to tears. 'No, indeed I do not.'

Davey stood undecided for a moment, then, with quivering lips, said, 'I know when I'm not welcome.' He stiffened his shoulders and marched away out of the park.

Betty threw herself onto the grass, banging her fists and feet into the ground and screaming loudly, 'Davey, Davey, Davey!'

'Please, sweetheart—' she bent over the child and pleaded '—please come and see the ducks.'

Betty lay prostrate and held her breath until her face was red.

'Please, be a good girl.'

The little girl arched her back. Her face turned purple.

'My brother used to do that,' Hugo said.

Kate felt tears running down her face. 'I just don't know what to do.'

'We used to leave him to it—' Hugo handed her a large, silk handkerchief '—please dry your eyes, I can't bear to see someone so pretty crying.'

'But she might die.'

'No, she won't die, not of a tantrum.'

'Are you sure?'

'Yes. My naughty little brother's still alive.'

52

'Is he a lot younger than you?'

'He's one and a half years younger and destined for Oxford next year.'

'And he used to do this?'

'Frequently.'

She dabbed her eyes with the handkerchief, saying, 'Thank you, thank you so very much for your help.' Then, looking at Betty who was now drumming her heels and whose face was no longer purple, merely very pink, added, 'She used to be a sweet little thing until my mother died.'

Hugo gave the little girl a cursory nod. 'I think she's over the worst.' He offered Kate his arm and said, 'Would you accompany me to that bench over there, Miss Barnes?'

She gestured towards her frantic little sister thrashing around on the ground. 'I think I should stay with her.'

'We can keep an eye on her whilst we sit and get acquainted.' He kept his arm crooked towards her.

She stepped towards him and put her arm through his. 'Thank you, Mr Harvey, I'd be pleased to join you.'

They sat on the bench in the spring sunshine for almost an hour watching Betty as she lay on the ground refusing to get up and sit with them. Hugo did most of the talking; saying how he enjoyed working in Harvey's Emporium and explaining how one day he would take over the management of his father's shop.

When he said he must return to luncheon, she insisted she too had to do likewise without explaining she had left a meal all ready for her to cook, or that she would need to change into her working clothes and stoke the range which was temperamental and might have gone out by now.

'I'll be here same time next week,' he said and walked away out of the park.

She dragged Betty home and later, when the little girl screwed up her nose and refused to eat the beef put on her plate, she shrugged saying, 'Suit yourself.'

Jack Barnes looked aghast. 'That's no way to speak to your sister!'

'I can't make her eat it. I have enough trouble dealing with her tantrums.'

'Betty—' her father looked solemnly at her '—what've you been up to.'

'Nuffin'.'

'So why's Kate annoyed with yer, bonny lassie?'

'Her not like Davey.'

'What does that mean, lass?'

'I don't *dis*like him, Dad, I just don't want to walk out with him.'

'I see. Does Mrs Dooley know about this?'

'I expect so by now.'

'Ah well, I canna say I'm sorry, they're a bit too fond of their ale in that house. Ye'll miss the help of Mrs Dooley, she was a good friend when yer ma died—' he stood up '—I'll be off up ter the house. Mrs Burns-Leon needs me for a while.'

She was surprised at his departure, firstly because his employer had never required his services on a Sunday before and also because he was wearing his best clothes, not his chauffeur's uniform.

That night, while closing her eyes, she thought of Hugo and longed for the days to pass until Sunday when there would be another chance to meet him before sliding into the dimly lit dwelling of her dreams.

Her mother crouched down beside the body, groaning as if in agony one moment and then banging the ground in anger the next. She looked wild and tormented in her grief, and very, very frightening.

Terrified of causing the fury to be turned against her, she kept to her sleeping shelf for the following hours, except when tending the fire which must be kept alive no matter what happened.

When at last her mother slept and all was quiet, she went and lay beside the small cold corpse that had been her grandmother. The pale flesh looked and felt the same as that of a plucked bird. She was a dead creature, not hunted for food it was true, but a creature, an animal without breath or heartbeat. This was the destiny of all living beings, perhaps it was this final truth her mother railed against whilst keening and moaning. She kissed the cold forehead and held the lifeless hand for a long while.

On awakening, her mother rose and picked up the body as though it was a child, then, bidding her pick up the old woman's sleeping fleece and knife, led the way out of the dwelling and into the cave.

Opening her eyes with the memory of the waterfall sparkling in the flickering candle light fresh in her mind, she lay for several minutes feeling at peace before recalling the events of the previous day and feeling her heart thump with excitement.

Remembering it was Monday and she must hurry downstairs to the scullery and prepare for doing the washing, she quickly rose and dressed.

Two hours later, having lit both the range which had gone out overnight and therefore delayed the breakfast and the washing boiler in the scullery, made breakfast, and seen her father and brother off to work, she walked into the backyard carrying the first basket of washing.

Whilst pegging her father's Sunday shirt onto the line, she heard the door open on the other side of the partition fence and her neighbour say loudly, 'I don't want you two girls speaking to anyone in that house; we're respectable folk here and I don't want you led astray by their loose behaviour. I knew there'd be trouble. Anyone can see she's a trollop, those short skirts and that hair, looking like a boy. I knew. Oh yes, I knew!'

Betty came out, still looking morose but evidently intent on seeking out her friends next door. She went to the hole in the fence and called, 'Coo-ee, coo-ee, coo-ee.'

Mrs Dooley shouted, 'Come along in, girls,' and the door banged shut.

Seeing Betty staring at the fence in disbelief, Kate ran to her and crouched down, saying, 'Poor baby, I'm so sorry.' She went to put her arms around her sister but withdrew as the little girl spat at her.

'Come along, dear—' she stood up '—sweetheart, come on, let's go in.'

When her sister screamed in fury and kicked her shins, she lashed out and hit the child's head; then, feeling about to lose control, she ran into the scullery and sank to her knees on the brick floor. None of this would have happened if her mum were still alive. Polly would know how to handle the situation with Davey, she'd talk Mrs Dooley round, and, above all, she'd know how to cope with the beautiful child who had turned into a monster.

*

55

At midday she turned from putting clean sheets on her father's bed and looked out of the window. Good heavens! There was a young man who looked exactly like Hugo Harvey sauntering past on the other side of the road. Could he be looking for her? No, that would be impossible, wouldn't it? With a thumping heart she hurried down the stairs.

Opening the door, she went and looked out at the street. Hugo was coming towards her. 'Good morning, Miss Barnes,' he said cheerfully, then adding hesitantly, 'I'm, I'm—' he studied his feet '—I'm on my way to deliver a letter for the manager, but I couldn't resist looking for you.'

'I can't ask you in, the neighbours would talk.'

'Of course, I do understand. Could you meet me at the park later, say, seven o'clock?'

'I don't know, I never go out, I have Betty to think of—' she saw the curtains move at the house next door '—I must go.'

'Please try to come,' he pleaded, 'I'll wait at the bench by the pond until eight.' He lifted his hat, saying loudly, 'So nice to meet you, Miss Barnes,' and walked off down the road.

That evening after she had cleared away the tea dishes and her father was sitting in the sagging old armchair, she said, 'I think I'll walk round to see Tilda. Betty's ready for bed and can play here beside you until I get back.' She knelt beside her sister who was sitting on the floor huddled up in an old shawl of Polly's. 'You'll be a good girl for me, sweetheart, won't you?'

Betty spat and pushed her away causing her to overbalance and fall sideways against her father's legs. She heard his explosion of anger, felt him move as he leaped for the child and watched in horror as he grabbed Betty and scooped her up, saying, 'Go and see your friend, bonny lass, but don't be long. I'll not have you out after dark—' he looked down at the little girl dangling from under his right arm '—I'll not have a child of mine behaving like that neither,' then turned and went up the stairs.

While putting on her coat and hat in the hall she heard Betty scream and hurried down the road with the sound of anguished cries ringing in her ears.

Hugo jumped up from the bench when he saw her and ran forward. 'What a relief! I'd almost given up hope and was feeling utterly wretched.'

As they meandered around the pond, he held her hand surreptitiously and, when another person came anywhere near them, he withdrew and kept one pace apart from her. On reaching the bench they sat down and he said earnestly, 'I've thought of nothing but you all day. I lied to you. I had no reason to be near your house.' He sat back as a middle-aged couple walked by arm in arm, and, when they were out of earshot, went on, 'I was desperate to see you, a driven man.'

'I suppose a lie is forgivable in some circumstances.'

'Yes, oh yes. When a chap is driven half mad to see a girl don't yer know!'

'I wonder how you knew where to look?'

He grinned shamefacedly. 'I've followed you lots of times. That's how I found you on Sunday with that uncouth lout.'

She was overwhelmed with delight but, pretending to be annoyed, said, 'I don't think you should have done that, or tell lies.'

'Only a small one, almost a white one really—' he looked around to make sure no one was near and leaned forward, holding her hand '—I'll never tell you another, I promise. Just say you'll forgive me.'

'Very well, I forgive you.' Her head swam as she squeezed his fingers.

'And you'll meet me here again?'

'I don't know, it's not easy to get away. I have my sister to care for.'

'Is there no one else?'

'Only my brother and he's not very keen to mind her. She's been really difficult since my mother died. You saw for yourself how she can throw a tantrum.'

Hugo grinned. 'I remember it well. I think your brother should do his bit and look after her from time to time—' he grinned sideways at her '—like, for example, every Wednesday.'

'Every Wednesday!'

'So we could meet like this.' He took her hand and pleaded, 'I beg you, please say you'll do it. Say you will.'

'I'll try,' she replied falteringly, 'but I don't know if he'll agree to do it.' She forced herself to stand up. 'I must go home now, my father thinks I'm with my friend Tilda and said I mustn't be out after dark.'

He stood close. 'You'll still come to the park on Sunday?'

'Yes.'

He stepped back as a man with a small dog passed by. 'And Wednesday?'

'I'll do my best. I must go.'

Hurrying home through the deepening gloom, she ached with excitement. Could Hugo, son of Mr Harvey the owner of Harvey's Emporium, be in love with her? Looking up at the moon rising over the rooftops she was reminded of her dreams. When the old woman gave her the ball of pink crystal, she had spoken of her mother. What had she said?

Stopping outside the gate of the house, she gazed up at the circle of light glowing through a thin cloud and remembered the words. 'Thy mother has no need of it for she prefers to call on the moon to help her'.

Raising her arms, she whispered, 'Oh, Mother Moon, please make him love me.'

Chapter Seven

A tea made from Chamomile flowers and leaves is calming and helps with insomnia, headaches, earache and toothache.

The sun had turned the paths to dust and the grass in the pasture to shrivelled hay, but under the willows, away from its burning glare, it was cool as she checked the traps for fish. Whilst pausing to savour the cool water swirling around her legs, she heard sounds of movement along the bank and stood still under the overhanging branches waiting to see who it was.

When the stranger walked to the river bank and stood gazing into the water she was not surprised by his presence. The woman who came regularly for comfrey salve had told her that the new Lord of all the land on the other side of the river had set his men to rebuilding the chapel. She had heard the sound of hammers as they worked the great lumps of stone and their laughter had reached her as she collected withies to make baskets, but, obeying her mother, had not ventured over the river to see the new building.

When he pulled off his clothes and waded into the water, sighing with relief and pleasure, she gasped in amazement. He was so beautiful! Until now she had thought all men looked as gross and ugly as the drowned man she had once helped her mother drag from the river.

The dust floating from him lay on the surface of the water as it swirled past her. For one terrified moment she thought his dark eyes had met hers through the dangling fronds of willow and held her breath, then, when he closed them and swam away, she breathed again. A few minutes later, when he climbed out and lay on the grass in a patch of sunlight, she gazed upon his

59

naked body in wonder and her heart lurched and thumped so loudly she feared he would hear it above the bird singing in the tree close by.

Each day she went down to hide in the clump of willow on the bend where trout were easiest to catch and lingered until either she watched the man bathe or until the light was fading. She thought only of him whilst awake and dreamed of him when asleep.

After the days grew shorter and colder he no longer came and she sometimes lingered by the leafless willows watching the water swirling and burbling below her, remembering his beauty.

When the first shoots of flowers were pushing up through the cold earth she walked at dawn to where tree trunks had been laid across the river. Although fearing her mother's anger, desire to see what the handsome man was making gave her courage and she crossed to the other bank then followed the path to the church.

The building was strange, the arches on doorways and windows curved into unfamiliar pointed shapes and there was a tower at one end with wooden ladders and walkways attached all around it. She was fascinated by the strange carvings lying unfinished all around and, whilst looking closely at one of an extraordinary face with large lips and bulging eyes, became aware that she too was under scrutiny. Gasping with shock, she saw three men watching her from within the building, two were older with greying beards, but the third, who now came out and stepped towards her, was the handsome young man who had filled her thoughts throughout the dark days of winter.

'Mademoiselle.' His eyes glittered as he smiled and doffed his hat to her with a flourish.

She inclined her head, then, panicking, turned and fled. Tearing her skirt on brambles and skidding in mud, she ran all the way back to the dwelling. Sinking down inside the doorway, she struggled to get breath back into her burning lungs ...

Betty was sitting on her chest, saying, 'Get up, get up, lazybones! Dad's calling for his shaving water.'

Later, after Eric had gone off whistling at six-thirty and her father had mumbled something about taking the Mistress somewhere that evening before leaving at seven, she was delighted to find a fat envelope lying on the doormat and, seeing her grandmother's handwriting on it, knew her birthday had not been completely forgotten.

Having opened it, she smiled down at the dried leaves that had fallen from it onto the floor. Then she unfolded the letter and read aloud, 'My dearest Kate, I enclose some rosemary to put in the rinse when you wash your hair. I hope to see you before too long, the years are passing and now you are a young lady of eighteen, no doubt as beautiful as your mother. I often think of you and wonder if you have had any special sights. Do not forget your promise to me. I am well at present. Albert sends his. Your loving Gran.'

Would Hugo approve of the sight? She'd never dared mention it: he might think she was mad. He wouldn't want to marry a lunatic would he? Not that he had mentioned marriage, not yet.

She showed the dried rosemary to Betty, saying, 'Look what Gran sent me from her garden.'

The little girl stared blankly at her.

It was her birthday and it was Wednesday, not even a miserable little sister could lower her spirits. She sang happily whilst turning the cuffs and collar of a silk blouse for an elderly lady and ignored the hunched little figure sitting on the floor close by.

This evening she would see him and they might kiss again behind the shrubbery; the last time they had done so she had been stirred into desperate, deep longings. His gasps for breath as he held her so close she could hardly breathe, had excited and stimulated her body in an inexplicable and unimagined way. She knew ladies acquiesced to men's base feelings when they married and this led to babies being born, she knew because her mother had told her. She hadn't known a lady might also have these same desires, perhaps *ladies* didn't and she was a trollop as Mrs Dooley had suggested. It was all very perplexing and exciting at the same time.

Eric came home and devoured the meat pie she had made whilst Betty ignored the sausage cooked especially for her and stared at the wall, kicking her heels against the chair legs. 'Cheerful little bugger, ain't she?' Eric asked, and they both laughed at their small sister.

Betty hurled the sausage at Eric.

He was a broad-shouldered young man of sixteen with arms strengthened by his work and he clenched his fists menacingly at

61

the child as he said through gritted teeth, 'I don't want to hurt yer, little lass, but if yer do that again, I'll bloody beat the living daylights out of yer!'

'You will still mind her for me this evening, won't you, Eric?' Kate asked anxiously.

He shrugged. 'I suppose I can't say no. I don't know how yer cope with her. D'yer think she's half-witted?'

'I don't know what to think. I suspect she's quite bright really, but it does wear me down. You will keep minding her for me, won't you?'

'Yeah. For a while, so long as I'm still living here I'll do it.'

'D'you mean you might leave home?'

He grinned sheepishly. 'I want to marry Daisy as soon as I can. There's something else too, but yer'll have ter promise not to tell Dad.'

'All right, little brother, what's the big secret?'

'We want to go to Canada.'

'You and Daisy?'

'Yeah, lots of her family are there already. They went there from Scotland; her father came to London instead. We want to go as soon as we can get married.'

'But, but, Eric, you're only sixteen!'

'I know it's young to marry, but there'll never be anyone else for me and we're old enough by law.'

'Not without Dad's permission. You have to wait until you're twenty-one to marry without his signature.'

'You could help persuade him.'

She sighed. 'I doubt he'd even hear me. I don't know what's got into him lately.'

Eric chuckled. 'I do. I saw them together on Saturday evening at the fair on the common. They were arm in arm and laughing together like lovers.'

'What? Who?'

'Our dearly beloved and respected father's got a lady friend. She looks a bit young for him I'd have said, but then who'm I ter talk?'

She sat silent for a few moments before exclaiming, 'That's disgusting!'

'Yer can't blame him, Kate love, he's a human being after all, ain't he?'

'Mm, I suppose so.' She looked at the clock on the mantlepiece.

'It's almost ten to six; you'll stay and mind Betty for me?'

'Yeah, I'll try not ter strangle the little perisher!'

On her arrival at their usual meeting place in the park, Hugo stepped forward, his brown eyes shining with delight as he exclaimed, 'What an age it's been since I kissed you! I've thought of nothing but holding you again.' He glanced around to make sure there were no onlookers and put his arms around her.

'People will see us,' she said nervously. 'If my dad knew what we were doing, he'd take a strap to us both.'

Hugo groaned. 'That's nothing to what my old man would do, but to hell with them all I say!' He bent and nuzzled her neck. Pulling her towards the bank of rhododendrons, he looked over her head. 'No one's about, quickly, come along.'

In between kisses, she asked, 'Why would your father be so cross?'

He ran his hands down her body and up under her skirt. 'Oh, he's got some silly notion about me marrying his partner's horrid little daughter.'

Although almost too overcome by the sheer pleasure of what his hands were doing, she just managed to control herself and pull away. 'What do you think,' she asked, whilst smoothing her skirt, 'of this horrid little daughter?'

'Oh, she's still a child really and very plain.' He pulled out a small package from his pocket. 'Here, I've brought you a little gift.'

'What a wonderful surprise!'

He laughed. 'I was hardly likely to forget. You did remind me it was your birthday, several times. Open it, please. I want to see what you think of it.'

She undid the string, unwrapped the tissue paper and, seeing the small, square, leather box, felt her heart thump with excitement. He had bought her an engagement ring!

'I'm afraid it's in the wrong kind of box,' he said, 'it's an old one of my sister's.'

Swallowing her disappointment, she lifted the lid and, gazing down at the small, oval silver locket, forced out the words, 'It's lovely.'

He opened it, saying, 'You can put a photograph of someone inside, or a bit of hair.' He put his arms around her. 'Do I get any thanks?'

'Of course you do.' She kissed him, then, although longing for him to caress her body as before, but, feeling she should appear ladylike, said, 'I think we should go and walk about. I don't think this is proper.' To her dismay, he solemnly agreed and they emerged from the shrubbery, having first made sure no one was watching, and sauntered along the path with a wide space between them.

They walked around the pond and sat for a while on the bench, where he said, 'The old folks are off to the theatre tonight, taking the sister and her ghastly young man with them.'

She was intrigued. 'What's wrong with the young man?'

'Oh nothing really, quite a good chap I suppose, just a mite boring. I knew him at school. His old man's a baronet. He's the first decent suitor she's ever had, so the old boy wants her married off soon. She's twenty-four and he doesn't want her left on the shelf.' He looked around, saw there was no one very close and held her hand. 'Listen, I've had a wonderful idea. There's an old summerhouse in the garden, would you like to see it?'

'The summerhouse?'

'Yes, do come and see it.'

'Whilst they're all out?'

'I just thought it might be a good opportunity to show you, you know, to see it.'

She was unsure how to react to this invitation and hesitated. What would a lady do?

'Come on,' he said, pulling her upright, 'come along, it's not far away.'

They walked quickly to the wide, tree-lined avenue close to the park where there were a few large detached houses behind tall impenetrable hedges. After looking about him furtively, he led her through a small gate, beside two wide wrought-iron ones that opened onto a gravelled drive and grimaced at the crunching sound of their footsteps as they ran to a narrow passageway between a large stone building and a tall brick wall.

Looking up admiringly, she whispered, 'Is that your house?'

He grinned. 'No, its much farther down the drive; this used to be a coach house and stables, but the old boy's motor lives in it now.' Keeping close to the boundary wall, he drew her along past a potting shed, several broken cold frames and two large dilapidated greenhouses, to where parallel privet hedges had been planted alongside the wall on either side of a narrow stone path leading to a ramshackle old summerhouse. Pulling the door open, he said, 'It leaks like a sieve when it rains. My mother plans to restore it when she has a Japanese garden laid out there.' He pointed to a tall jungle of conifers beyond which nothing of the house or garden could be seen. 'Then she and her friends can dress up like geishas and sit on the floor drinking tea out of tiny little bowls—' he grinned '—so far she's only bought the exquisite china and the kimono.'

She went inside and looked around her. All but two of the windows were broken and boarded up with rotten wood. The remaining glass, which was very dirty, allowed enough light in to make out a pile of broken old deck chairs and, in one, much cleaner corner, a neatly folded blanket. He had planned it. She should walk away. But the temptation was too strong and, when he put his arms around her then pulled her down, she offered no resistance.

After they had stroked and cuddled as usual for a few minutes, he took something from under the soft blanket behind her head. Thinking he was about to give her another gift, she waited expectantly as he turned away and fumbled for a moment before kissing her again.

He then manoeuvred himself over her and, leaning on his elbows, said, 'Don't worry, there won't be any babies.'

Suddenly understanding what was happening, she tried to push him off. 'No, we can't go that far yet, we must wait until . . .'

He was breathing heavily, kneeling between her legs as he pushed himself inside her, rapidly thrusting in and in and in again, until he shouted and groaned in ecstasy. 'There,' he mumbled, collapsing on top of her, 'I knew you were longing for it too. I just *love* a passionate woman!'

After a few moments he stood up and, while putting on his clothes, said, 'I think you ought to go, they'll be back soon.'

She stared up at him, transfixed with shock.

'Come on, you wanton hussy.' He grinned, and, grasping her hands, pulled her to her feet. 'Get dressed, my sweet.'

She stumbled and fell against the boarded window.

'I say! Steady on, old girl!—' he laughed '—I'm flattered to think that's the effect my performance has on you!'

Trying desperately not to cry, she buttoned her frock. Her

alluring, exciting petting was meant to make him long to marry her and consummate their union. He wasn't supposed to do one without the other; that wasn't what she'd expected. What should she do now?

'Come along, darling,' he said, his voice sounding more impatient, 'the folks will be back soon, don't yer know. I'll have to get back to the house.'

She peered at the dirty window attempting to see her reflection. 'Does my hair look all right?'

'Yes, yes, it looks fine,' he answered without looking.

'Shall I see you tomorrow?' she asked, fastening her shoes.

He bent and kissed her quickly on the back of the neck. 'I'll be waiting in the park as usual—' he patted her behind '—hurry up!' He opened the door and pulled her through it then hurried along the path to the passage by the garage just as a large black motor car drew to a halt outside the entrance.

'Damn!' He pulled her back into the shadows. 'The chauffeur always goes back to close the gates after he's driven the car into the garage. You'll have to wait until after he's come back. They can't see the gate from the house, so you'll be all right once he's gone—' he kissed her perfunctorily '—I'll see you in the park tomorrow.' Then turned and was gone.

She heard the car drive past and the banging of doors. No other sound followed. What should she do? He had said to wait, but not this long surely? She eased her way to the edge of the drive and saw a man in the same uniform her father wore leaning against the car talking to a maid. Feeling sick with fear, she retreated behind the bushes and waited until the sound of a car being driven into the garage was followed by footsteps crunching along the gravel, first one way then the other, and after that silence. Slowly and cautiously she made her way to the edge of the drive and, seeing no one, hurried to the small gate on one side of the main entrance and pushed through it out onto the pavement. Closing the latch she read the sign on the outside, TRADESMEN ONLY NO HAWKERS OR CIRCULARS.

Tears blinded her as she hurried home. This wasn't how she'd planned their love to be fulfilled. It should have happened in a hotel room – somewhere sophisticated like Paris. He should have removed a nightgown of white silk, one that echoed the design of her wedding dress. There should have been orange blossom in her hair and flower petals strewn on the pillows. Above all, there should have been a new gold band on her finger and, next to that, a diamond engagement ring.

Chapter Eight

The Wood Anenome or Windflower blooms when the swallows return. It may be used for headaches and gout. Bathing in water in which it had been boiled was once believed to be a cure for leprosy.

Her knife was nowhere to be found. How could she tell her mother she lost her most important possession? The leather holding the sheath onto her girdle had worn thin and must have given way as she ran from the church. She had nothing to sell or barter for another and without it she would have no way of cutting anything.

For many days she walked along the riverbank scrutinising every step of the way and looking in each clump of vegetation but found no sign of the knife. Now, knowing she must brave the men who were building on the other side of the river and seek it there, she went early in the morning to retrace her steps.

Desperation gave her courage as she walked, with head demurely downcast, up the slope towards them. One by one the hammers stopped until there was a sudden eerie silence. Turning to two men standing by large chunks of stone, she asked if they had found her knife.

They stared at her, then at each other and shook their heads. The shorter of the two was broad of shoulder and the hand he waved as he spoke his strange language was the largest she had ever seen. Others came and stood close, too close. She could smell their foul breath and malodorous bodies. One farted and the others laughed and gabbled in a strange tongue. As she stepped back a hand pushed between her buttocks and she instantly jumped forward, closer to the men facing her. The taller of the two looked

68

frightened, and the other shouted angrily and shook his fist. Two hands came around her from behind and clasped her breasts.

She screamed, 'Help me! Help me!' Before one hand moved up and covered her mouth and the other pulled at her skirt. The blood pounding in her temples drowned all other sounds as the shorter man stepped towards her.

They were staring down at her, offering a leather bottle. Sharp pains stabbed inside her lungs as she gasped for breath. How long had she lost consciousness? She sat up and took a gulp, almost choked on the strange red liquid and spat it out.

The men laughed and the taller one fetched a bucket from which she scooped some water and drank it. Then, looking around, she saw a large man lying close by with blood pouring from his nose and mouth.

'I thank thee, I thank thee,' she repeated many times to the one who she knew had saved her.

He bent over her smiling, saying, 'Up, up, sank see, sank see,' as he held out his enormous hands. She reached out and ...

Awakening to find her hand on Betty who had crept into her bed, she held her close and kissed the child's golden curls. It was only a dream! Frightening though it was, it was not real, not happening now. The problem of the present was more pressing. What was she going to do about Hugo? How could she make him understand he must marry her?

Every waking minute of the past weeks had been spent wondering what to do and she still wavered between a conviction on the one hand that he would immediately agree to their being engaged once he understood how he had compromised her, and, on the other, the belief he was biding his time in the knowledge he would need several months to persuade Mr Harvey that a girl who had been one of his own most junior shop assistants was a suitable match for his son.

Her earlier intentions of refusing any intimacy until after they were married had come to nothing. Each time she had attempted to broach the subject he had said how warm and loving she was in comparison with his sister who was cold as charity, his mother who never stopped nagging and his grandmother who had come to stay and was as mean as hell! As he unhooked her frock and pulled her down onto the blankets, he always said in a little boy voice, 'I need comfort, I need to forget my troubles. I need *you!*'

Sighing whilst getting out of bed, she admitted that all her resolutions dissolved on looking into his soulful brown eyes and was therefore unable to refuse him anything. While getting dressed she decided he would bring her a diamond ring one day, of course he would. His father would see the error of an arranged marriage, and would realise his son's happiness was of greater importance than business partnerships. He would love Kate too, like a daughter, a warm gentle daughter, who was so unlike the hard, cold, selfish young woman that Hugo despised. She'd be kind to his sister, she'd melt her icy heart and they would become friends. They would go on shopping trips together, they would be chums, bosom pals, as they went around town, the young Mrs Harvey and her sister-in-law.

Looking in the small mirror hanging on the wall, she smiled at her image as she brushed her hair. True love would conquer all; it always did, didn't it? In the meantime she would be patient and keep their romance a secret.

An hour later, whilst the family were eating their breakfast, Jack placed his knife and fork on the plate and pushed it away before saying, 'I'll be bringing a lady to tea this afternoon.'

She was remembering Hugo crawling around the summerhouse meowing like a cat the previous day and smiled. He'd said the rustling sound she'd heard outside was a mouse looking for a home now that summer was coming to an end and . . .

Jack asked sharply, 'Is anyone listening to me?'

'Yes, oh yes, Dad, a lady coming to tea.' She turned to her brother, asking, 'That'll be nice, won't it?'

Eric nodded and winked at her.

'She's a very special lady who I hope you'll all be nice and welcoming to—' Jack beamed benignly '—I'm sure you can do yer old dad proud, can yer not?'

Eric inhaled deeply and mumbled, 'Yes, of course, of course.'

Kate said brightly, 'Yes, I'll make a cake.'

At midday, as they were walking home from church, Kate and Betty met Tilda who asked, 'Are you going to meet you-know-who in the park?'

'No—' she shook her head '—we haven't met on Sundays lately. His grandmother's been staying since the middle of August and insists on him going to church with her and being at home for the rest of the day.'

'But you're still seeing him, aren't you?'

'Oh yes, Eric minds Betty on Wednesdays and Saturdays so we can meet.' She leaned forward conspiratorially. 'Actually, I ought not to stand chatting. I have to get home because Dad's bringing a lady to tea.'

'What! Walking out with her you mean?'

'Yes.'

Tilda's eyes widened as she exclaimed, 'You'd be able to come back to Harvey's if he married again!'

'Of course! I'd be free to go back to work. I'll have to make sure she likes us.' She chuckled, then added, 'How exciting! Just think I might be with you and . . .'

'And Mr Hugo,' Tilda hissed and they exploded into giggles. With a smile to the young man beside her, she said, 'It's such a lovely day, we're going for a walk. There may not be many more like this now it's nearly autumn.' Her face shone with happiness as she leaned forward, whispering conspiratorially, 'He's saving for a ring.' She looked down at Betty and frowned. 'I see you've got your miserable sister with you.'

The little girl poked out her tongue.

Tilda was outraged. 'The little madam will have to mend her ways if your dad gets a new wife!' she exclaimed and, with a toss of her head, led the young man away.

During the strained and stilted conversation that afternoon it transpired their father's friend, whose name was Violet Hendry, worked for Mrs Burns-Leon as a parlour-maid and she also came from Newcastle where she and Jack knew the same places and even had a few acquaintances in common.

When Miss Hendry rose to go, she smiled at each one of them in turn and, taking Kate's hand, thanked her for the hospitality.

For an instant the woman changed, her hair was no longer pulled back into a chignon, but cut short, and standing beside her was a small boy with golden curls and blue eyes just like Betty's. One blink and the image vanished. 'I'm so pleased to have met you,' Kate said, her heart singing with joy. Miss Hendry would set her free!

When Jack had escorted his friend out of the house, Eric muttered, 'It'll be a wedding next, you mark my words!'

71

'Yes, I'm sure of it, and soon I hope,' Kate replied happily. 'I'm longing to get back to work.'

Eric patted Betty, who was still sitting looking angelic on a chair at the table, and said cheerfully, 'You'll have a nice new step-mother soon, bonny lass!'

Betty stared unseeingly at him.

'Are yer deaf? I said you'll have a mother, d'you hear, a mother so Kate won't be forced to stay at home and put up with you.'

The little girl pushed her shoulders up either side of her neck and, with arms stiffly at her sides, walked out of the room.

'Oh, God!' Eric held his head. 'I've made it all worse for yer, not better.'

Kate smiled sadly. 'She goes into her own little world. I asked her once why she did that with her shoulders and she said, "I big."'

'How odd!'

'I suppose she wants to feel as big as the rest of us. She was only a baby when our mother died. Sometimes I think she's still looking for her. She often cries in her sleep, and she ran up to a woman in the Post Office one day and smiled at her, a most beautiful smile, Eric, you'd have been astonished, you really would.' She paused to remember the incident. 'The woman looked like our mum, with dark hair and a grey coat with a velvet collar like the one she wore for best, remember?'

'Yeah—' he swallowed '—I remember.'

'I had to drag Betty away. She can make herself really heavy so I couldn't lift her. It was awful, so embarrassing.'

'Did she cry?'

'No, just did that thing with her shoulders and didn't speak for hours.'

Eric opened his eyes wide, exclaiming, 'Oh my Gawd! Yer don't think she's like Uncle Albert, do yer?'

'I hadn't thought of that.' She was horrified. 'Something in the family you mean?'

'Could be. I've often thought she's strange. Mind you, that's no excuse for the way she treats you.' He shook his head. 'I still think she's an ungrateful little beggar. I really don't know why you're so patient.'

'But she doesn't know she should be grateful, all she knows is that her mother disappeared suddenly and she's got me instead.'

She kissed her brother on the cheek. 'Don't worry. Whatever happens, I want you to be happy.'

He grinned, 'I'll be that all right when I'm married ter Daisy. Her and me's going ter be just perfect together, I know it. I've told her the first girl must be called Katharine.'

'I'm very honoured. I'd like to be an aunt, I could make pretty frocks and take her to the ballet for her birthday, yes, that sounds a lovely idea.' She sighed. 'In the meantime we have to deal with Dad's wedding.'

'I'll bet you're looking forward to getting back to Harvey's, ain't yer?'

Glowing with excitement she agreed, adding, 'I just hope Miss Hendry's a better mother than I am!'

The following Sunday, when they were all sitting in the parlour, Jack Barnes held his shoulders rigid as he announced, 'It'll be a quiet little wedding. It's all arranged proper-like. Saturday, October twenty-first, eleven o'clock at the church around the corner from Mrs Burns-Leon's house.'

'Will she be invited?' Kate asked.

Her father gave a nervous laugh, 'Nay, bonny lass, she's far too grand for our little family—' he put his arm around his fiancée's waist '—but I'm sure she'll give us something special.'

'The housekeeper manages these things, and as I've never fallen out with her in the seven years I've been there, I should get something nice.' Miss Hendry looked at Jack across the table then cleared her throat. 'Ahem—' she smiled tightly at Kate '—I expect your dad's had a little chat with you about the future?'

'The future?' Kate repeated. 'Er, I don't know exactly.'

'The future, you know, with me living here.'

'Er, not exactly. What were you thinking of in particular?'

Miss Hendry's smile was fixed as she looked at Jack. 'I think you should explain, dear.'

'Er, yes, well, two ladies in a kitchen—' he gave foolish little smirk and shook his head '—not a good idea, bonny lass, definitely not a good idea.'

'Yes, of course.' Kate smiled reassuringly at her future step-mother. 'I'll be happy to hand over to you. I'm not really so keen on cooking and housekeeping. I love dressmaking and that's what I'd like to do eventually. I've already got lots of work,

73

doing little mending jobs and alterations.'

'Where do you do that?' Miss Hendry asked.

'Here.' Seeing the look exchanged between them Kate began to understand what was being said. 'I realise it'll be your house and you wouldn't want me working from home.' She leaned forward, eager to show consideration for her future stepmother. 'I'd be happy to go back to Harvey's; the dressmaking can wait.' A secret inner smile warmed her as she thought of Hugo; she'd be marrying before too long anyway, so all these arrangements would be unnecessary.

Miss Hendry looked pointedly at Jack as she asked, 'It's not always easy to get employment with accommodation, is it, dear?' Then, without waiting for his reply, went on, 'If you was wanting to find employment in a grand house, like Mrs Burns-Leon's, then I could put in a word. In fact there's a vacancy now for a housemaid, if you'd like me to arrange an interview.'

'Housemaid?'

'Yes, a coincidence. The poor housekeeper is very annoyed at two posts being vacated at the same time. The new lady's maid to replace me has already been selected. Her employer died, she was a friend of Madam's and very suitable.'

'Two, you said – is someone else getting married as well?' She was desperately trying to be polite.

Miss Hendry pursed her lips. 'No, more's the pity. She was found to be carrying on, not respectable, you see: Madam won't have anyone like *that* working for her.'

'Thank you, it was kind of you to think of me.' She swallowed uncomfortably.

'You'll have to be quick about it if you want it, there's many a girl after work in a house like that.'

Assuring her she was most grateful, Kate looked desperately at her brother who was slumped in the chair opposite paying no attention to this conversation, and enquired politely, 'What d'you think, Eric?'

'Pardon?' he asked pulling himself upright.

'I was saying how grateful I am to Miss Hendry for telling me about the post with Mrs Burns-Leon.'

'Which one?'

'Housemaid.'

'*Housemaid*! he shouted. 'What d'yer mean, housemaid?'

Miss Hendry's face reddened. 'I didn't mean no offence. We thought it'd be a good idea ...'

Jack Barnes clenched his fist. 'She'd be lucky to get in with such a good employer.'

'Yeah—' Eric sneered '—and she'd be living in, wouldn't she?'

Jack gripped the arms of his chair. 'She's my daughter and there's a home here for her, I'll not see her on the street, but ...' he hesitated.

'But?' Eric demanded.

Jack raised his arms and spread his hands in supplication, pleading, 'Two women in a kitchen, lad?'

'She's scivvied for you and struggled with that miserable little brat, and now you're saying that's all she's good for, is it?' Eric's eyes flashed with fury at his future stepmother. 'Our Kate's a lady, she worked at Harvey's, she's not a *servant*.'

Jack Barnes stood up. 'Eric, you'll apologise to Miss Hendry.'

'Whatever for?' He rose to his feet with arms akimbo.

Father and son glared at each other. In the small confines of the parlour there was no more than three feet between them and the smell of their sweat hung on the air.

'You'll apologise.'

'I will not!'

'Eric, you're in my house and you'll do as I say.'

'I won't be staying to tell no lies to no one!' Eric took the two steps across the rug to the door. Holding the polished brass knob, he turned and said, 'While I'm packing my things you can write me permission to marry Daisy Murdoch. You'll not be wanting me to smirch the family name by living in sin, I don't suppose.'

Kate stood up and held out her hands in supplication as she pleaded, 'Please, both of you, I beg you ...'

'Shut up and sit down,' her father shouted at her, 'I'm still master in this house. Good riddance to him!'

'I beg you, Dad, write him the permission, please, for our mother's sake.'

Violet Hendry coughed discreetly and said, 'He can't marry without it, Jack.'

'Very well, get the paper and ink.'

Kate rushed to obey him. Jack followed her into the kitchen and sat at the table, silently watching as she placed all the items in front of him. He wrote a few words, signed it and pushed it back to her, saying, 'Give that to the cocky little bugger.'

She put her hand on his. 'I don't want trouble, Dad.'

'Just give it him and be done with it. We must go. Violet has to be back by six o'clock.' He stood up. 'I know you liked it at Harvey's, best try and get back there, eh?'

Tears welled up in her eyes. 'Yes, Dad, I'll do that. I don't want to be in the way. Maybe I could rent a room somewhere near the emporium?'

He nodded and walked to the parlour. 'Come along, Violet dear, we must be getting along.'

She watched them walk to the front door and, as her father opened it, called, 'Wait, Dad, aren't you going to say goodbye to Eric?'

The door closed behind him and she was left staring along the little hallway feeling empty and wretched.

Her brother came down the stairs carrying a bundle of clothes and a canvas bag of tools over his shoulder. 'You can have my room now, Kate,' he said, putting his arm around her shoulders. 'Then you won't have to share a bed with Betty for the rest of your time here.'

'I don't care. I'd rather you could stay.'

'It's for the best. I don't want to watch another woman in our mum's place. You won't have to clean or do the laundry anymore and you won't have to go round with the little misery traipsing after you once they're married.'

'I'm very worried. Suppose she's no better with her step-mother?'

'That won't be your problem.' He held her close. 'I love you, big sister. I don't want you working as a servant for that lady muck. Can you get back to Harvey's?'

'Yes, I'm sure I can.' She sniffed, trying to stop the tears. 'You'll write to me, won't you?'

'Of course I will. I might be off quite quickly. Daisy's brother's going soon. He's been wanting me to go with him, but I thought Dad wouldn't agree.' He kissed her. 'So you see it's all working out really well for me – I can marry my girl and go to Canada!'

'What about your apprenticeship?'

'I'm as good a carpenter as I need to be.' He kissed her again. 'I wish I could take you with me. The only argument I can find against going is leaving you behind.'

Looking into his eyes, she saw him standing on the steps of a house and watching children pulling a sledge along in deep snow. The picture faded and she said reassuringly, 'You mustn't worry about me. I'll be all right.' She patted his cheek. 'It looks very cold, but I know you'll be happy.'

He walked to the door, opened it and turning to look back at her, asked, 'What d'yer mean, it looks very cold?'

'I heard the winters were harsh there, maybe I saw it in a book.'

He blew her a kiss and left the house, whistling cheerfully.

Chapter Nine

Marigold flowers have many uses. When taken in tea they are good for cleansing the blood and when in an ointment or lotion they help with rashes, wounds and burns.

That night Betty awoke screaming and lay shivering in fear of going back to sleep. As Kate held her close, crooning soothingly to her, she decided not to move into Eric's bed; she'd give the little girl as much comfort as she could for as long as she still lived in the house. There were three weeks left in which to somehow help the child get used to the new situation – in that time she must also get back to work at Harvey's and rent a room somewhere. She was sure Hugo would arrange for her to be re-employed. Perhaps he wouldn't let her go back to work at all, maybe he'd insist on their being married immediately. Whichever plan he decided on, Hugo would be delighted to find she'd be free to meet him in the summerhouse every day if he wanted, not that it was so comfortable now the evenings were drawing in and an autumnal chill was in the air.

Suddenly she remembered Eric had left. Without him she had no one to mind Betty whilst seeing Hugo on Wednesday evening and explaining what had happened. She'd write to him, he would understand, he would rush to see her and everything would be arranged to their mutual satisfaction. Her father would be pleased to know she had such a respectable and honourable man by her side. He'd seemed harsh today with Eric, but there'd always been friction between them. She, however, had proved herself to be a good obedient daughter in the past and he'd want her to be happy, of course he would!

Closing her eyes she slipped quickly into the other world.

Her mother had been watching like a hawk since the day she had returned and confessed that, not only had she lost her knife, but had almost been attacked by the foreigners. She no longer allowed her to go in search of a stray goat alone or leave the area around the dwelling without her.

The sun burned high in the sky, bright blue dragonflies hovered at the river's edge and clouds of butterflies flew over the flowers. There had been no rain for many days and cracks had appeared in the earth around the dwelling where they were stacking the sticks for kindling. Aware of someone approaching, they both stood watching until a figure appeared, shimmering in the haze of heat.

The woman came slowly up the narrow path carrying a child.

They went forward and greeted her.

She held out the small boy. 'His leg, his leg,' she cried, panting and gasping. 'Help me, I beg thee.'

They laid him on the ground with his head in the shade and looked at the hideously broken and twisted leg. Then, calmly and quietly they set to work whilst the woman sank down exhausted beside the child.

When all was done and the leg was tied within two pieces of wood wrapped in goatskin, mother and daughter looked at each other and then at the small pale face of the child who had lain motionless for some time.

'Be he dead?' the woman asked, kneeling beside him.

'Nay, 'tis the pain of it, he'll awaken soon.'

'Better he die than be crippled. My husband needs him to be strong to work the bellows.'

Her mother smiled for the first time in many days. 'Leave the boy here—' she paused for a moment '—leave him here for two full moons, by then he will be walking with a crutch but thy husband will see he is mending well. We will give him herbs to make the bone knit and help him take the pain.'

The woman kissed her son's pale forehead then stood up and said, 'I have a fine cheese I could bring thee, and a leg of pig, and a bag of ...'

'Nay.' The mother held up the knife she had been using to cut the goatskin. 'Can thy man make a blade such as this?'

'Aye.'

'Then bring one when you come for your son.'

The woman nodded and, after a lingering look at the small boy, hurried away towards the river.

On awakening and quickly dismissing the dream, Kate lay planning the letter she would write to Hugo.

Darling Hugo,

I am sorry to tell you that I have a serious problem. My father is going to marry again. This is good news because I can go back to work and I won't have to mind Betty all the time, which means we can see each other more. My brother who used to mind Betty has left home so I don't know what to do about Wednesday. I need to see you to explain the situation, please come and see me as soon as possible. I can go back to work at Harvey's when they are married, please will you arrange this for me or what ever you think is best for us and our future together. Please reply quickly, I am at my wits end.

With my love, your dearest Kate.

Getting the words right was difficult, especially how to both ask to return to the shop and also leave it open for him to argue that, as his wife, she should not work ever again. 'Whatever you think is right for us and our future together'. Yes, she decided, the wording was discreet, demure and undemanding, ladylike in fact! After posting the letter at midday she felt calmer and was composed enough to complete the last mending task in hand for the emporium. Once the work was wrapped in tissue paper ready for delivery there was nothing left to do. The afternoon slowly ticked by.

Betty, who had been unusually quiet and subdued until five o'clock, suddenly vomited all over her clothes and the rag rug by the range.

On undressing the child to clean her and seeing red spots on her chest she exclaimed, 'Oh no! It's the chicken pox! Oh damn! Damn! Damn!'

The baker had told her a week ago that two of his boys had the disease – normally she would have accepted the situation with equanimity, but the timing was the worst possible. How could she be available to meet Mr and Mrs Harvey when her little sister was ill? How do you explain to people used to servants and nursemaids that you can't leave the house because you have no one else to mind the child? She'd thought Hugo, knowing the situation and being so understanding of Betty and her tantrums, would insist on one of the maids taking care of the child whilst he introduced her to his family. Could a child with chicken pox be taken to the house and left with a servant? Of course not! Damn! Damn! Damn!

She carried Betty upstairs and put her into bed, then stood looking out of the window. Several men wearing bowler hats returned from their work as clerks. Two young shop assistants, both girls whom she had smiled at when similarly employed, walked past chatting and laughing. Seeing a large motor car draw up outside she was filled with joy. Mr Harvey had sent the chauffeur to fetch her, or perhaps Hugo himself was about to get out. The door opened and her father emerged, looking very, very nervous.

She ran downstairs to meet him and announced, 'Betty's got the chicken pox.'

'Never mind, bonny lass, she'll be over it by the wedding. I'm on my way to the station. Mrs Burns-Leon's sister's arriving for her annual visit to London. I had a few minutes in hand, so I called in to tell you the good news.'

'Good news?' she asked excitedly. Good news! Oh how wonderful! Everything was going to be all right. Hugo had been to see her father. Of course, that's what a gentleman would do! Why had she lacked faith? 'Tell me, Dad, tell me quickly. *Please, please* tell me and put me out of my misery.'

Jack Barnes smiled. 'Aye, bonny lass, you're in luck. I'm ter take yer along on the Monday after the wedding. You'll have to work hard mind. The housekeeper's firm but she's fair, and so long as you behave yerself and obey the rules, you'll be ...'

'The housekeeper!'

'You can start as soon as we're married. I'll need you to mind the bairn until then. I'm so relieved, I canna tell yer how worried I've been.'

'Oh no!' She felt sick, the hallway swirled around her and she reached out to steady herself against the wall.

'I'm sorry, lass, it's the only way. Violet, Miss Hendry that is, she thinks it would be for the best and so do I.'

'But why?'

'I think she feels she has to start as she means to go on. She needs to be mistress of the house, surely you understand that?'

'But I'd let her be in charge,' she cried desperately. 'I wouldn't interfere. I don't want to be a housewife. Why can't she just come and live with us as we are?'

'I suppose she has high standards after working for such a grand lady. She'd do things differently, that's all.'

'But she could do whatever she liked. I just need a week or two to get things straight. Once I get back to Harvey's, I could find a room somewhere ...'

'I'm sorry, bonny lass, no, you'll not be doing that.'

'Why not, Dad, why would you be so against me doing that? You could go and ask Mr Drew for me, like you did before. You know how I loved it and I only left because Ma died and there was Betty to care for and you and ...'

Jack put his hand on her shoulder and said pleadingly, 'Stop, lassie, stop.' His face was suddenly old and he grimaced as if in pain. 'I'd hoped not to tell you.'

'Tell me what, Dad, tell me what?'

'I went to see Mr Drew at Harvey's this afternoon. I was feeling bad about you being so unhappy. Playing on my mind it was. I'm in a bit of a bind see, love, I want yer to be happy, but I need a wife and Miss Hendry's made plain her terms.'

'So, what did he say?'

'Well, actually, it was the big fat foreign gentleman who spoke to me first.'

She stared at him aghast. 'You saw Mr Harvey?'

'Aye.' He fidgeted with the cap he was holding, turning it round and round between his hands. 'Just accept it'll be for the best, love. The housekeeper seems a bit strict, I know, but you'll have a roof over yer head and good food. They have quite a laugh in the kitchen yer know, nothing wrong mind, just some high-spirited larks.'

'What—' she swallowed and took a deep breath '—what did Mr Harvey say, Dad?'

Jack shifted his weight from one foot to the other. 'I really do have to meet the train soon, she's a right Tartar and I'll be in trouble if I'm late.'

'Please, Dad, what did he say?'

'I don't know the exact words like, with him being so posh and all, but it was something like, they're going to employ older assistants from now on, more steady and reliable, that's what he said. A new policy, is what he called it, very *definite* he was. I'm sorry, bonny lass, I did my best for you.' Taking a piece of paper out of his pocket, he went on, 'He gave me this. I don't remember exactly what he said. Then Mr Drew came and said as they wouldn't be needing any more mending from yer and he'd be obliged if I'd post what's in hand to him.'

Staring at the large white five-pound note in her father's fingers, she opened her mouth but, finding no words formed in her mind, watched silently as he replaced the note in his pocket.

Jack squared his shoulders. 'Let's make the best of things, Kate lass.'

'But ...'

He ignored her and continued, 'The housekeeper's really being very generous to you, she usually likes good references yer see.'

'Good references,' she echoed. 'Harvey's would give me that, wouldn't they?'

'I don't think so, love. Mr Drew made it all very clear. Apparently a lady complained about you for being impolite.'

'That old hag, Mrs Hartwell. All I said was ...'

'It don't matter what yer said, love, they've got yer down as not suitable and what with the giggling and gossiping and, and being a bit *flighty* like.'

'*Flighty*! Did he say that?'

'Well, yes, as a matter of fact that was the word Mr Drew used. I had a bit of an argument with him on that one. And, and I don't like to tell yer, lass, but they'd rather yer didn't go in being familiar with the staff, it makes for a bad impression, that's what he said.'

Uncontrollable tears poured from her eyes.

'There, there, lassie.' Jack attempted to hold her.

She pulled away from him and ran up the stairs into her room, slammed the door behind her and sank onto the bed sobbing.

Betty stirred and lay watching her with glassy, feverish eyes, but made no sound.

Chapter Ten

A tea made with Rosemary soothes headaches and is good for the digestion, poor circulation and chilblains. It is also used as an insecticide and hair-rinse.

Seeing the new Mrs Barnes smooth the skirt of her powder-blue dress and gaze fondly at her husband who was nervously fingering the starched collar of his shirt, Kate felt a sudden rush of emotion. This woman seemed to really love Jack and he was blushing like a young man, maybe they would be happy together. Glancing around the room and, seeing Betty standing quietly beside the small glazed china cabinet with the cracked glass door, she recalled her mother being carried from the room shortly before she died. Then, remembering her sister now had a stepmother to look after her, she smiled affectionately at the little girl. Soon she would be free to see Hugo again, everything was going to be all right now!

'Hang that up for me, there's a dear.'

Turning to find a middle-aged woman holding a fur coat towards her, she politely took it from her and carried it upstairs, where she laid it on the bed and then stood for a moment listening to the hubbub of voices as the guests arrived below. Glancing at the mirror of her mother's dressing table, she grinned at her reflection. Once this day was over she could leave her father and his bride to get on with their life together and she could begin to live hers.

Feeling more hopeful and self-confident than of late, she returned to the parlour and handed food around to the three servants from Mrs Burns-Leon's house, an old friend of Jack's and his wife, and the woman whose coat she had put on her father's bed, who was introduced to her as Jeanie and who talked very loudly about the weekend she had recently spent at a country house in Surrey.

On going into the kitchen to replenish the teapot she was followed by Jeanie who said, 'I hear you're going to work for Mrs Burns-Leon.'

'Yes.' She filled the teapot with hot water from the kettle gently bubbling on the stove.

'Been in service before have you?'

She smiled stiffly, feeling irritated by her manner. 'No, I worked in a shop. I gave it up to mind my sister.'

'Butchers, bakers or candlestick-makers?'

'Harvey's, d'you know it?'

The woman nodded and smiled while responding sympathetically, 'Bit of a comedown for you, is it?'

'I'm used to nice clothes and talking to ladies ...' She stopped, realising she'd said too much. 'Mrs Burns-Leon is a very good employer, my father worships the ground she walks on.'

'Yeah, I used to work there, before I bettered myself.'

'That's nice for you.' She was feeling increasingly disconcerted.

'Mmm, that was before I become a lady's maid.' Jeanie's lips curved in a smile, but her eyes remained cold and watchful. 'The grey uniform what the housemaid's wears is definitely a comedown when you're a bit la-di-da, ain't it?'

'No, I'd just prefer to be a shop assistant, that's all.' She was now very, very uncomfortable.

'Mm, I can understand that. I'd say serving in Harvey's is preferable to emptying chamber pots, any day of the week.'

She pretended to be engrossed in fitting the teapot lid.

'Not to mention the *restrictions*. Being below stairs is a bit *restricted* like, if you live in, that is.'

Although now thoroughly ill at ease, she felt compelled to reply, 'Really?'

'Oh yes, very restricted.' Jeanie sniffed and dabbed her nose with a lace-edged handkerchief. 'Mrs Burns-Leon don't like loose behaviour, did you know that?'

'I, er, I'll remember that.' She picked up the teapot. 'I really think I should take this ...'

'For instance, she wouldn't like no larks in her summerhouse.'

Feeling a cold thump of shock go through her chest she let go of the teapot, spilling its contents over the rag rug.

People came running from the parlour. Jack and his bride stood looking shocked whilst a young woman named Millie ascertained Kate was not scalded and offered to help her clean up the mess.

Jack herded the other guests back to the parlour and Violet said, 'Come along, Jeanie, you were going to tell us about Mr Harvey's daughter giving you the fur coat.'

Kate knelt on the floor mopping up the liquid.

Millie picked up tea-leaves whilst saying, 'I'll be seeing you soon then?'

'Yes, yes of course. I'll be there on Monday.'

'Yeah, I'll look out for you.'

'I'd be really grateful.'

Millie smiled. 'The housekeeper's a bit of an old dragon, but the rest of us is all right.' She pushed the armchair to one side causing the mending basket behind it to fall upside down on the floor.

A moment later Jack stood in the doorway, his face bright red except for a line of white around his mouth. Looking down at Kate who was still on her knees, he said through clenched teeth, 'This little brat has, has—' he reached back and pulled Betty into the room by the scruff of her neck '—let me down. Why did yer not teach her manners?'

'I've tried, Dad, I've tried.'

Betty held her breath and fell forwards, rolled onto her back and went purple in the face.

Jack shouted, 'Do something!'

'It's best to ignore her, Dad.'

'Are you mad? She's been ignoring everybody including my new wife, and yer say, ignore her!' He stood over Kate, his fist clenched. 'I'm that embarrassed, bonny lass, that embarrassed.'

She felt sick. 'I can't do anything with her, Dad.'

'I'm newly wed to a beautiful young wife and all me children have let me down. Eric's left his apprenticeship and gone to Canada, this little brat doesn't know how to behave in company, not even today of all days! I don't know where to turn.'

Violet appeared behind him saying, 'Most of the guests have gone, dear—' she surveyed the room then looked down at her silk dress '—I'll get an apron on and clean up a little.'

'But it's yer wedding day, bonny lass!'

Millie looked embarrassed and departed.

Focussing on the dusty mantelpiece, Kate admitted she had

scrubbed no floors, waxed no wood, nor polished any brass during the six weeks waiting for Hugo's response to her letter.

'Wedding day or no, Jack dear, this—' Violet gestured around her '—isn't what I'm used to.' Looking behind the armchair at the upturned basket and its scattered contents on the dirty floorboards, she gave a small sound of exasperation and began picking up reels of thread, balls of wool, needle cases and a pincushion.

Seeing several folded pieces of paper, Jack picked one up and read aloud, '*I collected some feverfew this morning, it being such a beneficial plant for headaches.*'

'Those are my letters from Granny.'

Jack looked furiously at her. 'I thought I told yer to stop this nonsense.' He sat down heavily in his armchair. 'Get out of my sight the pair of yer.'

Bending over Betty who was now lying quietly staring at the ceiling, she whispered, 'Come along, sweetheart, we'll go upstairs for a bit.'

Betty obediently followed her to the door where she rolled her eyes and poked out her tongue towards Violet.

A small nervous chuckle erupted from Kate's throat.

'Come here!' Jack shouted. 'Come here, both of yer!'

She returned to stand on the wet rug whilst Betty hung back in the doorway.

'That child's a wild animal and when she makes rude faces at her stepmother what do *you* do? Bloody laugh!' He turned to his wife and lowered his voice, saying in a placatory tone, 'I'm sorry, dear, I'm so sorry. You must be so shocked, not being used to such ill-mannered goings on.' He held his head as if in pain.

Violet's eyes met Kate's momentarily before she cast them down. 'I admit I am shocked, my dear. Very shocked indeed. I was also very shocked by something *very shocking* what my friend Jeanie said.' She stood by Jack and patted his shoulder 'You remember her, my dear, she's the one who used to work with us and has been lady's maid to Miss Harvey for at least three year now.'

Jack was surprised. 'Course I do, bonny lass, I'd hardly forget her seeing as she's only just left.'

'Well, I've just been chatting with my friend Jeanie, who must be mistaken I'm sure.' She simpered down at her husband. 'Apparently a young girl, very similar to your daughter in appearance, has been keeping company, well, I don't know how to put it ... Has been seen behaving in a very *unladylike manner,* let us say, with young Mr Hugo Harvey.'

'What d'yer mean?' Jack asked.

'Apparently, this girl, the one who looks like, er, Kate, has been the laughing stock of the Harvey household, below stairs, that is, for months. She's been going into the old summerhouse with him and behaving, well, I don't like to repeat what Jeanie said the gardeners saw. It's really not proper for a lady to know about such things.'

Jack stood up and looked into Kate's eyes as he demanded, 'Well, what d'yer have ter say for yerself?'

She opened her mouth, but no sound came out. She saw her father leap up towards her with his hand raised. She heard voices screaming in the distance and saw a burst of flashing stars explode in the darkness ... *the stars became circles of light around candle-flames illuminating the lady in the rocks with water trickling down the front of her. Kneeling down she dipped her hand into the pool as red as blood. 'I have a promise to keep,' she said.* Then, opening her eyes, found she was lying on the floor looking up at her father.

'I can't tell yer—' Jack swallowed '—I don't know how to explain. That Harvey must've known when he gave me the fiver.' He wiped his eyes with the back of his hand. 'It's been a terrible wedding day and no mistake.'

Betty walked hesitantly into the room and looking down, asked, 'Are you dead, Kate?'

Trying to smile reassuringly she sat up and replied, 'No, love.'

Jack sank into the armchair. 'I don't know what ter say, I don't know how I can bear it. The Harvey lad of all people! How could yer go and ...'

'But he'll marry me when he's persuaded his father, Dad, it's just a matter of time.'

'Dear God! Yer a bigger bloody fool than I thought!'

Violet stared unblinkingly at her while saying, 'I'd like a word, Jack, in the parlour.'

When they had left the room she pulled herself up into the armchair and lay back with her eyes closed trying to make sense of the jumbled thoughts crowding her mind. One idea kept returning amidst the muddle – she must make contact with Hugo.

Someone, somewhere, somehow had prevented him from receiving her letters. Once he knew her predicament then all would be well.

On their return a short while later, Jack Barnes said firmly, 'We've come to a decision, lass. We think the sensible solution is for you to go and stay with yer grandma.'

'What! I can't do that.' How was Hugo going to find her there? 'I'll go into service, I'll be any kind of maid you like!'

Violet pursed her lips then said primly, 'Mrs Burns-Leon has very high standards. She won't have no loose females in her house.'

'Yes—' Jack agreed '—it's out of the question.'

'And the other decision—' Violet smiled brightly '—is your sister can go with you for a while, just until we're settled.'

Chapter Eleven

Dandelion leaves may be eaten raw or used to make a tea. Good for kidney and bladder complaints.

'You said I'd come back, Gran.'

A fleeting look of anxiety crossed the old woman's face. 'You should be in bed, Kate, you've been very poorly. That blow to your head, what nobody has explained, but I assume was your father's doing.' She sniffed with disapproval. 'That *mysterious* blow, did you no good. By rights you shouldn't have travelled as you did. If you'd damaged your brain, there'd have been nothing I could do.'

'My brain!'

'Aye, you never know with the head. I've seen some bad ones in my time. I want you taking things quiet for a few days.' Nodding at her son who was sitting in the corner, she commanded, 'Bed, Albert!' She pressed her hands on the arms of the chair and pushed herself upright. 'These damp days do make my screws worse. I'm stiff as a preacher's collar!' When she was standing, bent forward with one hand on her lower back and the other leaning on the table, she said, 'I mun put the lamps out when you'm all upstairs, now let's get you each a candle.'

'I can do the lamps, Gran.'

'I don't want no accidents, my lover, that paraffin's a wonderful boon but 'tis very dangerous. I don't allow Albert to touch it since he near burned the house down.'

'I'll be very careful; that could be my task, whilst I'm staying with you. I want to be useful while I'm here.'

'You think you may not be here long?'

'I don't know, I mean, well—' she felt the hot blush colouring her face '—things may change.'

'Your father wrote there was a trouble of some sort; that usually means with a young man.'

'It may just be a misunderstanding—' she avoided her grandmother's steadfast gaze '—perhaps—' she hesitated '—perhaps he didn't receive any of my letters. He was away somewhere and . . . I don't know.' She pointed to the brass lamp with the glass funnel above it. 'I'm sure I could learn to do that.'

'Very well, tomorrow you can help me. And you—' the old woman looked down at Betty '—my little lover, can put the candles ready for us all on the kitchen table each night before you go to bed.' She opened a cupboard door and withdrew a china candle-holder decorated with a pattern of pink flowers, saying, 'This one is very special, you can have it just for tonight.' Smiling fondly at Kate, she added, 'I remember you had it the first night you came last time and you carried it like it was the crown jewels.'

'Yes, I remember it very well.' Kate bent towards her sister. 'It's so pretty, isn't it, sweetheart?'

Betty yawned and looked away.

The old woman kissed Kate's cheek. 'You used to like putting the candles ready for us all. That's why I thought she'd enjoy doing it—' she sighed '—but I'm beginning to think she's a selfish little madam.'

'She's had a difficult time, Gran.' Kate looked down at Betty who was staring fixedly at the floor and willed her to be more engaging.

'Losing your mother when so young is hard, but she's had you to look after her. I think she's a lucky little girl and she really ought to be grateful to you.' Seeing her son step forward to take his candle, an eager smile on his handsome face, the old woman patted his shoulder. 'What a good fellow you are, Albert.' Turning to Betty she said, 'Come along now, *early* to bed, *early* to rise, makes us all *healthy*, *wealthy* and *wise*!' and smiled brightly at her.

The little girl made no sign of having heard her and Kate crouched beside her saying, 'She's very tired.' Adding anxiously, 'Just say "goodnight" to Grandma and Albert, sweetheart. *Please* be a good girl and say "goodnight"'.

Betty stared unblinkingly at the wall.

'Is she half-witted?'

'I don't know, Gran. Eric thought she might be: she's certainly very, very awkward. I don't know what to do; I was hoping you might know how to handle her.'

The old woman nodded and said resolutely, 'I never had no trouble with none of mine and I don't expect none from my grand-child neither!' She held the pretty candleholder towards the child, adding firmly, 'You carry that upstairs for me, there's a good girl.'

Betty took hold of it and immediately dropped it onto the stone floor.

The others stared at the broken pieces of china, Albert's eyes filled with tears and his lips quivered whilst his mother's hung slackly open and Kate gave a low moan. Betty looked unmoved.

'I've carried that to bed with me for over forty years. Your Granfer won it at Pridden Fair before we were married ...' giving a strangled sob the old lady pointed at Betty, then croaked, 'Get her out of my sight.'

Kate half dragged, half carried her sister upstairs and, having quickly undressed her, put her to bed in the little room across the landing from hers. Almost falling over with exhaustion, she whispered, 'You horrible little ...' Unable to think of a word bad enough, she shut the door and crossed the expanse of polished wooden floor to her own room and sat on the bed wondering if the child really had dropped the candlestick deliberately. She had hoped her grandmother would form an immediate and inseparable bond with Betty and take over the burden of caring for her. It seemed the very opposite had happened and there was a deep antipathy between them. A sob escaped and she pretended to cough just in case anyone could hear through the walls.

Soon Hugo would send for her, he would arrange for a nanny to look after her sister after they were married and they would all live in harmony. He did love her. She had only to wait for him. The heavy lids slid over her eyes and she was instantly asleep.

The little boy was improving each day, but was still frightened of being left alone and therefore she and her mother took turns to forage for food.

On the fourth day, as the sun was sinking over the hills, she went to the river and waded towards the traps. Reaching down into the water, she suddenly scented the young man. Turning her head slightly she caught a movement in the willows and knew he was watching her as once she had spied on him. This was the moment to flee. She knew it but did not go. Instead she pretended to think herself alone whilst killing the brown fish and replacing the trap.

Wading back to the bank, holding her skirt high above her knees, she stared straight ahead at the roots of the tree close to where she had left her basket. On reaching the bank she climbed out, placed the fish in the basket and then cried out in fear as something landed with a thud beside her. Seeing it was her knife lying on the grass, she turned and looked towards the clump of willow. As the fronds of green parted to reveal the naked young man, she stepped forward.

Walking towards his glittering eyes she knew her body was part of the natural order of procreation. She wanted his penetration as the doe accepts a stag or the nanny receives a billy-goat.

He took her in his arms then pulled her down to lie with him beneath the willow.

In offering herself up to pain she found unexpected delight followed by exquisite ecstasy and, when he eventually shot his seed into her, she moaned aloud with pleasure.

Remembering the dream the following morning, she wondered if making love could ever be like that in real life. It certainly felt nothing like that with Hugo.

After climbing out of bed, she went to the window and saw heavy white clouds hanging like a pall of smoke over the hills above the cottage. There had been a time when she wanted only to see this view on getting out of bed every day, but now it meant nothing and she longed for the streets of London where she would be close to Hugo.

When both she and Betty were dressed, she reached for the door and, seeing the little doll wrapped in a white handkerchief lying on top of her suitcase, picked it up and carried it downstairs.

Her grandmother looked up smiling as she walked into the kitchen and greeted her lovingly, 'You looks a deal perkier than yesterday, my lover, but you'd best take it easy for a while. Sit down and I'll get the breakfast.'

She sank into the large Windsor chair and leaned back feeling light-headed.

The old woman put a large iron kettle onto the range and then indicated towards the window, saying, 'On mornings like this I'm glad to be here and not at the farm.' She placed a loaf of bread on the table, adding, 'It's nice up top when you'm able to see all the way to Glastonbury Tor but when they'm in mist I prefers to be warm and cosy down here. Your granfer were born at Pridden; he loved it whether he could see the valley or no.'

'It's sad he died so young.'

'Quiet and kindly he was, not a gentleman but a gentle man. Near broke his heart knowing there's no one to follow on—' the old woman sighed and looked out of the window to where Albert could be seen searching under the hedges for hen's eggs '—he never come to terms with our youngest being different.'

'Did he like my mother?'

'Polly was the apple of his eye. Her could twist him around her little finger, even more than Jane our firstborn and he *doted* on her.' She bit her lip. 'I thought his heart would break when her went to America and then when her died . . . He never got over it, never.'

'Did you give Jane a poppy-doll when she left home?'

'I did indeed.'

'Look, Gran, I've brought mine with me.'

'Oh my lor!' The old woman exclaimed, beaming with delight as she reached out for the doll. 'Here, let me see.' Then, having kissed it, she reached into an alcove behind the range and pulled out a linen bag, muttering, 'I knew, I knew.' She pushed the doll into the bag. 'Her can rest along mine and Albert's.'

Kate watched as the bag was replaced in the chimney then asked, 'Is that where you kept Mum's?'

'Aye. For all the good it did me,' her grandmother replied. Then, bending and opening the oven door, she added, 'The bread's ready, would you call Albert and Whatsername, please?'

'And Betty,' Kate said gently. 'Yes of course, I'll call them.'

During that day, whilst sitting on the sofa in the kitchen she watched her grandmother receive several visitors and either place her hands on them whilst chatting about their ailments, families and local gossip or fetch some dried herbs from the larder for them. All these callers left an offering of some kind and by three o'clock, a jar of Wortleberry jam, a fruitcake and a small packet of Indian tea had been added to the larder shelves, and a dead rabbit was hanging outside the back door.

When Alice arrived at half-past three, looking bloated and weary, they reminisced about the happy times they had had at the village school. After wistfully saying how they had whiled away the summers together during Kate's earlier stay with her grandmother, she looked down at her swollen body and added, 'When I heard in the shop that you're here I thought I'd call in before the baby comes.'

Kate chuckled. 'The news is out already.'

'Oh yes, it's the main topic of conversation. Everyone's agog to know you're back and wondering—' she blushed '—wondering how long you'll stay.'

The old woman's eyes narrowed and her mouth tightened as she said, 'You can tell that mother-in-law of yours, my granddaughter's not in the family way.'

Alice looked uncomfortable for a moment and then, obviously wishing to avoid the subject, smiled brightly at Betty who was sitting at Kate's feet looking miserable.

The little girl ignored her.

Alice stood up, one hand on the table and the other on the small of her back. 'Would you come and see me in Pridden, when I've had the baby?'

Kate promised she would visit her soon.

A few moments later, watching her friend waddle down the path in her shabby old coat, she murmured, 'Poor Alice.'

'Aye, you can say that again!' The old woman replied. 'She's tied to that young ne'ere-do-well, silly girl.'

'Teddy Nelson was considered rather dashing when we were at school.'

'*Dashing* bain't much use for putting bread into children's mouths. But I has to admit he stood by her when her was in trouble and he do seem to be settled down now they'm married. He's working for the tenant of our farm up top and they'm living in the tied cottage out by the old lead mine.'

'That's very isolated, poor Alice, she'll be so lonely!'

'Her'll be glad of a friend like you, my lover, her life's not going to be a bed of roses.'

Kate nodded sadly, realising as she did so that for just a short while she had forgotten her own problem.

That evening, the old woman looked across the kitchen table at Betty who was staring fixedly at the floor, and asked, 'Are you going to bed soon, my lover?'

The child gave no sign of hearing her.

Looking up from the letter she was writing, Kate said brightly, 'Grandma's speaking to you, sweetheart.'

There was no response.

'Please, dear, try and be a good girl. Be nice for me, dear, please.'

Her sister continued to ignore her.

A red spot appeared on both the old woman's cheeks. 'I think her needs a good walloping. I've been ashamed all day at the way her's behaved when people have come to see me. Mrs Parsons looked very put out. I'd have larruped one of mine if they'd carried on like that.'

'I don't know what to do, Gran. I've tried smacking her and Dad took a strap to her once, but it did no good.' The memory made her wince with horror.

'I told Mrs Parson as you'd been sewing in London and her said as the mistress was wanting some dressmaking and so—' the old woman smiled proudly '—I've said as you'll go next Monday morning to see her.'

'Where's that, Gran?'

'The Grange.'

'That's where the kind man lived.'

'Mrs Parsons don't call him that. Her's told me a few tales of drinking and such like, when he's at home that is, goes away a lot, to America I think. Very fond of her mistress, Mrs Parsons is, says her's never been the same since the boy died.'

'Oh no! Was he ill?'

'There was an accident, drowned in the pond whilst his father was away at the War. Terrible it was.'

Remembering the kind gentleman saying how loath he was to leave his little boy and his beautiful wife, she felt very sad until, with her mind returning to her own problems, she looked down and read what she had written. 'Dearest Hugo, I am in Somerset now and very, very miserable. I think you have been away and may not have received my earlier letter. I wonder how you are and long to hear from you. Grandma is being very kind to me and Betty is being difficult as usual. With my deepest and undying love, your Kate.' Raising her eyes and seeing her grandmother watching her, she asked, 'Are they very rich?'

'Them Wallaces? Well, they was once 'tis true, but I don't know so much nowadays.' The old woman sniffed disapprovingly. 'Been selling off the land for three generations they have. Only the house and thirteen acres left, and most of that be the woodlands up behind us. Hankeys Land be no use to nobody, nothing but goats ever done well there, 'tis all so steep and stony.'

Remembering Eric shrieking with laughter and calling it 'Handkerchief Land' she wondered if he was happy in Canada and imagined him tobogganing in the snow.

Her grandmother opened the door of the black metal range and put a shovel of coal onto the flames. 'Mind you, they'm rich enough to pay for you to do their sewing so that's good enough for me.'

Chapter Twelve

A tea made with Eyebright can be used as a lotion for inflammation of the eyes and conjunctivitis.

Emerging from the cottage into the wintry sunshine, Kate inhaled the scent of a few pink roses still in bloom outside the door and, thinking of her dead mother who had loved them, ached with grief. Wiping away the sudden tears, she went through the gate and turned right along the lane beside the tall hedge enclosing her grandmother's garden.

To her left, open fields bordered by hedges formed a pattern of interlocking rectangles stretching for many miles with little sign of habitation other than a few clusters of farm buildings. On her right side, at the end of the hedge, a high wall marked the corner of the Wallace property, and rising above it, could be seen thick and tangled woods that joined with the vegetation on the hillside above Old Myrtles. On reaching the wide wrought-iron gates she opened a smaller one at the side, remembering a similar arrangement at Hugo's house and how, time after time, she had stood fearfully waiting to leave without anyone seeing her.

Walking along the drive following a curving line of tidily clipped yew, she thought of her lover and wondered how soon he would reply to her letter. And also, how long she would have to stay here. Rounding the end of the hedge, she gasped with pleasure at the beautiful stone house festooned with Virginia creeper on each side and wisteria dripping from a long balcony at the front, before knocking on the enormous wooden door.

A maid wearing a black frock with a starched white apron and a frilled cap on her head led her through a spacious hallway into a large sunny room overlooking the garden, and told her to await the mistress.

Standing by the carved stone fireplace, she looked around her in wonder at large oriental vases, a chaise-longue with a vividly embroidered silk shawl thrown over it, several beautifully upholstered chairs and a Persian rug that she longed to kneel on and stroke with her hands. Seeing two portraits hanging on the walls either side of the doorway, she gazed admiringly at them. One was a lovely fair-haired young woman in a white frock reaching her ankles, and the other was the man she had met by the oak tree on Hankeys Land four years earlier, who looked out from the canvas with smiling, deep-blue eyes beneath shining brown hair and his long fingers curled around a riding crop.

Turning to examine the two ornate silver frames on the mantelpiece, she knew the photographs – one of a tiny baby in a flowing lace gown in his mother's arms and the other of a small boy in a sailor suit smiling roguishly at the camera – were pictures of the son who had died and felt sad.

The door opened and a small slender woman, looking vulnerable and frail, crossed the threshold and introduced herself as Mrs Wallace. 'I need silk blouses and small things, nighties, undies, those sort of things. Can you do that?'

'Yes,' she responded eagerly, 'and I can make little drawings to show you the style, if you'd like to explain what you had in mind?'

The faded face bloomed into a smile. 'I think we might get on, you and I.' A gold chain bracelet with a padlock shaped like a heart jingled as Mrs Wallace patted her short fair hair. 'I've been unwell for some time, but now I'm so much better, I've resolved to be more in fashion. We made an expedition to Bath in the motor car, not a pleasing experience. I find it makes me queasy.' She frowned. 'Where was I?'

'Bath?'

'Ah yes. I had my hair cut off, very long it was. My husband was so upset; my crowning glory he calls it, well, *called* it I should say. We did visit a dressmaker there, but although I'm so well now, I really can't be forever traipsing.' She shook her head and tightened her mouth in disgust, saying, 'The train is so dirty and one has to change at Evercreech as there's no direct line to Bath. And—' she looked hopefully at Kate '—I do so hate the motor.'

'I can make anything you wish, anything at all. We'd need to get fabrics and threads, but if I went to Bath I could get samples for you to choose from. Would that suit?'

'Such initiative! Yes, yes that would be perfect.' The bracelet jangled as she clapped her hands and called out, 'Lee, Lee where are you?'

A large plump woman of middle years with an agitated expression appeared through an open door, as though she had been hovering in attendance. 'I'm here, madam, I'm here.'

'Arrange with the housekeeper for this young lady to have the train fare to Bath.' She turned and inclined her head gracefully then left the room.

After receiving the money for her expedition, Kate hurried out of the house then walked along the gravelled drive imagining herself living there with Hugo and sauntering through the gardens hand in hand. When a motor car drove through the gates disturbing this delightful dream, she stepped to one side and then, seeing the driver raise a shining metal hook at her, stood transfixed in horror. She had known he was injured, had expected him to have lost his hand, but nevertheless the metal glinting in the sunlight where the long fingers should have been still shocked her. On reaching the gate she turned and saw Mr Wallace standing by the car. He had seemed so strong and kindly under the oak tree, and so sad when he said, 'We're soulmates, you and I.' Was that only four years ago? It seemed like another lifetime and now here she was desperate to get back to London and he, poor man, had not regained the happiness he left behind.

On her return to the cottage, after describing the interview with Mrs Wallace she asked, 'Did you know her before the child died, Gran?'

'I didn't *know* her, like, not being of the same class as you might say, but her come to church of a Sunday and was always civil. She's rarely left the house since, poor lady. Very tragic! They say he drinks and he's been seen in his car with a woman from Wells.' She shook her head. 'All I knows is he roars about the lanes in that monster, churning up the mud in winter and the dust in summer, frightening us all out of our wits. They say the poor lady do suffer with her nerves, but her wouldn't come to the likes of me.' She sniffed and looked askance. '*Ladies* go to the doctor in Wells.'

Having seen several smartly dressed women sitting at the kitchen table in earnest discussion with the old woman, she said, 'Some

100

ladies do come to see you, Gran, don't they?'

'That's true, my lover, but they don't come for the remedies, as a rule.'

'For a look into the future?'

'Aye. Whether they'll be married to a rich man, poor man, beggar man or thief!' She sighed. 'I could tell them a lot more'n I do. Sometimes I wish I didn't have the sight, sometimes 'tis a burden, the knowing of what's in store.'

'I can't see my own future, Gran, that's the one I really want to see.'

'Seeing your own's the most difficult of all and not to be tried for.' The old woman smiled. 'I recall saying much the same thing years ago when you was playing the fool casting spells with your friend Alice.'

'We wanted to see our one true love on May morning.' She ached, thinking of Hugo. 'I'd really like to know what's going to happen.'

'I know, but we don't see our own future, not deliberate, though sometimes we get a little taste of it so to speak. You has the gift born in you, Kate, and the right way for seeing into others' future will come. I sees looking at hands but my gran said her grandmother used to scry in a pink marble ball, talked about it often her did on account of it being lost when her grandmother died. Her way, my gran's that is, was that fishing float—' she pointed to a green glass ball tied around with string hanging in the window '—her looked in it and told me my fate when I was leaving to marry your granfer. I hadn't found myself yet, just past fifteen I was.'

'What did she tell you, Gran?'

'Her said as how I'd come back here to this house and I'd know much pain and sorrow but happiness also. One child would stay by me, that's what her said, *one will stay by you, my lover*. Her didn't say all the others would leave me, or the one who stayed would be simple, *just one would stay by me*. Do you see what I mean?'

'I think so. My mother didn't have the gift, did she?'

'No, my Polly didn't, well, that's to say her wouldn't admit to it. 'Tis my belief there's degrees of it, and I think her was more *knowing* than most people. I never felt I had the gift like my grandmother did, her truly was a wise woman. The only one I've known since who had the full knowing, was our firstborn, Jane. Her could

101

hold something belonging to a person, a ring maybe, or anything they'd worn regular and her'd know their past and future like an open book. The dearest, sweetest girl her was, and you'm the image of her, the very image.' She held Kate's hand. 'Accept whatever destiny holds, just as my dear Jane did. Take happiness and enjoy it while it lasts. The years of youth are so quickly over, gone in a flash. Aye, a long life means there's plenty of time for looking backwards later.'

'That sounds rather dramatic! Do you think I'll run off with a handsome stranger like my mother did?'

'No, no, your future's here. I knows you thinks love be far away, but bide your time. Remember you belongs here, my lover, right here!' She looked at Betty who had fallen asleep on the sofa and put her finger to her lips. Then standing up, led Kate out into the garden and down the path towards the dell. On reaching the stone slab jutting out at the bottom of the ivy covered cliff to their left, she stopped and said, 'I showed you this place before you left, remember?'

She nodded.

'This be our secret. Do you swear?'

'I swear, Gran.'

Pushing into the ivy the old woman parted it and stepped through into the darkness.

Following behind, she heard her grandmother fumbling with matches and on seeing a flame ignite a candle, gazed around the domed cave.

'My gran remembered her grandmother keeping cheeses here on account of the even temperature. That was when they still kept goats of course.' The old woman walked to the far corner and fumbled with the rocks until one slid sideways then stepped through the gap and lit six candles which she placed on rocks at intervals around the edge of the cave. Then, taking Kate's hand, she led her to stand looking up at the female figure kneeling before the pool as red as blood. ''Twill be your turn to keep the secret next and maybe your daughter after that.'

'But what if I don't have a daughter?'

'Then it'll be some other girl from the family, I dunno for sure, all I knows is that's what we'm sworn to do.'

'I don't really understand why we go on keeping it secret. I mean, there's no foreign invaders nowadays is there?'

'I suppose folk would ruin it and make a circus of it, I dunno. All I know is we'm sworn to keep it.'

Scooping some water in her hand, Kate said, 'It's not at all red, it's just the rock that makes it look that colour.'

'Aye, that's why nobody knows 'tis what I gives them in their remedies.'

The old woman pointed to a long oval piece of rock lying on the ground, saying reverently, 'Under there be all they women going back and back into the long ago.'

'Why are they buried there?'

'I suppose so their spirits keep watch, I don't rightly know, I just knows that's what we do.' She looked into Kate's eyes. 'I wants to be put there too when my time comes. You understand?'

'But how?'

'You do as I did for my mother, you buries the coffin in the churchyard all regular like and then—' she patted the large flat slab of stone '—you puts me in here and we'll all be happy. D'you promise?'

Thinking of Hugo in London, she said, 'Suppose I'm not here when you die?'

'You'll be here, my lover, you'll be here.'

Chapter Thirteen

A tea made from the Deadnettle or Archangel may help with both women's menstrual problems and men's prostate problems.

Dalrymple's Physic Garden – what a strange title! Kate pulled the large book off the shelf and laid it on a table nearby. This was the first time she had ventured into the reference room of Wells public library and she looked around nervously before opening it. Inside the thick cover, protected by a sheet of tissue paper, was an engraved picture of a portly gentleman with flowing white hair and moustaches. On the next page was written, 'A herbal of sorts wherein the good housekeeper may find plants from which cures for many ailments can be obtained. Published London 1808'. The book was over one hundred years old!

Turning the pages she was entranced by the beautiful engravings of familiar plants and read with increasing excitement the accompanying descriptions and medicinal uses of each one. Remedy after remedy was similar to those made by her grandmother. Feverfew was one of Gran's most popular remedies and there it was with the words: 'An infusion of the flowers or leaves may be taken for the relief of headaches, colic, indigestion, cold, influenza, alcoholic poisoning and release of women's courses'.

The purple loosestrife growing by the river was one of her favourite flowers and she was excited to read: 'An infusion of dried flowers in hot water will ease a sore throat. Also can be used in the cleaning of wounds.'

The raspberry leaves Gran collected for pregnant women were listed as 'beneficial in childbirth and women's pains'.

Knowing she still had shopping to do and had also left Betty with her grandmother, she reluctantly left the room and took the books she wished to borrow to the desk. Smiling nervously at the librarian, she asked, 'I was wondering if there might be a copy of Dalrymple's Herbal that I could take home to read. Is that possible?'

The small woman looked with interest through the thick lenses of her gold-rimmed spectacles and replied, 'No, that is far too valuable to let off the premises, but you may come and spend as much time as you like reading it.'

An hour later, having fetched her bicycle and put shopping in both the basket fixed to the handlebars and the one on the little rack over the back wheel, she was about to ride home when the librarian appeared at her elbow, saying, 'I do hope you will come and see the Herbal again, it really is so fascinating. I hope you don't think me presumptuous, but I see that you always take my favourite authors.'

Looking down at the books in her basket, she answered, 'I've only just discovered Harrison Ainsworth and I'm looking forward to *The Tower of London*.'

They talked about other historical novels for a few minutes until the librarian coughed nervously and said, 'I am a little intrigued. I hope you'll not think me forward, but you are the first person who has ever shown any interest in Dalrymple's Herbal and I wondered if you share my fascination with nature?'

Feeling in awe of someone so knowledgeable and well read, she nodded. 'Yes, I love to walk up top and to help my grandmother in the garden.'

'Up top?'

'Yes, that's what we call the hills above my grandmother's house. I walk for miles sometimes, up through Hankeys Land and beyond to Pridden, then back down again through the valley to the old mill. You can see the cathedral here in Wells, and across the moors to Glastonbury; sometimes, when it's been wet and then warm, the Tor rises out of the mist like an island.'

'That sounds delightful. I wish, I mean, I should love to see that.'

'It *is* delightful, especially at this time of year. There are wind-flowers in the woods and primroses and the bluebells will soon be blooming. I walk for miles sometimes without seeing another living soul, apart from my little sister who I have to take with me.' She hesitated before adding, 'You'd be most welcome to join us on one of our Sunday walks. We go out at two o'clock for about two hours. I collect plants for my grandmother and just walk, sometimes I feel could go on wandering round the earth forever, it's so beautiful.'

'I could ride on my bicycle to your house.' The small thin face bloomed with colour, then her animated expression faded. 'I do have Mother to consider – if she needs me to stay with her, I shall be unable to come.' She held out her hand. 'So remiss. I did not introduce myself, Margaret Simpson. Please, call me Margaret—' she gave a small squeaky laugh '—except in the library, of course. It wouldn't do there, no, the head librarian would not approve of such familiarity, but in private, let us use Christian names.'

On her return to the cottage she found her sister waiting at the gate looking tear-stained and fretful. Taking the child's cold little hands in hers, she asked, 'Were you worried about me, sweetheart?'

Betty nodded and clung to her.

The old woman was sitting at the kitchen table, kneading dough. Her mouth was working anxiously and there was a red spot on each cheek. Without looking up, she said flatly, 'None of my family ever carried on so. Either children today be different, or her's not right in the head, just four years old and answering me back! I'd take a belt to her if her was mine. So embarrassed I was. There's Mrs Fraddon comes asking me to lay out her mother. Old Kate's been hanging on by a thread for twenty year, out of her wits for most of that time as well, but it still comes hard to lose yer mother and I'm trying to give comfort to the poor soul and the little minx is sat under the table whining and screaming.'

Betty ran up to her bedroom, slamming the door behind her.

Guessing the little girl had misunderstood the conversation, and thought it was her own sister who had died; Kate followed and sat on the bed holding her until she fell asleep.

Returning to the kitchen, she sank onto a chair, saying, 'I'm sorry I left her with you for so long, Gran. I forgot the time.'

The old woman looked across the table, her lips becoming fuller and eyes softening. 'I was getting anxious, 'tis not like you to be so late.'

'I found a book in the library called a Herbal. I wondered if you'd seen it.'

'A book, my lover, why should I see that?'

'It has some of the plants you use in it, and there's a description of remedies, almost the same as yours.'

'I don't know why anyone would write such a thing, we all just *knows* it, we don't *read* about it.' The old woman chuckled. 'Come to think of it, I don't know as my old granny *could* read!'

That night before falling asleep and dreaming of the earlier life-time she imagined a book of her grandmother's remedies illustrated with paintings of the plants.

Day after day she had waited by the river but the beautiful man had never returned. Longing to see him had almost overcome her fear of the other builders, but not quite, and she had therefore not crossed the river to seek him out.

This was the second full moon since the small boy had come to them, his mother would return to fetch him before long and bring the knife to replace the one she had confessed to losing but which had lain hidden in a hollow tree near the river since the foreigner gave it to her. The days were shorter now and she spent every waking moment collecting berries, making cheese or drying fish for the cold hard winter ahead.

Soon she would bring the goats down to their winter paddock by the dwelling and already she had stored all the rough feed they would need until spring. All this she had done with her mother's knife, for, although she had tried to tell her mother about the hand-some man, she had been unable to do so, and, whilst wishing to pretend she had found the knife, somehow the moment for telling such a lie was never quite right.

The woman came early in the day to fetch her son. Her face shone with delight as she saw the little boy hop forward on his crutches and cried, 'Jan, my baby, my love!'

When the boy had shown her how he could now milk a goat and make a basket of withies, the woman made ready to leave. 'Here—' she handed each of them a leather bag '—thee's earned my husband's gratitude. Should thee ever need more he has set up a smithy close by the new church.' She shook her head sadly. 'He'll miss the foreigners, they were always wanting one thing or another made. He'll be relying on local trade now the building's finished and the masons have gone.'

The green trees, the rock face and the stone dwelling built against it all merged into a grey blur. 'Gone?' she asked.

'Aye, only our own men be left. All they foreigners be gone to work on the girt big one in Wells.'

'Wells?' Her spirits rose.

When the woman had left, proudly following the boy as he hopped along ahead of her on the narrow path, mother and daughter stood in the sudden silence and looked at each other.

'Our lives will be quiet without his merriment, Mother.' She swallowed rising tears then added, 'I grew to love him like a brother.'

'Aye, and I confess he was like a son to me—' the older woman stepped forward and held her close '—but there'll be a girl-child to take his place come spring.'

On awakening, Kate found her face was wet and knew it was from tears of joy. Then, remembering her meeting with the librarian the previous day, hoped she would keep her word and come for a walk. How wonderful it would be to have a friend who was so educated and so clever!

When the librarian arrived at two o'clock on the following Sunday afternoon, Kate was delighted and eagerly led her up to Hankeys Land.

While passing by the great oak tree, Margaret said, 'I'm so glad you find the Dalrymple interesting.'

'I had no idea people studied plants like that.'

'Oh yes, there have been many herbals. The first one I know of was printed in the seventeenth century.'

'The seventeenth!'

'Yes, that was Mr Culpeper. I could try to borrow a copy of the eighteen twenty-six reprint from another library for you to examine. It's much more complicated than Mr Dalrymple's.'

'I might not understand that so well,' Kate replied. 'People like me just need a picture of the plant, with a description of where it grows and how to use it. Actually, that gives me an idea – I love drawing flowers, shall we take some home and draw them together?'

Margaret shook her head. 'Sadly, I have no aptitude. I prefer to write poetry. But I'd like to see your artistic endeavours.'

'They're not as good as I'd like and I'd be rather embarrassed.' Kate smiled shyly. 'I'd like you to come home with me and taste

108

Granny's elderflower cordial, that I do know is good!'

'Your grandmother might not like a stranger coming into her house.'

'She wouldn't turn a hair. People come and go all the time, she holds court in the kitchen with the stockpot bubbling and the bread baking.' Hearing a loud scream she looked around for Betty and then, seeing the small girl lying at the foot of a tree in a clearing nearby, she ran to her. Kneeling beside the unresponsive child, she saw a man come crashing through the undergrowth from the other side.

'Has she fallen?' Mr Wallace asked, kneeling beside her and, keeping his right arm close to his side, placed his left hand on Betty's wrist.

Struggling to control her agitation, Kate answered, 'I don't know. I feel so awful, she must have run ahead while I was talking. I should have been watching her.'

Margaret joined them and, leaning over the child, blew gently on her eyelids. Sitting back on her heels, she said, 'Nothing wrong with her. She reacted to that, you see. If she was truly unconscious, her eyelids wouldn't have moved.' She picked up Betty's wrist and tickled her under the arm.

The little girl sat up, red in the face with fury and screaming, 'I hurt! I hurt!'

The three adults rose to their feet, looking embarrassed.

Kate could only keep repeating, 'I'm so sorry, I'm so sorry, I'm so sorry.'

Mr Wallace grinned. 'Don't worry. I'm very pleased she wasn't injured.' Raising his hat, first to Margaret and then to Kate he bade them good day and walked away into the woods.

When he was out of earshot Margaret said, 'Bounder!'

Betty brightened and stood up, obviously interested in this information.

Kate was intrigued. 'Why d'you say that?'

'Because that's what he is.' Margaret's mouth formed a tight straight line. 'I don't gossip.' She looked in the direction in which Charles Wallace had departed and sniffed disapprovingly. 'Let's get on with this walk, shall we?'

On arrival at the cottage, Kate introduced her to the old woman, who was eagerly awaiting the comfrey leaves she had requested. 'I need to make some salve and 'tis the only ingredient I lacked, bless you, my lover!' She pointed to a pot of molten lard on the range. ''Twill make a potent strong smell, I fear.'

Kate fetched the elderflower cordial and the two young women, followed by the sullenly silent Betty, went into the hallway that now served as Kate's workroom.

Margaret looked at the array of garments in various stages of completion, and then at the drawings pinned to the wall. 'I had no idea,' she enthused, 'I didn't know how talented you are!'

Kate set a small posy of wild flowers on the table. 'I'll draw these before they droop. They last such a short time once they've been picked.'

'I've an idea for a poem. Might I trouble you for something on which to write?'

Ignoring the loud snort from Betty, who had positioned herself under the table, she produced pencil and paper for them both.

After almost an hour and a half Margaret looked up, yawning. 'I must go home, Mother will be wondering where I am. I'll finish this little piece and bring it to show you next Sunday, if I may?'

'Oh yes, please do. I've so enjoyed today,' Kate said. 'I've started drawing these primroses and I'll be planning all week what to do next; there are so many flowers beginning to show themselves.'

'Yes—' Margaret smiled '—at this time of year everything is beginning to bloom in such profusion, you will have an *embarras de choix*, *n'est ce pas*?'

Having no idea what the words meant, Kate nodded enthusiastically, hoping it was the correct response and then, when Margaret had departed, went to her room and picked up the dictionary she had bought in a second-hand bookshop on her last visit to Wells. The room was too cold to sit for long and, having been unable to find the word immediately, she decided to continue the search in the warm kitchen.

When the old woman, who had been dozing on the sofa, awoke and went to put the kettle onto the range, she looked to see what Kate was reading and exclaimed, 'Dictionary!'

'I'm looking something up, Gran.'

'What?'

'Ombera.'

'I never heard of that. What do it mean?'

110

'I don't know—' Kate felt the embarrassed blush flood her face '—it's the only word I can remember in a kind of expression of some sort and I felt foolish for not knowing.'

'When you was with Margaret, I suppose?'

'Yes.' Seeing her grandmother's mouth tighten, she explained, 'Sometimes I wonder what I'd be doing now if we hadn't gone back to London and I stayed at the school. I only wish to seem more educated, Gran. I feel so ignorant sometimes.'

'Aye, my lover, you might be a teacher now—' the old woman sighed '—but then there's no undoing the past. If there was, my Polly might be alive and Whatsername wouldn't be hanging like an albatross round your neck.'

Betty emerged from under the table and threw herself at Kate who, shocked by the sudden impact on her windpipe, gasped for air and began to choke. Unable to speak or do anything other than struggle for breath she accepted a drink of water from her grandmother. A few moments later, hearing a door slam upstairs and footsteps stamp on the floor above, then the metal frame of the bed clang as her sister dived onto it, she swallowed painfully and croaked, 'It was an accident. She banged my throat. She didn't mean to hurt me. I think she was showing me she loved me.'

In the following silence it was apparent that the old woman now disliked Betty even more.

Chapter Fourteen

A tea made from Cleavers helps with any illness where the glands are swollen such as mumps or tonsillitis. Also it is good for skin conditions and cystitis.

The tiny baby was the most beautiful creature she had ever beheld. More exquisite than the pale pink rose, more delicate than the white blossom on blackthorn or the windflowers in the woods. This fruit of coupling with the stranger was her jewel and her treasure, and, looking into her mother's tearstained face, knew that she too was in an ecstasy of joy. 'Shall we name her Caitlin, Mother?' she asked.

'Aye, the name of thy grandmother will do her well.' The woman stood up, saying, 'I shall cook the afterbirth for thee to eat.' Looking down at her daughter and granddaughter, she bent and touched the baby's head, then added, 'Being born under the new moon be a good portent.'

Awakening to bright sunlight shining through a gap between the curtains and the scent of bread baking, Kate realised she had slept longer than usual, quickly arose and went down to the kitchen.

'I dreamed I had a baby last night, Gran. A little girl named Caitlin.'

'That's a good name. I'm glad you still gets them dreams of long ago. I had them too when I were young; and one in particular that were powerful strong. I still recall it well.'

'Tell me, Gran.'

'I were in the cave lying beside the pool. My daughter had lit a fire for me and brought me food. but I could not eat. I lay looking up at the lady in the rocks and I knew I was dying of a plague and

112

all I could think was that my girl must live for if she died then there'd be no one to carry on. I watched myself from above. I looked down on my poor body and knew I were dead. Then, I sort of floated upwards into the sky and went into a dark tunnel all velvety and black. There was a little star shining at the end of it that grew bigger as I got nearer to it and then I woke up.'

'D'you think that's what dying's like, Gran?'

'I do, for I've seen it in other dreams of other times also. 'Tis why I never have been feared of death.' The old woman turned, opened the door of the oven and removed a loaf which she then placed on the table. 'One thing I can say is, living in that time were not easy. No, not at all. There'd be no range to cook on, only a fire pit in the little hovel—' she tapped the crust on the loaf '—and no oven to make bread neither.'

An hour later, whilst Kate was collecting the breakfast dishes in order to carry them to the scullery for washing, her grandmother looked up, saying, 'Bye the bye, The schoolteacher came yesterday while you were at market. You remember her?'

'Miss Gregory?'

'Aye, had a terrible winter with her chest she has. I've tried everything I know but that cough don't ease even now and 'tis the first day of June.' She nodded her head towards the little girl under the table, adding, 'Her said as Whatsername could start school next spring. I warned as the child be difficult.'

Peering down at her sister, Kate said, 'Yes, Betty will be five in March.' She'd be back in London by then of course, but it was best to humour Gran. Hearing a loud knock on the door, she went to find a young man in dark-blue uniform holding a yellow envelope towards her and gasped. Hugo had responded at last! The months of waiting were over. Taking it from him, she ripped it open and stared at the words in horrified silence before handing it to her grandmother who read aloud, 'Father took bad Stop Come soonest Stop Violet Barnes.'

When the telegraph boy had left on his motorbike and whilst the machine could still be heard whining into the distance, she said, 'I'll have to go and help his wife.' Turning to her grandmother, she asked, 'Can I leave Betty with you for a few days?'

The old woman's face fell. 'I don't know. Her's upset poor Albert.' She shook her head doubtfully. 'I don't know; I really

113

don't know.' Adding, with averted eyes, 'I suppose we *could* manage for a day or two.'

One and a half hours later, settling back into the seat on the train she thought about the telegram. What could be wrong with Dad? Influenza maybe? Bronchitis? This wasn't the time of year for either complaint. His leg might be playing up. A man in the village had shrapnel lodged in his back; maybe it was the same problem? Whatever it was, this was a perfect opportunity to make contact with Hugo. Once he knew she was back in London he might have the courage to stand up to his father and declare his love for her. Looking at her reflection in the window she frowned – her hair had grown in the eight months since leaving London and was now tied back in a bun. What would Hugo think of her old-fashioned appearance?

On arrival at the house that evening, she was disconcerted when her stepmother opened the door and looked blankly at her.

'It's me, Kate.'

'My goodness, I didn't recognise you! Come in.' Violet led her into the kitchen and sank, with a sigh, into the sagging armchair. Placing both hands over her swollen belly, she said, 'It's come at a bad time.'

'The baby?'

'No, the accident.'

'What sort of an accident?'

'The motor car ran off the road. He was taking the mistress to see her sister, in Surrey somewhere, Hindhead, it's called. She goes every year in the spring, well, it was a bit later this year; usually it's April but ...'

'The accident?'

'She's all right. Madam, Mrs Burns-Leon, I mean. Her leg was broke they said, but she's all right. Bertha, her maid's all right too.' She sniffed and looked at her hands, apparently studying them very carefully. 'Funny really, I've never liked her, not good enough for Madam in my opinion. I always think ladies' maids should be a cut above the rest. Take my friend Jeanie, she was my superior for three years before she went to the Harvey's, really ladylike and genteel, taught me a lot she did.'

Trying not to sound impatient, Kate said gently, 'You were telling me about the motor car.'

'It went over an embankment or something, down into a place called the Devil's Punchbowl. Jack said it's famous. Have you heard of it?'

'No.'

'Nor me neither 'til I worked for ... it's no good.' Violet's eyes were dull and her face blank. 'It's no good pretending.' She pointed upstairs. 'He went an hour after I sent the telegram. They brought him home—' she waved her hands in the air '— I don't know when. A week ago, I think, maybe less. He was all cuts and bruises, but he hadn't broken nothing, his bad leg was giving him gyp, but that was to be expected, wasn't it? He seemed all right, well, not *all right* if you see what I mean. He was poorly and stayed in bed, said his head hurt a lot, yes, he kept saying it hurt and got very crotchety with me. Very nasty indeed he was, shouting and calling me names and that, then yesterday his eyes went funny, then he went to sleep and was snoring very loud. I didn't know what to do. Mrs next-door was very kind, she sent for the doctor, but he couldn't do nothing for him – said his brain was damaged and gave me a bill. How'm I going to pay that?'

Feeling a cold, hard, tightening in her chest, Kate went to the bedroom and looked at the figure lying in the big bed. The left side of the waxen face was bruised and his mouth hung open. She'd had a sight of him. He'd fallen into a valley of trees just as she'd seen it. My Daddy, my Daddy! A deep well of tears rose up within her and she knelt beside him weeping. He'd stopped her going to school, had been difficult and demanding at times, and he'd hit her before sending her away, but, when all was said and done, he was her father and despite everything, she loved him.

Mrs Dooley came in the following morning and helped lay out the body; she also arranged for the undertaker to come and measure for the coffin. She was very helpful but politely distant and formal until, as she was leaving, she said, 'My Davey's engaged to a nice girl. Very respectable she is, really respectable.'

'I'm so pleased, I hope he'll be very happy.'

For a second the old kindness flashed in the neighbour's eyes. 'I once thought it'd be you, Kate.'

'I wouldn't have been right for him. He deserves to be happy. He's a good, kind man and she's a lucky girl.'

115

Mrs Dooley swallowed, brushed some hair away from her eyes and departed.

Violet ate when food was put in front of her and did whatever was suggested to her, but otherwise she either slept or sat staring into space. When told that the coffin was ordered and the burial was arranged for two days later, she nodded vaguely, and when asked what she would do or how and where she would live, she shrugged and went back to sleep.

Kate began cleaning the house, and, whilst dusting the mantel-piece, moved some letters behind the clock. On seeing there was one addressed to her, she tore it open and read the familiar rounded hand with delight, 'Dear Kate, I'm very happy now I'm here and a married man. The winter is colder than you can imagine and the snow is deeper also. We are staying with family until the spring when we shall build our own house. Everything is made of wood so I am sure of work and Uncle Jim owns a timber mill. Please write to me soon. Eric.'

She found the writing paper and ink in the usual place and wrote a reply. 'Dear Eric, I am so sorry to tell you Dad died. I am staying with Violet until after the funeral and then I shall have to hurry back to Somerset because I have to care for Betty.' Until now she'd clung to the possibility that her father would one day send for the little girl leaving her free to be reunited with Hugo. She paused and read the words aloud, 'I have to care for Betty.'

She chewed the end of the pen before adding, 'I don't know what will become of Violet, she is having a baby soon and will not be able to afford the rent of this house.'

Writing helped her to think what she must do and she continued, 'I shall try to help her before I return to Somerset. Perhaps she can go back north to her family. I shall go and see Dad's employer. I am so pleased you are happy. Please keep in touch. Your loving Kate.'

She looked at the clock, it was already five minutes past five and Hugo would be leaving the shop soon. Without stopping to think she grabbed her coat from the hall and went out into the street unaware of the leaden sky or spots of rain spattering the pavement. Her head cleared as she walked along through the gloomy drizzle – should she be staying in, withdrawn and in mourning? She *was* grieving, definitely she was, but the desperate need to see Hugo

116

was even stronger than the painful loss of her father.

By the time she arrived outside the staff entrance to the shop soon after half past five, the rain was falling steadily and, ignoring her lack of umbrella or mackintosh, she waited doggedly, despite the rivulets running down her neck.

Several members of staff who came out through the door at six o'clock looked at her, exchanged whispered words and averted their eyes. Then Tilda emerged, put up her umbrella, stopped still for a moment, hesitated, squared her shoulders as if in resolution and walked past as though she was invisible until, after several paces, she turned and walked back again. 'Kate! Listen to me.' She looked around anxiously before continuing, 'He's engaged to be married.'

Rain was running down onto her nose and then dripping off the end of it. 'Engaged?'

'Mr Hugo's going to marry the daughter of the shop owner, W.D. Driscoll. You know, the ladies' outfitters.'

Staring at Tilda through the rivulets running down her face, she echoed, 'Driscoll's!'

'Yes, they'll be amalgamating. Harvey and Driscolls they'll be called, so Mr Drew says, he's absolutely overjoyed. I must go now.' Touching her wet shoulder, she added, 'I'm truly sorry about your dad. Everyone's really shocked and sad. I must go now. I'm meeting my fiancé tonight to plan our wedding.'

For a moment Kate saw a plump woman gazing fondly at four children whilst a large man carved a joint of meat on a table laden with food.

Tilda looked anxiously into her eyes as she asked, 'You won't make a scene, will you?'

Shaking her head she turned and retraced her steps through the rain-soaked streets. Then, standing in front of the small garden gate, she looked up at the leaden sky in which there was no sign of the moon she had asked to make Hugo love her. Had the request been granted? Possibly it had and he still loved her while accepting that duty and happiness do not always go together. Should she have asked for him to want to marry her? Might she now be engaged to him if so? Had she condemned the poor man to dream of her for the rest of his life?

Leaning her head back she allowed the raindrops to run down her face for several moments. Making a wish to the moon might

117

be more complicated than she had thought, or, possibly, it had no effect at all on anything. But whatever the truth of it was, her own dream was over. Gran was right: her destiny awaited her in Oakey Vale.

Chapter Fifteen

Garlic is good for the circulation of blood, for colds and for treating worms in children.

Oakey Vale 1928

The little girl had lain with eyes like glass as the fever raged and wracked her body for three nights and days.

Distraught with fear and worry she held the limp little body close to her heart, willing God to take her own life and spare her daughter.

When her mother first tried to take the child from her she resisted, but eventually, in desperation, she relented and followed her as she carried the child into the cave. Then, obediently fetching dipping rags into the red pool when told, she watched her mother place them on the child. Hour upon hour throughout the night the cloths were dipped in the cold water until the shallow breathing deepened and the fever was gone.

She carried Caitlin back to the dwelling and laid her on her sleeping shelf wrapped in fleece. The child, flesh of her flesh, born from her own blood four summers since, would live.

Awakening from the dream to find herself drenched in sweat, Kate got out of bed and poured cold water from the china jug on the washstand into a matching bowl. Then, whilst washing her body, went over and over the agonising experience of watching her daughter go to the brink of death.

The sky was still dark and the birds were not yet singing. Knowing she would not go back to sleep and feeling the need for fresh air, she crept downstairs and out through the glory hole. Without thinking where she was heading she went up to Hankeys Land and then down to the gorge by the old mill where she had often collected roots from the marshmallow growing by a spring that fed a tributary of the river below. Walking aimlessly a little way along the gully, she ached with loneliness. The suffering in her dream had left her feeling drained and isolated. If only she had someone to share her present life, someone to father a daughter who could carry on. Looking up she saw the full moon above the trees and, on impulse, held up her arms and called out, 'Oh, Mother Moon. Where is the love I long for?'

The sky began to lighten and a lone robin sang its first song of the day in a nearby tree. Lowering her arms, she sank down onto a large flat rock beside the stream. In winter after heavy rainfall it would become a gushing, burbling torrent running off the land down into the valley and onwards to the sea, but at this time, after an unusually dry May, it was shallow and slow.

The peace and tranquillity of the place with only the sound of birds awakening and singing all around her, fed her spirit, and, gradually, she relaxed. Her eyelids grew heavier and she yawned, leaning forward resting her elbows on her knees. Her eyes were out of focus as she looked sleepily into the almost motionless water. Suddenly lightning flashed overhead and thunder reverberated from the other side of the hill. A shape formed amongst the reflections and for a moment she saw the figure of a man. Her automatic reaction was to look behind her, but she was alone. Turning back to the water, she briefly saw the image of a broad, square-shouldered figure with a mass of white hair, before it was disturbed by splashes of rain and was gone.

On returning to the cottage, she found her grandmother standing by the range stirring a saucepan of porridge and quickly told her about the experience by the stream.

The old woman's eyes were milky with memories as she said, 'That'll come true, my lover, you mark my words. 'Twill be when you least expect it. I saw my man long before we ever met. I never tried for it, mind. The sight of him just come to me one day when I were twelve.' She continued stirring for a minute, her mouth working in private pain, then, looking up, she went on, 'You'm doing well with the sight, I never seen no one do better with the tea-leaves and there's nothing I can tell you about the plants.

120

And—' she carried the saucepan to the table '—as for the healing, well, you'm better'n my old granny and that's saying sommat!' Hearing Albert approaching through the glory hole she gave a small smile and whispered, 'Remember the fireweed, remember that.' Then, loudly and cheerfully, she told him to come and eat his breakfast.

Three hours later, having left her bicycle in Wells for a puncture to be mended, Kate was walking towards Oakey Vale when a car screeched to a halt and Charles Wallace offered to give her a lift home. After climbing in and explaining she had been delivering an evening frock to a client when the front tyre had suddenly gone flat, she attempted polite conversation, saying, 'Everywhere is so lush, so green.'

'Including my lady oak?'

Her heart lurched. He remembered that day. Soulmates he'd said they were then – did he remember that too? 'Yes.' her voice sounded strained and she took a breath 'Yes, she's in full leaf now,' then sat silently as they drove along the lane to the village.

On arrival outside the cottage, he stared ahead out of the windscreen and said, 'Not very communicative today, sorry about that.' He climbed out, walked around to open the car door and explained, 'Alcoholic poisoning, I'm afraid.'

She thanked him for the ride.

He doffed his hat and opened the gate for her. 'I've been away for a while and it's nice to be back. I hate to miss the summer here.'

She had a sudden intense desire to hold him. His throat seemed very beautiful and she longed to place her lips beneath his Adam's apple. 'Did you go far?' she asked, gripping the wooden gatepost.

'America,' he replied, 'I have an old school friend there . . .' He closed his eyes and groaned, 'Lacrima Christi! I have the mother and father of all hangovers.'

Seeing the beads of sweat on his pale forehead, she took the white handkerchief from his breast pocket and caressed his brow with it. Then, realising what she had done, stepped back, saying briskly, 'My granny could give you something to help.'

'Really?' He reached out his left hand towards her, held it in mid-air for a moment and raised it to his head. 'I knew, I mean, I've heard you both do fortune telling and our housekeeper comes to you for help with her indigestion.' He swallowed, looked into her eyes for a moment and then down at her hand holding his handkerchief and asked, 'D'you really think she could help a drunken sinner like me?'

She nodded, thought she could listen to his deep voice for eternity and turned away to hide the blush flooding her face.

'I'd be grateful if you could ask her.'

Opening the gate, she said, 'Gran'll probably tell you off for drinking in the first place; she's not one to mince her words.'

He slammed the car door behind him and grimaced at the noise. 'No mincing,' he agreed and followed her along the path to the door where he stopped and waited.

She walked into the kitchen, saying breathlessly, 'Mr Wallace is outside.'

The old woman raised her eyebrows. 'What be a fine gentleman like him doing here?'

'He's got a most frightful headache.'

'Hangover?'

'Yes. I said, well, I wondered, that is, if you'd do something for it?'

'You know as much as I do.'

'I'd rather you did.'

'Aye, send him in.'

She hurried through the glory hole and beckoned to him.

His eyes were wistful for the instant before he gave his lopsided smile and commanded, 'Lead me to my fate!'

She giggled and knocked against Albert's gumboots causing them to fall over and they both bent to pick them up. She could feel his breath on her neck whilst replacing them and, as she straightened her back, was aware of the closeness of his body and his hand lightly touching her hair.

The old woman's mouth curved slightly as she watched them enter them enter the room. She then welcomed the visitor and made him sit by the table whilst she fetched a jar of herbs from the larder and placed a handful in a saucepan of water. 'Thyme's what you'm in need of, or more to the point, that liver of yourn.' Turning to Kate, she added, 'You go and get some please, my lover.'

Remembering there was plenty freshly picked that morning, she opened her mouth to remind her, saw the old lady's expression and knew she wanted to see Mr Wallace alone.

After collecting a bunch of the herb, she sat on the rock feeling the ivy hanging down behind her and ached for Charles Wallace. Closing her eyes she imagined lying by the river close to the willows with him leaning over her. Opening up her body to his embrace she reached up ... This was ridiculous! The man was married! She drew in a deep breath and stood up to calm herself, then smelled the bonfire smoke wafting across from The Grange, where *his* gardener was cutting the hedges and burning the clippings. Desperately trying to stop the pulsating desire throbbing within her, she concentrated on her surroundings and wandered around the garden until, feeling more in control of her mind and body, she walked slowly back up the path to the kitchen.

They were leaning towards each other over the table, deeply engrossed in conversation and, as she walked through the door, they moved apart, both looking at her with smiling eyes.

Mr Wallace said, 'I must say I was doubtful about it, but I took it like a man, well almost, and here I am, reborn thanks to a cupful of ditchwater.'

'Ditchwater indeed! I growed them herbs special,' the old lady reproved him with mock annoyance, adding, 'come and see me again soon.'

'I shall, this arm feels so much better.' He raised his hook and departed.

'He do drink too much and he do drive that rackety thing too fast and frighten Percy my cockerel, but I have to admit—' she grinned, her eyes shining '—I does like Charlie Wallace!'

'Mmm—' Kate picked up a newspaper and pretended to read the advertisements on the front page '—he's quite nice.'

'Come put your hands on me knees, my lover, me screws be troubling me something terrible.'

She put down the newspaper and obeyed.

'You're a good girl, Kate, a very good girl—' she sighed '—ah that's better!'

They sat silent for several minutes before the old woman said, 'There's some folk as would make trouble for us what does the healing, but if that's what you're born to then you mun do it.'

'Have you ever made spells to get what you wanted, Gran?'

'I can't deny I did once or twice when I were young. Just as you and Alice did. Trouble is you never knows how t'will turn out in the long run. 'Tis not easy to see what pitfalls there may be. Like Alice got her man, 'tis true, but be she happy with her lot?'

Remembering the dark smudges under her friend's eyes, Kate admitted she did sometimes look sad, but pointed out that when looking at her children her face bloomed with affection. Then she asked, 'D'you think the women used spells long ago?'

'Aye, I daresay they did and I wouldn't blame they for making a few pennies by giving a charm to local girls wanting a man to like them when they was poor as church mice. I don't see no harm in that. What I don't hold with is '*ill-wishing*' for, as my old gran used to say, "Thee'll get back threefold, both good and ill." 'Twas her golden rule and I've always followed it.' The old woman chuckled. 'Though I may have been tempted from time to time, I never have stuck no pins in nobody!'

'And the poppy-dolls?'

'They'm how we care for people. We makes one for all the family and keeps they safe in the chimney where 'tis warm. I know folks think they'm for doing evil but no, 'tis the opposite with us. We gives healing to the doll when the person be away from us. I only give yours to you 'cos I knowed you'd bring it back.' She shook her head sadly. 'Times have changed. My daughters went too far for too long and though I tried t'was no use to them.'

'Eric kept a lucky rabbit's foot in his pocket for years—' Kate grinned '—he probably took it with him to Canada.'

'Aye, there's many a person both poor and gentry in these parts what's believed in some lucky charm or other. My old Gran told me as the hands of a hanged man was once much sought after.'

'Whatever for?'

'Put 'em in the wall to keep away the devil or summat, so she said.'

'They wouldn't still do that, would they?'

The old woman shook her head. 'I doubts it. I reckon they'd be hard to come by on account of they don't hang so many people these days. Specially not witches.'

Their eyes met and they both laughed.

Chapter Sixteen

Hemp Agrimony helps to purify the blood and the fresh leaves when placed on bread will prevent it going mouldy.

On returning from a walk with Margaret three weeks later, Kate found Charles Wallace sitting with her grandmother and, seeing the old woman's face blooming from recent laughter, was reminded of Polly in rare moments of joy.

Margaret, who was following in her wake, stepped over the threshold, nodded at Albert who was leaning forward in his chair beaming happily, then, seeing Mr Wallace, stopped, turned and rushed outside.

Kate went out after her, asking, 'Aren't you coming in today?'

The young woman's small face was suffused with red, as, shaking her head, she took hold of her bicycle and exclaimed 'Certainly not! I'm surprised your grandmother allows such a man into her home.'

'Gran gives him healing for his arm. I don't see the harm in that.'

Margaret pursed her lips and tossed her head. 'He may think the scandal's been forgotten while he was away, but I can assure you it's not.'

'What scandal?'

'Surely you must have heard. Everyone knew the reason for his sudden departure last year and why that young accountant and his trollop of a wife left Wells.' She pushed her bicycle to the gate before adding, 'I know he's renowned as a ladies' man and can charm the birds off the trees, but he's a bounder and a cad, that's what he is!' And, placing her foot on the pedal, she rode away without looking back.

Kate watched her depart down the lane then went back to the house feeling cold and sad. Charles Wallace was a womaniser as well as a drunk! She attempted to walk into the kitchen as normally as possible, but was aware immediately of all eyes upon her. 'My friend decided to go home early today, I, er—' she took a breath to calm herself '—I think her mother was entertaining guests to tea.'

Mr Wallace looked uncomfortable. 'I hope she didn't leave because of me. I'd hate to cause any unpleasantness here.'

Albert, evidently sensing the tense atmosphere, began rocking in his chair and humming a medley of hymn tunes.

Looking at the man beside her grandmother, whose handsome face expressed such pain that, for a flick of a second, she wanted to put her arms around him and comfort him, she said, 'No, I'm sure it has nothing to do with you.' Becoming aware of the bunch of ragwort clasped tightly in her hands, she added, 'I must put these in water, I want to draw them before they droop.'

'I'd no idea there was an artist in the village.'

She blushed. 'It's just a hobby. I like doing it, that's all.'

The old lady said proudly, 'She'm writing down my recipes and drawing the flowers and plants what's in 'em for a book.'

'That's fascinating. I'd like to see them sometime, if I may.'

She gave a cursory nod before going into the scullery to fetch a jam jar of water, and while standing at the sink, heard her grandmother say, 'Aye, Thursdays is better. Aye, that's right. Best not come on a Sunday again, my lover.'

On returning to the kitchen and finding the old woman alone, she placed the jar of flowers on the table, saying, 'I think this should only be used externally, don't you, Gran?'

''Tis powerful strong, I grant you. My mother used to call it St James's Wort. Her said 'twas the best cure for the King's evil.'

'The what?'

''Twas called that on account of a foolish belief that 'twould be cured by the King touching it. 'Tis not so common nowadays, but I do remember seeing a poor soul with a terrible sore in her neck when I were young. Terrible bad it was—' she reached over and crushed a leaf in her fingers '—the juice of it be powerful strong for treating nasty ulcers in private places, but best not mention that in your book, just say 'tis for the wounds and ulcers on the body and good in an ointment for soreness of the eyes.'

126

Taking up a pencil and paper, Kate began sketching the flower and then, feeling displeased with the effect, drew a man with a shock of white hair beside it.

Betty walked into the room, saying, 'I'm starving. Me and Billy've been looking for conkers but they're not ready yet.' Looking over Kate's shoulder she asked, 'Who's that?'

'Nobody,' she responded. 'It's just a doodle. And you should say, *"Billy and I."*'

That night, whilst lying in bed thinking over the events of the day, she wondered who the man in her vision could be. He certainly bore little resemblance to Charles Wallace who had no sign of grey in his shining brown hair. Could he perhaps be a figure from the past? Might she meet him in her dreams of that earlier life long ago? She closed her eyes.

All living things die in their time. She knew this, but knowing made the pain no less nor the loneliness easier to bear. The moon had reached fullness four times since the first signs of pain and weakness. Now her mother lay still and cold with the yellowing skin clinging to her bones.

She knew where to put her having helped to bury her grandmother there long ago. Now she must take the frail remains and place them with those who went before.

The coldness made her slow as she carried a burning stick through the snow and clumsy as she lit many rush lamps around the cave. On her return to the dwelling she made sure the child had skins securely tied to her feet and was warmly covered, then told her to follow closely behind.

Taking the body in her arms, she carried it to the narrow hole in the cliff and looked around the unusually still and silent landscape in which the river was a solid block of ice and birds lay dead in the woods. Having neither heard nor seen anything untoward, she stepped through the ivy curtain and laid her mother down on the bare earth before turning and smiling down reassuringly at the little girl. 'Remember what we do, my love. One day thee must do this for me.'

The following afternoon, whilst a young woman smoothed the gold fabric over her hips and posed before a long cheval glass, Kate looked around the room at solid oak furniture and Persian rugs on polished wooden floors and, breathing in the scent of beeswax and freshly arranged flowers, admitted this would be her ideal home. She imagined Charles Wallace walking in and putting his arm around her – yes, it would be a perfect place to live with the man she loved.

Cycling along the lanes towards Oakey Vale she remembered Hugo and grimaced with shame; what a fool she'd been. Was she in danger of doing the same thing with Charles Wallace? Could she be imagining he felt the same way about her? Might he simply like her as a friend and have not even thought of her from one Thursday visit with her grandmother to the next?

By the time she cycled past the village school her mind was set on controlling her silly crush on a married man. The whole thing was too ridiculous for words! It was high time she found someone more suitable to think about. Remembering the reflection in the water she smiled – perhaps the man with white hair would come to her soon and put an end to her girlish fantasies?

A young woman was standing by the cottage gate. 'I'm looking for Mrs Lamcraft's house,' she said nervously.

Kate dismounted and invited her into the house. Once inside the kitchen she greeted her grandmother who had obviously been dozing on the sofa, then turned to face the visitor and suggested she should sit at the table.

Looking anxiously around the room the woman said, 'I'm given to understand you help with a – er – *ladies* special – er – problem—' she pointed to her stomach '—you know.'

The old woman looked at her appraisingly as she asked, 'You'm not from these parts?'

'No. No, I'm from up north. I've been working near here and soon I've to go back.' She swallowed and twisted the handkerchief nervously around her fingers. 'I heard you have the knowledge.'

The old woman frowned and said, 'Put the kettle on, Kate, there's a good girl.' She stood up and placed her hands on the slouched shoulders. 'So, you'm in need of help?'

'Yes—' she sniffed '—I'm desperate, I just don't know where to turn. You're my only hope.'

'Bain't there no one where you lives?'

'No, no one at all—' her mouth quivered '—I'm desperate, I even thought of, you know—' she ran her index finger across her throat.

128

'Wait here . . .'

'Gran!' Kate exclaimed. 'Gran, we must be. . .'

''Tis all right, my lover, I'll deal with this,' the old woman said firmly before going into the larder and quickly reappearing holding a twist of blue paper. 'There you are, boil these up and drink the liquid.'

The woman jumped up, saying, 'I'm so grateful. How much money do you want?'

'Nothing.'

'Thank you, I must go.' Pulling her coat around her she hurried out of the house.

Kate went to the window and watched her run to the gate and turn right up the lane. 'There's something fishy about her, Gran, I really don't think you should've . . .'

'Don't you start questioning me, my girl. You'm not always as clever as you might think.'

'But we've no idea who she is or where she's from—' she saw the two red spots appear on the old woman's cheeks, but was too sure of herself to stop '—I think we should be more careful about who we give those herbs to.'

The old woman clenched her jaw as she spoke. 'So you'm saying as I can't judge rightly, is that it?'

'No, no of course not. I just didn't think we should give her what she wanted so easily. I'd have asked her how late she was for one thing. And for another, you just said to boil them up and drink the liquid . . .' she stopped as her grandmother pushed past her and crashed through the glory hole knocking mackintoshes off hooks and causing an old straw hat to fall from the shelf above them.

'You'll see, you mark my words. You'll see!' the old woman shrieked before slamming the door behind her.

Feeling miserably unhappy, she went to her sewing machine and tried to work, but, after half an hour, admitted it was useless and went outside, longing to make peace.

She searched the outhouse, the small lean-to beside it, the pig pen, the hen coop and around the vegetable patch without success, then, stopping by the porch and feeling dizzy, she forced herself to inhale slowly for several breaths until the buzzing in her head had cleared. Taking a step forward and finding an unruly tendril of the climbing rose had caught her skirt with its thorns, she yanked it free and immediately shivered at the memory of holding her grandmother's hand in London long ago.

Panic surged through her and, hearing the thump of her own heartbeat and feeling her lungs burning as though on fire, she ran down the garden path, until, seeing the crumpled figure lying on the ground outside the cave, she sank to her knees and cradled the old woman in her arms.

Chapter Seventeen

The Horsetail has many uses. A tea taken internally three times a day is good for urinary problems, weak lungs and varicose veins. When used externally it is effective for skin complaints such as eczema and acne.

Kate's head ached and her eyes felt alien to their swollen lids as she escorted the undertaker out of the house. Returning to the parlour she stood beside the coffin and, after stroking the white hair tightly tied back from her grandmother's temples, gently teased a few strands free. Once the wisps the old woman had always brushed back before speaking were framing the sunken face as usual, the corpse looked more like the woman she had loved and she bent to kiss the cold forehead.

On hearing a loud knock on the back door, she went to open it and found a policeman looking very solemn. Her immediate thought was of Betty. Had she done something stupid like stealing from Woolworths?

'I'm looking for Mrs Lamcraft and Miss Barnes.'

'My grandmother died yesterday, but you may speak to me, I'm Kate Barnes.' She ushered him into the kitchen. 'I do hope there's nothing seriously wrong?'

He frowned, saying, 'It *is* a serious matter, that's to say, a serious allegation—' he pulled out a notebook '—and that's all it is at present, an *allegation*.'

The pit of her stomach churned as she asked, 'What are we alleged to have done?'

'A neighbour of yours has accused you of providing a young woman with the means of an illegal abortion.'

The room spun around her and she grabbed the table. 'Who was that?'

The policeman consulted his book. 'A lady by the name of Joan Baker came to see you yesterday afternoon.' He looked at her. 'Do you corroborate that?'

'A young woman came to see us, but I didn't know her name.'

He made a note then asked, 'Do you admit you gave her poisonous herbs that would induce an abortion?'

'No, I gave her nothing.'

'And your grandmother, did she give her poisonous herbs that would do harm to an unborn child?'

She took a deep breath. 'I saw her give the young lady a packet but didn't ask what it contained.'

The constable made more notes and then said, 'I'm instructed by my superior to inform you that the herbs in question have been sent to a laboratory in Bristol and if they prove to be as alleged then you may be asked to come to the police station in Wells for questioning.' He gave a small cough. 'The old lady's died, you say?'

'The doctor says she had a heart attack.'

'I'm sorry to hear that, Miss. I'll let you know as soon as we get the result.'

'How long will that take?'

He shifted his weight from one foot to the other. 'I don't rightly know, a week or so, I expect. I'm sure you'll be told immediately.'

When he had pedalled off towards Wells, she sank down at the table and flopped over it sobbing uncontrollably until, becoming aware of a hand on her shoulder and a handkerchief being held close to her face, she said, 'Betty? Oh, sweetheart—' she sat up and mopped her face '—something so terrible has happened.'

'I know, I heard.' Her sister grinned sheepishly and indicated towards the sofa as she said, 'I dived behind that when I saw him through the window.'

Guessing her first reaction to the policeman was correct, she began, 'I've told you a thousand times not to ...'

'Listen—' Betty held up her hand, '—listen to me. I know where that beastly person came from.'

'You do?'

'I saw her at The Grange.'

'What! You mean she lives there?'

'Not exactly. She's the maid of a horrible old hag who's been

132

staying at The Grange since Christmas.'

Kate sat staring at her sister. 'We're in a terrible mess, sweetheart. Gran's told me time and time again how careful we have to be and she just fell right into the trap.'

Betty frowned. 'I think it's very odd Gran didn't smell a rat.'

'You've heard her do this sort of thing before?'

'A few times. Everybody thought I was just a little girl playing with her dolly, so they didn't take much notice of me. She could tell just by looking at someone if they were having a baby, she always asked the same questions and I'm jolly sure she wouldn't give them anything over the two weeks, well, maybe three at the most if they weren't regular as clockwork.'

Feeling a pulse throbbing in her temple, Kate said, 'We had a row about it. I've never argued with her before and now I feel—' she had to voice the thought, had to force the words from her mouth '—I feel like I killed her.'

Betty put her arms around her and said consolingly, 'Of course you didn't. Oh, Kate, darling, you mustn't think that.' After a few moments she asked, 'Have you checked the larder?'

'What for?'

'Evidence, you know like Charlie Chan would. If we were in one of his films he'd be looking for clues to see ... Actually, what we need to do is *remove* the evidence isn't it? Come on!' She pulled at her arms. 'Oh, do come on. The police might come back at any moment and take all the jars and then when they find that special mix on the top shelf, you'll be done for.'

Feeling light headed she allowed herself to be dragged to the larder and watched Betty fetch a chair then stand on it while searching the highest shelf and announcing, 'It's thick with dust up here.'

Kate's knees gave way and she grasped the chair to support herself. 'She can't have given her the special mix. She couldn't have reached it without standing on something and I know she didn't ...'

Betty handed a jar to her saying, 'This looks empty to me.'

She unscrewed the lid and nodded. 'She gave her something else, something harmless because she *did* smell a rat.'

Betty jumped off the chair and brushed dust off her skirt. 'Crikey blimey, look at the state of me!'

'Oh, sweetheart, I'm so grateful to you.'

Betty blushed with pleasure and asked, 'Can I go and tell my friend Billy?'

'Good heavens, no! We'll have to keep very quiet and wait for this test to be done on the herbs.'

'But we know it can't be anything dangerous.'

'That's right, and also it was a very small amount in that twist of paper.' Seeing a dried flower lying on the floor, she stooped and picked it up then exclaimed, 'Chamomile! It's soothing and calming and would do no harm, thank God!'

The following morning, having lain awake all night either remembering her argument with the old lady or worrying how to make the coffin feel as though it contained a body, she decided to deal with the one problem she could do something about and went into the lean-to beside the house in search of potato sacks that she could fill with earth and use to substitute for the corpse.

Hearing a cough, she turned round and gasped in horror at finding a police sergeant standing in the doorway watching her. Could he somehow know what she was doing? Would this make the case against her stronger? Had they found a way to make her look guilty? Could they even think she'd killed her grandmother?

'Sorry to trouble you, miss. I thought you'd like to know straight away,' he said, then indicated with his head towards The Grange. 'She's withdrawn the allegation.' Then, after a small cough, he added, 'I'm afraid the inspector's already sent the sample.'

'That's all right,' she said calmly, 'I'm sure it was only chamomile flowers.'

'Phew! That's a relief. My old auntie used to come to your grandma for comfrey ointment. I can remember her saying there's nothing better. I reckon she'd come back and haunt me if we'd taken her to court.' He smiled. 'You can call at the station to see the results from the laboratory when you're in the city and they'll notify you in writing too.'

She thanked him and, having waited for him to leave, sank to her knees on top of the sacks feeling unsure whether to laugh or cry.

A few moments later, Betty came excitedly to her saying, 'There was a big black motor car at The Grange. I think it was the cops!'

Kate explained what the sergeant had said.

'Smashing!' Then, looking at the sacks, Betty said, 'I wondered about using potatoes to make the weight, but then I realised they might grow in the grave and that'd really give the game away!'

They walked into the house together and found Albert humming and rocking in his corner. Seeing the glazed expression in his eyes, Kate decided to let him deal with the grief in his own way and left him alone.

The Reverend Bretton arrived at four o'clock, saying mournfully, 'She has gone to a better place, a far, far better place.'

Nodding in agreement, whilst signalling to Betty she should make some tea, she ushered him into the kitchen where Albert was now calmer and humming quietly whilst rhythmically stroking the small black cat on his lap.

When the vicar suggested they should pray together, Kate knelt on the stone floor wishing she could sink a bit further and go to sleep, and Albert slowly removed the cat, bent one knee and said, 'Amen,' then began to get up again.

The Reverend Bretton cleared his throat and intoned mournfully, 'We pray, dear father, you will take our dear sister to your heart in heaven.'

Albert went down again.

'She was but a humble sinner and we beg you to forgive her. We too are sinners who pray you will likewise forgive us all our sins.'

The sound of a porcelain saucer smashing on the scullery floor, was followed by Betty shouting, 'Damn!'

Albert looked up. 'Amen,' he said cheerfully.

The vicar's voice sounded strained as he continued, 'We ask you, Lord, to help the grieving family in their time of need.'

Betty, still in the scullery, said loudly, 'Bleedin' eck, this milk's gone off all-bloody-ready.'

Albert said hopefully, 'Amen?'

'Amen.' The vicar struggled to his feet and sank into the nearest chair. 'Ah, splendid!' he said, as Betty, smiling angelically, carried in a large fruitcake. 'I suggest,' he said after swallowing his first mouthful, 'I suggest for the service tomorrow we sing an appropriate hymn such as ...'

'Peril on the sea,' Albert interrupted eagerly.

'Well, no, not that one.' The vicar pursed his lips and screwed up his eyes. 'There are several that suit the funeral service well and ...'

135

'I like "peril on the sea,"' Albert insisted.

'I'm sorry, Albert, but it really is *not* suitable. I could understand if we were burying a nautical man, or even the widow of a sailor, but we are not. Perhaps you could think of a favourite of hers, "rock of ages" perhaps, or "Guide me oh thou great redeemer", for instance.' He looked at Kate. 'You understand, do you not?'

'Er, I think perhaps the vicar has a point, Uncle,' she said tentatively. 'Gran did like that one you're fond of, you know, "thy hand oh God has guided"?'

Albert's mouth set into a straight, hard line and his eyes narrowed.

Betty leapt to Albert's side and rested her hand on his shoulder. 'I think dear Granny would want Uncle to sing his favourite hymn one last time for her.' She smiled sweetly at the vicar and ran to Kate. 'Please,' she begged, sinking to her knees and crossing her eyes, 'please, let my darling uncle have his favourite hymn, Kate, *please*.' She allowed her eyes to return to normal and winked.

Fascinated by the performance, Kate said, 'You're right, it would be Grandma's wish, sweetheart.' She turned to the vicar. 'I'm sure we'll be pleased to be guided by you in the choice of the *other* hymns.' She stood up and went to hold Albert's hand, saying brightly, 'We must carry out your mamma's wishes, mustn't we?'

Her uncle looked up at her, grinning silently. The cat returned to his knee and began purring very loudly.

Seeing the Reverend Bretton had lost his customary air of superiority and knowing his passion for carved wooden screens in churches, she said, 'I was reading in the paper about a scheme to reinstate ...'

The vicar interrupted her, 'The Italianate screen in Yelmerton? Yes, it was removed by the bigoted partisans of the nineteenth century under the misapprehension that they are of Roman origin, which is quite inaccurate. Some of my fellow clergy regard the restoration of a screen as a superfluity of naughtiness, but their number decreases year by year.'

She opened her mouth to ask if that was because the dissenters were dying out, but, thinking this might be tactless when speaking to such an old man, closed it again.

The Reverend Bretton, having regained his composure, then ate another piece of cake while talking at length about the weather, the local bus service and the new hospital in Wells before taking his leave.

Whilst getting into bed that night she wondered if her grandmother had been watching over them that day and had approved of the way in which she had prised open the coffin and replaced her body with sacks of earth after the undertaker had called and made ready for the funeral.

Laying her head on the pillow, she smiled at the memory of Betty arranging for Albert to sing his favourite hymn. If Gran had seen her, then she might look down on her more favourably than she had while alive! She closed her tired eyes and relaxed into sleep ...

The child had made a daisy chain and hung it around a young kid's neck and the little animal skittered and skipped until the flowers fell off and she ate them. The shrieks of her daughter's laughter drowned the sound of footsteps approaching and she jumped when the young man suddenly appeared.

'I need help, my lady,' he said.

'Aye,' she said, looking at the pustules on his handsome young face. 'There's a remedy, I can give.' She pointed to some young shoots of stinging nettles. 'Make a soup of these.'

'What! My lady, how can thee suggest such poison?'

'Do as I say and all the young maidens will be eager for thy embrace.'

''Tis not so now. None will let me near.' His pouch swelled as he spoke.

She felt the itch between her thighs and took a deep breath. 'Eat the soup each day until the plants are tall and in flower.' She averted her gaze from his large brown eyes. 'That alone will not be enough. Come back later and I will give thee a potion also to help clear thy skin.'

He nodded. 'I mun hasten back to the flock, but—' he licked his lower lip '—I could leave a boy to mind them after sunset.'

'Aye, shepherd, that will do well.'

After he had gone, she went to the cave and selected the dried flowers of red clover and some roots she knew would clear the boils, and, having fetched water from the pool in the secret cave, she heated them in a clay pot on the fire.

137

The child came in carrying the fish they had caught earlier and they cooked and ate it. As the sun began to sink in the sky they placed clods of earth around and on the top of the fire to keep it from dying in the night and the little girl then went to her bed and fell sleep.

He came soon after dark and stood waiting by the entrance until she lifted the leather flap and beckoned him inside. There was little light within until she bent and uncovered a small area of the fire beside her sleeping place. As she straightened and looked up she saw his eyes glisten and his lower lip shine. They reached towards one another and, while his hands pulled at her skirt, she grasped his naked penis with one hand and ran the other around him to feel the small buttocks tighten as he pressed towards her.

This was lust. Desire of the flesh. A primitive need for mating that must be satisfied. She sank back into her bed eager to feel his searching hands explore her. Then, when he knelt between her gaping thighs, she arched her back to welcome him into her body.

He was young and strong, proud of his virility. He grunted when she moaned with pleasure and laughed quietly as she restrained her scream of ecstasy but could not contain his own roar of triumph.

Awakening in the dawn light she lay remembering the pleasure of her dream, then, hearing Albert's bed creak as he got up, she felt the dull ache of grief return followed immediately by a gnawing anxiety in her stomach. It was the day of the funeral and although she knew all was ready, she felt sick with fear. Suppose the undertaker opened the lid of the coffin before he took it to the church? What would happen then? And if he didn't open it, might it come undone if the pall-bearers tripped on the uneven path and dropped it on their way out of the cottage?

Five hours later, she held her breath as the four men lowered the coffin into the hole, then, when it was lying beneath her, she threw the white rose on top of it.

Betty teetered over the open grave and snorted.

Kate quickly put her arm around her sister's shaking shoulders.

The vicar, who had been reciting in a singsong voice all the while, continued intoning for a few moments before turning and walking away followed by all the mourners except Kate, Betty and Albert who remained huddled together with their arms intertwined.

Betty wiped her eyes, saying, 'When he said ashes to ashes and dust . . .'

'Hush! It's all right.' She looked around and was relieved to see no one was within earshot.

'I just thought of the earth in the coffin going into the earth . . .'

'I know, I know.' She linked arms and patted her sister's hand.

'Can I still have the bike you promised?'

'Of course you can. Providing you can be nice to all the people who come back to the house, and—' she turned to look at her '—you promise to keep the secret for your whole life.'

'I promise to keep Gran's secret for my whole life.' Betty looked around her. 'I've just realised. We all die, don't we?'

'Yes, I had the same thought looking at our mother's grave.'

Betty giggled nervously. 'At least I'll know what to do when you die, won't I?'

They walked back to the cottage and gave tea and cake to the many kindly neighbours who came to pay their respects and say complimentary things about her grandmother, and then, when the last of them had finally gone, Kate took the canvas bag out from the chimney behind the range and laid it on the kitchen table. Betty and Albert moved closer and watched as she pulled out four dolls. The old man picked up the one with trousers and hugged it.

Kate took the oldest and dirtiest one with black hair. 'This must be Gran's.' Then, seeing a smaller one with yellow woollen hair, she turned to her sister, saying, 'Look, sweetheart, look at this.'

The young girl stared in disbelief. 'I didn't know, why didn't she say?'

'I don't know, but she did love you. She wouldn't have made you a poppy-doll otherwise.'

'D'you think I could keep it for a bit?'

'Of course you may, it's yours.'

They made their way to the cave carrying the old woman's body wrapped in a sheet and laid it beside the large slab of stone, then Albert gave a low moan and stood to attention humming his favourite hymn tune whilst Kate lit the dozen candles already placed in position.

Betty gazed around her and held out her hand to catch a glistening droplet of water falling from one of the long slender pink stalactites above her and whispered, 'It's a fairy castle!'

Kate knelt before the figure in the rocks and watched the water

139

trickling steadily down over sparkling pink crystals into the pool glowing like a ruby in the golden light until, seeing her uncle bend and push the slab of stone sideways, she picked up a candle and joined him. Then, looking down into the fissure in the rocks, she gave an involuntary sob on seeing pale bones and skulls gleaming below her.

Albert took his mother's old knife from his pocket and placed it under the gnarled hands folded on her chest, Kate tucked the poppy-doll in the crook of her arm, Betty scattered dried rose petals on her and then all three of them carefully lifted her and dropped her onto the remains of her forebears.

Leaning over the hole, Betty whispered several words, one of which sounded to Kate like, 'Forgive,' and another, 'Whatser-name.'

Albert pulled the slab back into position, muttered something unintelligible and, picking up a torch, hurried out through the exit hole.

Kate crouched in front of the pool, cupped her hand and scooped some water from it, then Betty immediately imitated her, saying, 'I thought it would be red, but it's clear.' And, looking up at the glistening crystal, she added, 'It looks like it's made from fondant icing coloured with cochineal.'

When they had both taken a drink, Kate held her sister close and, feeling the tears on her cheeks, whispered, 'I'm so glad we'll have this moment to remember all our lives.'

Chapter Eighteen

Feverfew is a good cure for headaches and the fresh leaves can be eaten with bread or when dried made into a tea.

The solicitor peered over his spectacles at her as he explained, 'It's all very straightforward, Miss Barnes, there is a covenant which means that you may never sell any of the property because it's entailed on your children or next of kin and, there is also an unusual stipulation that the cottage known as Old Myrtles must go through the female line to a daughter or nearest female relative. But—' he smiled brightly at her '—both the farm and the cottage belong to you and the rental income from the farm is yours to use as you wish. Your grandmother also trusts you will care for your uncle and never let him be put into an institution.'

'Oh yes, of course,' she responded quickly. 'I'd never do that.'

'There's also a generous insurance policy that will mature on your sister Elizabeth's twenty-ninth birthday.' He picked up an envelope and handed it to her. 'And this is for you.' Then he escorted her out of the building.

Stepping out into the sunlit square, she heard the sound of an Irish jig and, seeing a tramp playing a tin whistle in Penniless Porch, went over to him and opened her purse to take out a penny, then, on sudden impulse, emptied all the silver and copper into his hat.

A deep and beautiful voice behind her, said, 'That's a very generous gesture, Miss Barnes.'

She turned and smiled. 'I wanted someone else to feel good too, Mr Wallace.'

'I'm glad I've caught you alone. I'm so dreadfully sorry about

141

the—' he hesitated '—the appalling accusation my wife's cousin made against your grandmother and you. I wish I'd known about it sooner. As it is, I believe it was stopped in time.' They gazed into each other's eyes for a long still moment.

Summoning the strength to look away, she said, 'Yes, I'm hoping it's all over, in fact, I'm going to call and see if the report on the herbs has arrived.' Leaving him, she walked along the pavement to the Police Station where the sergeant recognised her and asked, 'Can you guess what the contents of the packet were, Miss?'

'Chamomile flowers?'

'Yes, your grandmother was a wise old lady. I'm afraid we have to keep all such information for the record, but that should be the end of the matter.'

Having thanked him with great relief, Kate stepped into the street and, coming face to face with her friend Margaret, said, 'I've been meaning to contact you. I expect you'd heard about my grandmother?'

The small face was suffused with fury as she spat out the words, 'I've heard about her and you!'

'Gran died.'

'I'm sorry for that, but I know what she did. It's all been hushed up, of course!' She tossed her head indignantly and hurried away.

Kate cycled home and, feeling overwhelmed at knowing this property now belonged to her, walked along the path between rosemary and lavender to the rock seat outside the cave.

Sitting with her back against the ivy hanging down the cliff, she took the envelope the solicitor had given her out of her pocket and opened it. Inside, wrapped in a piece of faded blue velvet, was a cameo brooch set in a gold frame. Holding it to her chest she closed her eyes and saw her grandmother standing before her. 'Oh, Gran, I'm still in trouble. Margaret knows about the allegations to the police and therefore so does the whole population of Wells.'

The old woman whispered, 'Fireweed!'

Feeling herself sucked down and down, back to the past, she relaxed and waited for the dream to evolve.

The girl stood by the dwelling with her hands outstretched as she pleaded with her, 'I beg thee, mistress. Give me a spell to make the man I love come to me.'

'He loves no other?'

The girl shook her head. 'I never saw him with a girl.'

''Tis not a thing to be lightly done nor lightly taken. A spell may not always work as we would wish.'

'No harm can come from helping a man to follow his heart.'

'He likes thee?'

The girl blushed as she replied, 'Aye. He looks kindly upon me.'

'Thy father knows him?'

'He wishes for it also—' she swallowed '—he needs help to work the land since my brothers all died of a pestilence.'

She turned away to avoid the girl's desperately beseeching eyes. Although she had made such magic of her own, she had never done so for another.

'Mistress, I beg thee, help me.'

She weakened. 'I could give thee a little help.'

The girl's face bloomed and her eyes shone. 'I could bring a cheese for payment.'

'When the moon is newly forming, think of him and raise your arms in supplication. Ask Mother Moon to aid you. Ask that his love will grow as she grows each night. Ask this of her thrice on each of three new moons.'

'And he will love me then?'

She spread her hands in the air. 'If there is love within him for thee then it will out. But take care, young mistress, for if he does not hold thee dear and has been spelled against his heart, then, though he may fall for thy charm, he will not be faithful nor kind in time to come.'

She opened her eyes, blinked in the sunshine and, remembering how she had stood by the front gate of the house in London with her arms outstretched towards the moon, gave a rueful smile. Then, thinking how little the desires of young girls changed over the centuries, she pinned the cameo brooch to her blouse and walked up to the cottage where she began making a cake for tea.

Looking up when her sister arrived home an hour later, she said, 'I went to hear the will today.'

'I bet she didn't leave me anything.'

'Yes, she did. She left you a special insurance policy she'd been paying into for years.'

'Crikey!'

'It'll be yours when you're twenty-nine.'

'*Twenty-nine*! I'll never be that old!' Betty poured a glass of milk from the jug on the table and asked, 'What did she leave you?'

After clearing her throat, Kate replied, 'Her property.'

'All of it?'

'Yes.'

'Oh, that's nice. I'm going to play with Billy now.' She looked at the brooch on Kate's chest as she passed her. 'And that?'

'Yes.'

On reaching the door, she turned around. 'What about the farm up top?'

'Yes, she left me that as well.'

'Crikey blimey!'

'She wanted to be sure the properties are in my name because I'll manage the rent from the farm that keeps us all, and the house provides a roof over our heads. I can't sell either of them.'

'Why not?'

'Because it's all tied up legally so I can't.'

'What if you don't *want* to stay in this miserable, boring, deadly dull village? What if you want to *sell* it all and go and live in *London*? Why can't we do *that*?'

'Because we're ordinary people, for one thing, and we're not rich for another, and anyway I just can't.'

Betty's lower lip drooped.

Kate tried to sound enthusiastic as she said, 'Let's think about your bicycle, shall we?'

'What for?'

'So we can start looking forward and be a little more cheery.' The headache that had hovered behind her eyes all day was increasing by the minute.

'Billy says you could easily sell the farm and ...'

Kate hit the table hard with the flat of her hand and winced from the pain in her head as she shouted, 'You mean, *you* think I could, and you're wrong.'

Betty shrugged and examined her fingernails. 'I don't see the point of staying in this—' she gestured around her '—this ... this, this *pigsty*!'

Kate slumped at the table and leaned on her elbows. 'I'm sorry you think it's that bad, but we've no choice. We're very lucky to have this place, we really are very, very lucky, but if you want to go into domestic service and live in a big house then I'm sure we

144

can arrange it soon. I'd like you to stay at school until you're fourteen but I daresay there's ...'

'I didn't say I wanted to go into *service!*' Betty shouted. 'I only want to know what's the point of staying here, when we could go back to London and live in a nice house?'

'The point is—' Kate wanted to lie down and place her aching head on the cold stone floor '—I can't do just what I like. The point is I have responsibilities, I'm tied to this place and Uncle Albert who needs my care for the rest of his life.'

'How long is that?'

'I don't know, years and years. He's younger than our mother, so he's probably getting on for fifty.'

'Bleedin' 'eck!'

'Betty! Where on earth did you hear that expression?'

'Billy Nelson's dad says it sometimes. He says bloody *all* the time.' She grinned. 'He says our grandma was a *bloody old witch.*'

'That's ridiculous!'

'He says there was one lived here a long time ago too.'

'One what?'

'A *witch.*'

Kate felt suddenly cold. 'That's just a legend. Everyone knows the story about her living in a cave. What else does Mr Nelson say?'

'That she was very, very wicked. So bloody evil and bloody bad and bloody wicked, that monks from Glastonbury came and exercised her.'

'Exorcised!'

'Mmm, I dunno, something like that.' Her eyes widened. 'Maybe that's what I'll be. I'll fly through the village at night on a broomstick!' She laughed with delight and exclaimed, 'Gosh! What a wonderful idea! I could put spells on people like that horrible schoolteacher and the vicar. Oh yes, a smashing idea! I'll go and see Billy now, all right?'

Kate remembered the spells and love potions she made when the other children told her the story of the witch and, holding her head, she gave a small, careful nod and said, 'If you promise not to turn me into a toad.'

When the door had banged shut, she went and picked some feverfew leaves from the garden and ate them in a piece of bread, then walked down the path to the rock outside the cave and sat leaning back against the ivy-covered cliff until her uncle returned from work half an hour later, whereupon, feeling refreshed, she resumed her preparations of the evening meal.

Betty walked through the door at six o'clock and sniffed the air, declaring, 'That smells good! I showed Billy I can ride a bike, he didn't believe I could!'

Kate, who was holding a large casserole in mid-air, noted the bloodstained handkerchief tied around her sister's left knee and the black oil stains on her torn skirt, decided against commenting on either and exclaimed, 'That's wonderful, you clever girl!' She placed the dish on the table, saying, 'It's Saturday tomorrow, we'll go into Wells first thing in the morning and buy a bicycle for you. What make does Billy have?'

'Actually, it's his dad's bike, that's why I fell off, 'cos it's more difficult than yours, it's got a straight bit on the top.'

'A cross bar's difficult to negotiate with a skirt.' Kate smiled, adding, 'Mr Nelson was very kind to let you ride it.'

Betty shifted from one foot to the other and looked at her badly scuffed shoes, 'Mmm.'

'Oh dear! He didn't know, did he?'

'He was working in the garden at the Grange and me and Billy ...'

'Billy and I.'

'Yes, well, we thought it would be a good idea to practise ready for when I get mine and as he's not supposed to talk to me any more we couldn't ask, could we?'

'Oh no!' Kate muttered, 'Mrs Nelson's heard the rumour.'

''Fraid so. Actually, I might as well tell you. I fell off by the bridge and then Mr Wallace came along in his new motor car and helped me put the handlebars straight 'cos they were crooked. He said I'm the image of Mary Pickford in *Daddy Longlegs.*' Betty wound a blonde curl into a ringlet around her forefinger. 'His new car's green, it's smaller than the other one, but he likes it better 'cos it's easier to drive with one hand. He said to give you his regards.'

'How kind,' Kate said, wondering if her face looked as red as it felt.

Chapter Nineteen

The large Royal Fern can be used both as a balm in ointment or drunk in a tea for broken bones and bruises. The common Fern, known as Bracken, is not recommended because it is a strong purgative and can induce abortion.

He was standing by the river waiting when she came to check the traps. 'I had to tell thee—' he looked around nervously '—I cannot stay.'

She called to the child, 'I'll be with thee soon.'

Her daughter waved and climbed down the bank.

She reached out and touched the pitted cheek, whispering, 'My poor lover, what ails thee?'

He stepped back into the shadow of a tree. 'I'm, I'm to be at the church door on Sunday.'

She stared at him, speechless with shock.

'Her's willing and thee baint.'

She steadied herself on the strong trunk of the oak.

He put out his hand to touch her breast. 'I could come sometimes?'

'Nay.' She shook her head. 'Keep only to thy wife.'

'If I could marry thee ...'

'I've told thee nay so many times. I can never leave this place. I mun stay ...'

'But I do like thee,' he moaned, pushing her against the tree and pressing his hand between her thighs. 'I knows thee likes me.' He glanced at the girl wading in the river. 'We could go into the withies.'

Blood was pounding in her temples. Her body was responding to

147

his touch as it always did. Just once more? Yes, yes, yes! She sank down onto the soft grass and, looking up at his face framed by the canopy of willow, welcomed him into her body for the last time ...

Awakening with a start and finding she had fallen asleep whilst leaning back against the oak tree in Hankeys Land, Kate stared up into the bare branches remembering the erotic dream and wondering again if such feelings were possible.

Looking around her at the bright green grass illuminated in the sudden sunshine of early spring she knew that, although still grieving, life was sweet and she was glad to be living it. Looking back on the past three months, she admitted disappointment that many of her dressmaking clients no longer required her services due to the gossip from The Grange, but acknowledged that since she now received the rent from the farm up top, her income from sewing was no longer so necessary.

She felt a sense of achievement in knowing that her grandmother's corpse was buried in the cave and a coffin filled with earth had been given a decent Christian burial in the graveyard by an unsuspecting vicar. Although surprised by Albert's apparent lack of grief after emerging from the cave, she was pleased at his acceptance of her in his mother's place. She took great pleasure in seeing Betty cheerfully riding round the local environs on the most expensive bicycle in Wells, and, to her astonishment, she was proud to be the new owner of Higher Tops Farm at Pridden and Old Myrtles on the outskirts of Oakey Vale village.

Smoke from the chimney of a small factory far away in the valley below rose upward in a straight white column. A hawk was silhouetted against pure, clear blue sky as it hovered, hanging motionless in the still air. A motor bus rumbled through the village towards Wells. The bird dropped suddenly and lunged out of sight.

Several guffaws of laughter floated up the hillside and she smiled – someone somewhere was having fun. She looked across the strange flat moors to where, in the distance, the Tor in Glastonbury was clearly visible. Half closing her eyes, she lay back against the ribbed bark, listening to the twittering birds. Voices murmured in the far distance with an occasional laugh or shout. A motor car hooted far away and a steam train sounded its whistle as it approached a level crossing on the moors.

Allowing her eyes to slide out of focus, she was overcome by an overwhelming tiredness tugging at her and sucking her down and down and down into a dream of being chased through the woods by drunken men. They were singing, 'La-dee-doo la-dee-day-dee. The gypsy rover came over the hill, the gypsy rover came over. The gypsy rover came over the hill and he won the heart of a lady. Good Lord!'

'Kate!'

Opening her eyes she stared up at the two dark forms against the light.

'I do apologise, I'd no idea you were there, Miss Barnes.' The taller man sank to the ground and sat close by, saying, 'Climbing and singing take one's breath away,' whilst mopping his brow with a large white handkerchief.

She sat up and, shading her eyes, recognised her solicitor. 'Mr Parville!'

He grinned and gestured towards his companion. 'Wallace and I are taking a break from our duties.'

Both men were dressed in very muddy long stockings and plus fours. Charles Wallace looked down at his torn and badly stained white shirt as he explained, 'I've been digging a hole in a cave.'

Her heart lurched. 'A cave?'

Mr Parville nodded. 'Yes, believe it or not, we've made such an exciting discovery. The archaeologists have gone into a huddle so we thought we'd take a little walk before tea. I haven't been up here since we were boys; we used to run wild here when we were lads.'

Charles leaned towards her, saying, 'We used to have such larks in the cave and here we are discovering its secrets. Such a fascinating, exciting experience, I'm absolutely thrilled to be involved. You'll be amazed, Miss Barnes, absolutely amazed, to know that only a short distance from your house, there's a cave with a body in it.'

She experienced a fizzing sensation in her head and whispered, 'A body?'

'I was being too light-hearted about it. I do apologise, it really isn't *so* shocking as I made it sound.'

'Not shocking?'

'No, not at all.' He grinned, his eyes looking into hers. 'The person's been dead for many, many, possibly, hundreds of years.'

The breath came out of her lungs in a long sigh, 'Ahhgh,' before she repeated his words, 'hundreds of years?'

149

'Yes, all our lives we've been hearing the legend about some old witch who lived here, and now we think we've found her.'

'Oh no!'

Mr Parville's eyes shone with enthusiasm. 'I expect you've heard the story?'

She nodded.

'Of course, we really want it to be the remains of the witch.' He grinned. 'Well, that is, Wallace, and me are hoping that's the case, but the archaeological buffs are more scientific than us and they won't commit themselves to such fanciful notions. We found some goat's bones in the same place, so they're calling the deceased the goatherd, but we're not convinced.'

'I've heard,' she said, hoping her tone was convincingly dispassionate, 'that the witch was turned to stone by the monks from Glastonbury, because she put bad spells on people.'

'Yes, that's one version of the accepted folklore and I suspect the story has a seed of truth in it.'

'What are the other versions of the story?'

'Oh, you know the sort of thing, when the people refused to give in to her demands for something or other, money or land, I forget what, she poisoned all the crops and the animals. I have my own theory about that. The clean water from the reservoir was first piped into this area a hundred years ago, before that they'd have relied on the water coming down off the hills into the valley.' He pointed across the hilltops as he went on, 'Up there about three miles away are the remains of Roman lead mines and I believe the water would be contaminated with lead spoil.'

'Not only that kind of pollution,' she agreed, 'but also in summer, if a dead sheep or some other animal fell into the river, it would've been a breeding ground for goodness knows what bugs. So they'd blame her when their babies were ill. They'd think she'd ill-wished them, despite all she'd done for them, and when none of her charms or potions helped . . .' Seeing their fascinated expressions she paused and added lightly, 'Sorry about that, I was getting carried away.'

'You certainly were!' Mr Parville exclaimed. 'I was beginning to think you knew something about it.'

'Only the legends that everyone knows.'

Charles Wallace said, 'We added a few extra bits when we were lads after we'd found the cave in the dell.'

'In the dell?' she echoed with relief.

'Yes, it's been covered up with brambles for years. We used to go in there and light fires so we could see inside.' He chuckled. 'Rocks can take on all sorts of strange shapes in the flickering light of a fire if you've a fanciful imagination, and there's a strange formation that looks a bit, just a bit, like a woman with a big hooked nose.'

The solicitor smiled. 'We did rather overdo the description to the local children I'm afraid, and, what's worse, we damaged a few stalagmites in the process.'

'I wonder—' Kate hoped she sounded politely interested '—why these scientific people wish to investigate the caves.'

'Mr Hayes invited them,' he replied. 'He's interested in opening it up to the public and wanted to check what was in there before doing so. Actually I think these hills are honeycombed with caves.'

'My Granfer said the dip in one of the fields up there was a huge crater formed when the earth suddenly subsided when his granfer was a boy and he'd maintained it had been an entrance leading to many large caverns of amazing beauty.'

'That's fascinating.' Mr Parville looked at his wristwatch and exclaimed, 'I say, Wallace, we really ought to go and join the ladies!'

'Yes, yes of course. We mustn't keep them waiting.' Charles Wallace gave her a lopsided grin and his eyes held hers for a moment before he departed.

As they walked away towards The Grange she heard him say, 'We met here once during the Great War.'

When they had disappeared from view, she stood up and looked at the land below her. Most of the view was obscured by summer foliage, but she could see the upper part of the river valley sweeping down to the mill. This investigation was fascinating, but also most unfortunate. The dell, where the cave they spoke of was situated, ran along the end of her garden and, most worryingly, it also adjoined Hankeys Land that belonged to Charles Wallace and under which was the cave where Gran and numerous of her antecedents were buried. If these men dug their way through and discovered the lady of the rocks, they'd also find the tomb and the recently deposited body of her grandmother. What might happen next? Could she be sent to prison for fraud, or whatever the crime of deceiving the vicar might be called? She walked home to the cottage feeling anxious.

The following morning, feeling tired after worrying throughout the night, she was baking in the kitchen when she heard Betty call, 'Kate, Kate, where are you. Kate!'

Wiping the flour from her hands on the large white apron tied around her waist, she went to the kitchen door and opened it to find her sister in the arms of Charles Wallace.

'I fell off my bicycle,' Betty explained, pointing to a bleeding knee protruding from her torn stocking.

'Oh my goodness! Oh dear me!' Feeling flustered and awkward, she fetched a bowl of water from the scullery and bathed the leg, then, having dried it, gently rubbed some marigold salve onto the wound and wrapped a clean piece of cotton around the knee.

Mr Wallace said, 'You seem to be accident prone, young lady.' Adding as he looked towards Kate, 'Fortunately for you, your sister's a good nurse.'

'She does seem to fall off rather a lot.' She smiled and thanked him for bringing Betty home.

'A pleasure, Miss Barnes, a pleasure. I couldn't leave a damsel in distress, especially not one looking like Mary Pickford waiting for the hero to rescue her.' He picked up the pot of ointment with his left hand and asked, 'Are you following in your grandmother's footsteps?'

Gesturing at the bunches of herbs hanging around the room in varying stages of dryness, she replied, 'I'm still collecting, but ever since—' she faltered, remembering it was the maid of his wife's relative who had made the accusations against her '—er, since my grandmother died not many people have asked for remedies.'

He reached out to touch a bundle of lemon balm and sniffed his fingers. 'What d'you use this for?'

'We make a tea of it. It's good for indigestion and headaches. I rub the leaves on insect bites, it stops them itching.'

They stood in silence for a few moments until, saying the first thing that came to mind, she pointed to a flower pot, 'I'm afraid I took that root of wood anemones from Hankeys Land. I wanted to paint them for my collection. They fade so quickly when you pick them so I dug up the root and then I thought I'd return it and I haven't got around to it yet. '

'You're welcome to dig up anything you want, apart from My Lady Oak, of course!'

She felt her face redden.

Betty mumbled, 'I'll get changed,' and limped exaggeratedly from the room.

Charles pointed to her forehead. 'You have flour in your eyebrow, Kate.'

Feeling her whole being fizzing with excitement, she pulled up the apron and, wiping her face with it, said, 'Gran used to say the messier the child, the more she'd enjoyed herself. I suppose I must be having a good time.'

He gave a small laugh and stepped closer. 'You've made it worse.' His finger touched the arch above her eye.

She gripped the corner of the table and steadied herself. 'The p-pie, um . . . It, it will b-burn,' she stuttered and stepped backwards towards the range. 'I must get it from the oven.' With her back to him she invited him to take a seat at the table then placed the pie to one side and, after taking a deep breath, returned to join him.

'You must miss her, most terribly,' he said.

'I turn sometimes and speak to her, I'm so sure she's there. I even hear her walk up the stairs and across the floor above to her room.'

'I asked if you were taking over from her for a reason—' he hesitated '—I miss my healing sessions and wondered if you would . . .?'

'I don't think, I mean, after what happened about the herbs.'

'I thought that was all resolved satisfactorily?'

'Yes, but there was talk nevertheless.' Her heart ached as she looked down at the metal hook projecting from his brown tweed sleeve.

'I suppose you're right. I wouldn't want to cause any further gossip.'

Albert could be heard singing 'Abide with me' as he came in from the garden and moved objects about in the glory hole.

Charles asked, 'How's he coped with the situation?'

'Surprisingly well. He hardly mentions his mother, but when he does it's as though she's in the garden or gone to the shop. I seem to have taken her place.' She fumbled for a handkerchief.

'Here, take mine.'

She accepted the large white square of fine silk and, dabbing at her eyes, remembered an identical one wrapped around her poppy-doll.

'You have a great responsibility on your shoulders.'

'Yes, I know, but I love him dearly.' Loud bangs and thumping footsteps overhead reminded her of Betty and she pointed upwards,

153

saying, 'There's the biggest of my worries at present. She'll leave school in two years and I don't know what she'll do then. She shows no interest in studying, in fact she plays truant rather a lot with your gardener's son.'

'She seems a very bright girl to me. I'm sure she'll get on all right in the end.' Charles inspected the metal hook resting on the table as he spoke. 'Actually, I'm more worried about you.' He bit his lip. 'I couldn't come and speak to you for fear of setting the tongues wagging, but things have quietened down now and also my wife's gone to stay with the cousin whose maid caused all the trouble.' He looked directly at her. 'I'm wondering if she did irreparable harm?'

Although longing to tell him that many people shunned her, she said instead, 'I expect people will forget eventually.'

'I suppose the word went round the village?'

'Several times and with many additions.'

'Such as?'

'That you hushed it up.'

He gave a small nervous cough before saying, 'Three separate sources have already told me of your good fortune. I'd put money on there being several bachelors within a radius of five miles just waiting for a decent interval to pass before coming to call.'

'You're changing the subject.'

'I know. It's because I feel ashamed of my wife. It only happened because her cousin's an interfering bully. Within three days of arrival she wanted to know why I came here on Thursdays. Then she sent her maid to try and trick you.' He looked upwards. 'I'm so grateful to that little madam upstairs, otherwise I'd never have ...' His jaw dropped and he exclaimed, 'Oh, damn!'

'Betty told you, didn't she?'

'Kate, sweet Kate, you might be in the middle of a very expensive legal wrangle by now if she hadn't.'

'So the story that it was hushed up is true?'

'I spoke to a friend of mine who has influence.' He shrugged. 'I suppose one might argue that because the stuff you gave her was harmless it would have happened anyway, but if the local press had got hold of it who knows? And—' he grimaced '—if my wife's cousin had thought of suggesting her maid had been deceived into thinking the strawberry leaves, or whatever they were, would induce an abortion instead of rushing off to the police immediately then there's a whole other case to be argued.'

154

She looked up at the herbs drying over the range. 'I'm going to be very, very careful.' Then, understanding the full implications of the situation, added, 'In fact that's the end of it, isn't it?'

'I think you'd be wise to avoid giving anyone anything for a while unless you're really, really sure of them—' he grinned '— like me for instance?'

'You're the last person I should give anything to.' After a long pause she went on, 'There's one very good outcome of inheriting the property.'

'And that is?'

'I don't have to wait until I'm thirty to vote.'

'Of course. Congratulations!'

'My father wouldn't be so happy. I remember him saying the suffragettes were all mad women who broke windows and should've been content to mind their bairns and let the menfolk do the voting.'

'Well, I'm glad those *mad women* joined in the war effort and won your battle.'

Albert opened the door cautiously sniffing the air and sat at the table looking expectantly at her.

Charles stood up and patted the old man on the shoulder. 'I must be going. I'm invited to an archaeological dinner at Valley View tonight. I'm sure it won't smell as good as yours.' He walked to the doorway and paused, before adding, 'If you wish to come and see us at the dig tomorrow you'd be most welcome.' He raised his left hand. 'Until we meet again, Miss Barnes.'

Betty reappeared a few minutes later and, as she sat at the table, said, 'Mr Hayes says I can go and see the cave any time I like.'

'You've promised you'll never ever say a word to anyone about the secret cave and Gran and ...'

'I've sworn a solemn, cut my throat and hope to die, oath,' Betty retorted indignantly. 'I haven't even told Billy Nelson and he's my blood brother and Romany, er, friend.'

'Very well, sweetheart. We've sworn the oath for life. You won't forget that, will you?'

'I'll keep it for my *whole* life,' Betty said solemnly. Then added with a grin, 'And I'll know what to do when I bury you in there, won't I?'

Chapter Twenty

*Dried Coltsfoot can be smoked as herbal tobacco. A drink made
by boiling the leaves is good for asthma and breathlessness.*

Hearing a vehicle approaching, Kate closed the small front gate
behind her and stood in the lane waiting for it to pass by, then felt
the familiar thump of excitement when Charles Wallace parked the
car beside her and jumped out, saying, 'Good morning, Miss
Barnes, what a beautiful day! Allow me to introduce our two
archaeologists from London.'

Smiling politely at the two men, she asked if they had found the
remains of the wicked witch.

The older man shook his head as he replied, 'I doubt it, myself.
We've no way of knowing either how old the bones we've found
are, or who they belonged to. Mr Wallace would like us to believe
the romantic notion, but no I fear not.'

'We can show you the cave.' Charles opened the car door. 'We
just can't be sure the legendary wicked witch lived in it or, for that
matter, died in it. Jump in the back with Jim and we'll show you.'

She squeezed into the remaining space on the seat beside several
items of photographic equipment and the younger man who was
holding the camera.

Charles drove over the bridge and turned left down the lane until,
reaching the old mill ruins, he parked the car and they made their way
across the small wooden bridge, along a narrow path between large
boulders and up to the hole in the rock face above them.

The young archaeologist gestured around him. 'We had a lot of
clearing to do before we could get into the cave.'

Looking at the familiar cliffs of rock, sheer in places and hidden by undergrowth in others, she recognised they were part of the same formation as that behind Old Myrtles and, attempting to hide her apprehension, said, 'I've often walked this way down from up top and I'd no idea the entrance was here.'

After lightly touching her elbow, Charles suggested she should follow him then led the way along a path and showed her the entrance to the cave. He held out his left hand and warning, 'Take care, it's slippery and I don't want you to fall.' His eyes met hers until she lowered her gaze to the muddle of excavated rock and earth.

After several minutes of walking through first one cave, then another, they stopped in one very similar to that in which she had left her grandmother's body.

Pointing up at the pink and white stalactites overhead, Jim said, 'I never get used to them. To think they've been formed over years and years from that steady fall of water just amazes me every time.'

'It's very, very beautiful,' she agreed.

The older archaeologist pressed his ear against the rocks. 'There's probably other caves beyond this one, in fact I can hear water here—' he beckoned to her '—listen.'

She climbed across several planks of wood covering a hole and did so. Hearing what she guessed would be the sound of water falling into the pool in the secret cave, she said, 'I suppose it runs down through cracks in the rocks off the land and into the river.'

He nodded in agreement. 'There's a story, probably another legend, that there's a lake under the hill.'

'Yes, it's a common belief around these parts.' She grinned and added, 'Mind you, my sister told me there's also tales a fairy castle and treasure-trove too!'

Charles Wallace smiled as he suggested, 'Maybe they're all true. Jim's heard some good stories, haven't you?'

'Oh yes—' Jim chuckled '—quite a few. One chap in the pub told me there's a magical pool of blood in a sacred cave where the Holy Grail is hidden and Tom Hayes met a man in Glastonbury who believed Jesus Christ is buried under these hills and will one day emerge to save us all.'

The older man said, 'And I was told King Arthur's knights used to come here and drink from a holy well before they went on their dragon-slaying quests.'

Charles looked shamefaced. 'I think I probably started that rumour when I was nine!'

157

'Creative little bugger, weren't you, Charlie?' the older man responded and laughed.

'I do apologise, Miss Barnes, for my friend's appalling language.' Charles's deep, lovely voice was close, very close.

She could feel his warmth and smell his shaving soap, and, as she turned her head to speak, her lower lip brushed the tweed covering his shoulder. 'I'd like to believe all the stories,' she said breathlessly. Then, moving away, continued in what she hoped was a casual manner, 'My sister said you'd found a knife. Is that right, Jim?'

'That's a bit of an exaggeration. It's a piece of metal that looks as though it might have been the blade of a small knife, but we need an expert metallurgist to look at it.' Jim smiled at Charles Wallace as he added, 'There's always the possibility it might have been dropped by mischievous little boys about thirty years ago, but if it is old then it's an important find.'

'I imagine a knife would have been a precious tool to someone living in a cave.'

'Indeed, it would have been vital to their survival. '

'And the bones,' she asked, 'what about them?'

He shrugged. 'Who knows?' Pointing to the disturbed earth at his feet, he said, 'We found two goat skulls mixed up with the human remains and I suspect it was an old goatherd who'd taken shelter and died. He'd probably tethered his animals and they'd have starved to death alongside him.'

She sighed with relief and, realising what she had done, quickly said, 'How sad, and how very lonely that sounds.'

'My money's still on the witch—' Charles Wallace's mouth was just behind her ear, his breath tickled her neck '—I'm sure females have a wider pelvis so we could tell if it belonged to a woman.'

The younger man bent to light a second lamp and his shadow loomed on the rocks ahead.

Seeing the grotesquely distorted shape, she felt overwhelmed with panic. Blood was drumming in her ears and sharp pains pierced her lungs. 'I must get back,' she said, desperately trying to keep calm. The atmosphere was suddenly thick and oppressive, the space seemed to be shrinking and she was suffocating. Turning to escape she slipped and lost her balance, then, falling against his solid square chest, she felt Charles' arms enfold her.

'Take care, Kate,' he said huskily. 'We don't want any more witches dying in here.'

158

With an enormous effort she pulled away from him and led the way out into the daylight where, turning and meeting his concentrated gaze for a moment before focussing on the left lapel of his brown tweed jacket, she thanked him for showing her the cave. Then, trying to breathe steadily and deeply to restore her rapidly thumping heart to its normal pace, she walked along the path beside the river and onto the lane towards the village shop.

Three days later, after another sleepless night in which she could think of nothing other than Charles Wallace, she cycled wearily home from Wells beside the hedges hazed with the green of newly opened buds. On rounding a bend and seeing the village with a few brash yellow daffodils still blooming in the gardens and her favourite wild narcissi gleaming from the grass verge beside her, she felt her spirit lift and smiled with pleasure.

On her return to the cottage, she walked up the steps in the cliff and all the way to the oak tree in Hankeys Land where she sat at its base looking up into the dark lace of twigs and saw the buds ready to open. Spring happened no matter what else was going on. No war, no plague, no heartbreak could stop the new growth beginning again.

She heard the cough to warn her of his presence on the other side of the small clearing.

'May I join you?'

Knowing this moment would affect the rest of her life, and in years to come she would remember the feeling of inevitability as he stood hesitantly before her on the path between two young oaks, she nodded and beckoned him to her.

He walked several paces and stopped. 'That's almost where you were the first time we met.' He took another step and sat on a root nearby, then looking at the ground, went on, 'You were white as a sheet and I experienced a level of panic I didn't know existed. I'd seen all sorts of indescribably terrible injuries on the Somme and yet the sight of a young girl lying at the foot of a tree completely unnerved me. Odd isn't it?'

'I suppose you only expected to find death and injury in stinking horror and I took you by surprise.' 'Indeed you did. I've never forgotten it, in fact it was one of the most memorable events of my life.' He turned to look at her. 'Your grandmother told me you had a premonition that day —' he held up his hook '— of this.'

159

She nodded.

'I knew something strange had happened. Your eyes became milky for a moment.'

'It was the first time I had the experience.'

'So it was a memorable day for you also?'

She agreed and, remembering the young man in the train to London, asked, 'the smell in the trenches was so terrible after the action, wasn't it?'

He nodded, 'Yes, an absolute nightmare, but you helped me to bear it. I often thought of you when I went back after we'd met. If I wanted to take myself away from the harsh reality of it all, I only had to think of this tree and immediately there you were, curtseying to it like a creature from fairyland.'

'A rather muddy and untidy fairy!' she exclaimed and grinned before adding seriously, 'you said we were soulmates, both leaving the place we loved.'

'Yes, indeed. And here we are back again—' he smiled wryly '—badly changed in my case, but beautifully so in yours.'

She felt her face redden. 'You were very sad to be leaving your lovely wife and, and. . .'

'My poor wife suffers most terribly, that's why I must make allowances for, well,' he frowned, 'things like attempting to ruin your grandmother and you. She's in such pain and I'm consumed with guilt.'

'But your son died while you were away. Why should you feel guilty?'

'Because I'm helpless and can do nothing to ease her suffering. Because my grief doesn't match up to her *agony*.'

Looking into his troubled eyes and at the deep lines either side of his mouth, she wanted to take him in her arms and rock him like a child while telling him he was a normal natural human being who had suffered terrible loss. Taking a deep breath, she said, 'I don't know, Mr Wallace. I've never lost a child. I imagine it must be the worst thing that could happen to a mother, poor Mrs Wallace.'

'Indeed. Poor Mrs Wallace,' he echoed, leaning back against the tree.

With her body aching for his touch, she forced her mind to think of his wife. She was sorry for the woman, but she'd already said that. What else was there to say? 'I hope she enjoys her stay with her cousin.'

'I hope so too.'

She sought words to fill the silence and said the first that came to mind, 'I'm going to Bath tomorrow to get fabric for Betty's ...'

'Really! That's a coincidence.' He raised his head and brightened. 'I have to go there tomorrow. I could give you a ride in the motor car.'

'Oh no, I couldn't trouble you, no, I can get the bus, it's so much quicker now. It used to take most of the day what with changing trains at Evercreech ...'

'Nonsense—' he interrupted'—I'll be driving the archaeologists there anyway and the wicked witch too, well, her bones that is, but there'll be plenty of room.'

'I really don't think ...'

'Nothing to think about. It's all settled, we'll call for you at half past nine.'

She stood up. 'I'll see you tomorrow.'

He rose and placed his left hand on her shoulder. 'Sweet Kate,' he whispered.

A man's voice called, 'Mr Wallace, sir, are you there?'

They jumped apart. Charles exclaimed under his breath, 'Bloody gardener!' then strode away towards The Grange.

That night, she lay awake looking up at the shadows on her bedroom ceiling and wondering what might have happened if Billy's father had not come in search of his master. Would they have embraced? Might she have given herself as she had once to the shepherd under the willows?

Slipping quickly into the other time and other life, she lay on her sleeping shelf listening to the even breathing of her sleeping child. *She had seen the shepherd in the marketplace that day walking with his wife and had quickly hidden behind a cart to avoid meeting him. Now, remembering how the girl had come to her asking for a spell to make a man love her, she gave a wry smile to think that she had helped her take him from her. Then, admitting she could never have married him for fear of his finding the secret cave, knew she must accept his going and no longer think of him or ache for his embrace.*

Eventually, knowing the moon would soon be ready for her, she rose and went to stand outside the dwelling and took long deep breaths of the sweet night air. She had a beautiful bright daughter who ran along the paths before her, laughing with the joy of life. A

161

child who gave her such pleasure as made her heart fill with over-whelming love. She had the cave and the beauty within it to feed her spirit; and she had enough food to feed her body. From time to time she had the local women come seeking her help with birthing or healing. All these things she had for which to be thankful, and yet she wanted one more thing. She longed for another child.

Looking up at the thin crescent of light shining in the dark sky she raised her arms and called, 'Oh, Mother Moon, send me a lover soon.'

Chapter Twenty-One

Raspberry leaf tea helps in childbirth but should not be taken in the early weeks of pregnancy.

She was aching under the heavy burden of wood whilst encouraging the weary child to walk faster. Soon they would rekindle the fire and cook the pigeon they had trapped, then they could sleep.

On approaching the dwelling she saw a figure sitting on a log nearby, and, placing her bundle on the ground she hurried forwards. Her own child was tired and in need of food, but she could see the little boy in the woman's arms had greater need. 'What ails him?' she asked.

'He keeps no food inside him. I'm desperate. Canst thee help me?'

She looked at the grey pallor of his skin stretched across his bones and said sadly, 'I fear it is too late.'

'I beg thee to try. Please, please, at least try.'

She knew it was hopeless. 'I can make no promise of cure. He has the summer sickness.'

'Thee saved the Miller's babe a twelvemonth since.'

'Aye, but she was stronger and not so near death.'

'Just try, I beg thee.'

'Very well.' Realising the woman needed to feel she was doing something to save her child, even though there was no hope, she fetched some herbs and handed them to her, saying, 'Boil these in water. Make sure there is much steam from the pot and the water is reduced by half: then when it is cool moisten his mouth with it until he can drink a little. If he ... When he has taken some of the liquid for one day, add some honey to it the next day and—' she

163

gulped back her tears '—on the next morning give him goat's milk to drink. If he holds that down then he will get well.'

'I thank thee. I shall repay . . .'

'Nay—' she held up her hand '—I need no payment.' She watched the sad figure walk away into the lengthening shadows, knowing there would be grieving on the morrow.

Turning away she entered the dwelling and saw her own healthy daughter had already plucked the bird and was rekindling the fire from the embers under the clods of earth she had placed over it that morning. They would sleep well with full bellies that night.

Awakening to the sound of Albert humming in the next room, she lay reliving the sad experience in the dream, until, remembering that this morning she would go to Bath with Charles Wallace, she felt her heart lift. What would she wear?

An hour later she was trying to decide whether panama hat would look better with the cream raw silk outfit or perhaps a white straw might be better, when her sister said, 'I'd like to come with you today, I could help carry things and . . .'

'No, Betty, I explained yesterday, you must go to school or we'll be in trouble.' Kate threw a blackened piece of toast into the dustbin, thinking she was too nervous to eat it even if it wasn't burned.

'We never do anything sensible in the beastly place. *Please, please, please* let me come with you.'

'Sorry, I'll be getting a visit from the Attendance Officer if you miss any more days. You can come with me in the holidays. Please, sweetheart, you really should go now.'

'It's a complete waste of time. The teacher hates me . . .'

Kate took a sixpence and placed it on the table, saying, 'There's a little extra pocket money. I'll probably catch the three o'clock bus and be home soon after five.'

'She does hate me, honest!'

'Please, just go to school *now*!'

'All right, keep yer hair on!' Betty picked up the coin and, in a sudden movement, jumped up and hugged her before running from the house leaving the door to close with a loud bang.

A few minutes later, while dithering between the two hats, she heard the car draw up outside and, jamming one onto her head, ran to the gate where Charles was waiting with the two archaeologists who were sitting on the back seat.

The older man patted the container on his knees, saying, 'We're taking a few of the bones we found to Oxford, for some scholars to look at.'

She sat in the front passenger seat and reached back to touch the plain flat wooden lid of the box, then recoiled as her fingers burned with intense heat. Turning back to face the windscreen, she heard voices far away calling, '*Catch her! Catch her! String her up now!*'

Charles Wallace looked quizzically at her as he asked, 'You look awfully solemn, Miss Barnes.'

'I was wondering whose bones they might be and how they got there, that's all.'

The younger man on the back seat leaned forward as he spoke. 'I'm sure it was just a goatherd who used the cave as a shelter and was either ill or died of old age.'

'My money's still on the witch,' Charles said and drove the car down the lane, across the bridge and through the village.

Seeing several lace curtains quiver behind cottage windows and Mrs Nelson pause on the threshold of the shop to watch them pass by, Kate guessed the local population would soon hear she had not only narrowly avoided going to prison for giving an abortion, but had been seen with Mr Wallace in his motor car.

Although now used to travelling in the charabanc operating between Bath and Wells and Mr Wallace had given her occasional short rides home from Wells, this was an exciting adventure and she was entranced as they hurtled through the undulating, green and golden land past the occasional farmhouse and through tiny hamlets where old men gaped, children waved, dogs barked and chickens scattered out of their way.

On arrival at the station, Charles Wallace climbed out and helped the two men extricate themselves and their boxes, then, when she placed her hand on the shiny door handle, he told her to stay seated and, unwilling to argue in front of the others, she complied.

After the archaeologists had departed, Charles turned the starter handle in the front of the motor car and, after several minutes and three false starts he climbed into his seat and pressed the accelerator. 'She's very temperamental, starts like an angel when no one's looking and it really doesn't matter how long I struggle to get the damned thing running, but give her an audience in a public place and she goes to pieces.' Having revved up the engine to his satisfaction, he let in the clutch and drove the car to the main street. After parking outside the drapers he said, 'I'm meeting my sister for coffee. Will two hours be long enough for you?'

'But I can catch the bus ...' she began.

'Nonsense, meet me here.'

The doorman was opening the car door and once again, being unwilling to have a public dispute, she agreed.

An hour later, having bought fabric for Betty's two new summer frocks, she left the shop and found Charles standing beside his car talking to an elegantly dressed middle-aged woman whom he introduced as his sister, Mrs Faires, and who, with the same slightly askew smile as his, suggested they might visit the tea garden in Victoria Park as a pleasant change from the Pump Room, and then departed.

She sat in the front seat of the motorcar whilst Charles turned the starting-handle, getting hotter and hotter with each attempt until, by the time the engine burst into life, sweat was pouring down his red face.

'God knows why I don't employ a chauffeur to do this for me,' he said, climbing in beside her. Then, shaking his head and pushing the gear lever forward, he grinned as he added, 'Because I love her, that's why!'

She relaxed and laughed.

Staring ahead through the windscreen, he said, 'Yours is the loveliest laugh I've ever heard.'

Unable to control either the smile of joy or the blush burning her face, she dared not look at him until they arrived at the tea garden where two elderly ladies eyed them with interest as a waiter ushered them to a table in the dappled shade of a huge tree.

Feeling light-headed, and regretting having missed breakfast, she said, 'This is a rare treat for me, I'm shy of eating out alone.'

'This is a *very* rare treat for me too.' The only person I usually meet in Bath is my sister and the main topic of conversation is always her financial situation. Today it was whether she can afford to stay in her favourite hotel in Biarritz this year or not. She's a widow and the house she inherited costs a fortune to maintain, almost more than the income from her investments. But—' he smiled and gave a sigh '—that's all about to change since my friend in New York has agreed to help her out.'

'You must be so relieved,' Kate said.

'Johnson's a financial wizard,' he explained. 'He was at board-
ing school with Parville and me and offered to help us both. I've
done very well since I became his partner two years ago but Par –
sorry, I should say, *Barnet* Parville was far too cautious and
wouldn't join us. He won't admit it, but I suspect he's wishing he
had now.' He grinned. 'We still call each other by our surnames,
I'm afraid – even after all these years. My wife finds the school-
boy tradition very irritating and insists we should grow up and use
our first names. I do try, but old habits die hard. After all, we were
seven years old wen we first met! As I was saying – Johnson, I
should say Hilary ...'

Kate made a desperate attempt to hear the words as they floated
far away over the treetops towards a bird flying high in the sky.
Why had she not eaten that burnt piece of toast?

'... and so you see he took the chance and now he's made a
fortune in the States.'

Her mouth was dry as she forced out the words, 'You must find
life dull in the village compared with New York—' her voice
seemed as though belonging to a stranger '—especially now the
archaeologists have left.'

'I'm sure I'll find interesting things to do—' he leaned towards
her '—actually, Jim wants to come back and investigate all the
other caves ...'

A sudden thump of shock echoed through her body and swarms
of bees buzzed around her head before she awoke to find herself
on the ground, looking up into the same anxious blue eyes as she
had done years ago under the oak tree.

'I'm so sorry. I'm so sorry,' she repeated several times as
Charles helped her to stand.

'It's the heat, madam,' the waiter said as he held the cast-iron
chair for her to sit down.

The two ladies hovered beside her for a few moments and then
returned to their table and Charles Wallace sat on the edge of his
seat, holding her hand.

'I, I feel terribly, terribly foolish,' she stammered.

'Eat,' he said, placing a sandwich before her. 'Please, please eat
and drink.'

Having watched her silently consume three smoked salmon sand-
wiches and two cups of China tea, he nodded with approval. 'You

look as though you've come back to join the living. D'you feel better?'

'Yes, but still rather daft.' She looked over the balustrade at the exotic forest of camellias and rhododendrons growing below her and at the patch of cloudless blue sky above a glimpse of rolling countryside in the distance, then up at the majestic trees towering overhead before returning her attention to the man sitting across the round, cast-iron table and seeing him pull a small green leather box from his pocket.

Handing it to her he said, 'I saw this in an old junk shop and, well, I'd like you to have it.'

Lifting the lid she stared in wonder at two heart-shaped opals surmounted by a gold lover's knot. 'I can't accept such a ...'

'I showed it to my sister, she thinks it's pure Victorian sentimentality, and she's right of course, but then I *am* sentimental and I was born in eighteen eighty-eight which makes me *Victorian*.'

She looked down at the stones flashing a myriad of colours in the sunlight and murmured, 'It's the most beautiful thing I've ever seen.'

'I've no idea what shape a soul would be, so I thought a heart would do quite well. What d'you think?'

'Soul-mates?' She took the ring from its box and slipped it onto the third finger of her right hand. 'It's lovely, but I can't possibly accept it.'

A couple walked past their table and hesitated. Looking up, Kate exclaimed, 'Mr and Mrs Hayes! Good morning.'

Charles slipped the empty box into his pocket and said cheerfully, 'Tom and Lydia, how delightful! Do join us, won't you?'

Polite conversation followed in which the weather was discussed and Tom Hayes explained the dig had been very successful and a wooden door had now been fixed into the entrance to the cave and was securely locked to prevent any possible accident to inquisitive sightseers.

After ten minutes, Kate said, 'If you'll excuse me I really must go now.' She smiled politely at Charles. 'Thank you so much, Mr Wallace. That was most enjoyable.' Then, after bidding them all good day, she left the café and walked to the bus stop on the road to Wells where she stood looking at the ring sparkling in the sunshine while praying he would come and find her.

When the bus arrived without any sign of him, she sadly climbed on board and stared out of the window wondering what might have happened if Mr and Mrs Hayes had not joined them. Then she remembered her shopping was still in his car and felt her heart skip a beat. Might he bring it to her that evening?

The following morning, reaching under her pillow for the opal ring, she held it up to catch the early morning light and kissed it. If only Mr and Mrs Hayes hadn't arrived when they did, they might be lovers by now. But he could have come to her later, couldn't he? Maybe she had misread him. Maybe his intentions were purely honourable and she had been saved from making a huge fool of herself by timely arrival of the Hayes. But, on the other hand, maybe he would come to her this morning!

Placing the ring onto her finger she waved her hand this way and that. It was the most beautiful thing she'd ever owned and, unless she could think of a plausible explanation for having acquired it, she'd have to keep it hidden away. Mrs Faires had said the ring was *'pure Victorian sentimentality'*. Well, the grandparents were Victorians weren't they? All she had to do was move into her grandmother's room and pretend to find it there.

When her uncle and Betty had left the house after breakfast, she changed into a linen frock with buttons all the way down and, feeling giddy with anticipation of Charles' arrival, began changing the bedrooms around.

Hearing the clock at the bottom of the stairs chime twelve, she sat on the bed and admitted he would not be coming. How wise he was to keep away. This was the best outcome. It would have been lunacy, utter insanity! Thank heavens Mr and Mrs Hayes arrived when they did! Then, lying back with hands behind her head on the pillow, she smiled up at the cracked ceiling. He really was very romantic. He had been in love with her all that time. On the other hand, he was a married man and she'd had a lucky escape.

The knocking on the back door, rat-a-tat-tat broke the silence. Her heart stopped for a moment. Again, rat-a-tat-tat. He had come, as she hoped he would. She ran downstairs and opened the door. 'Charles!'

'Your shopping,' he said, handing her the bags.

'Won't you come in?'

He shook his head and looked at the stone floor. 'No, must go.' He turned to leave.

'I'd like you to come in ...'

He swivelled round to face her. 'I didn't dare come yesterday, I thought if I waited I'd be calmer and more ... more ...'

'Prudent?'

He nodded.

'I'd rather you were reckless.'

They reached for each other and kissed.

'It's madness,' he said, closing the door behind him.

'Madness,' she agreed and kissed his throat. 'I've wanted to do that for so long.'

'And I've wanted to do *this* for so long,' he murmured, deftly undoing the buttons with his left hand.

Chapter Twenty-Two

A tea made with Angelica may help indigestion and was an old remedy for both the plague and the ague.

She could hear someone coming along the path and waited sadly, expecting to see a mother carrying a dying infant. There had been three such women in recent days, all with ailing babies and only one of them likely to survive. When the figure of a man emerged through the trees she rose to greet him with surprise and relief, then stood waiting and watching the dust rise with each step he took towards her on the parched earth.

She greeted him politely and looked up into the smiling blue eyes.

'Good day, mistress.' He bowed low, adding, 'A boy across the river told me of thy skill with herbs.'

'Aye.' She was wary of such a man. Why would one who was so richly clad in leather and silk come seeking her aid?

'My horse has a wound that does not heal and I have far to go.'

'I work no miracles.'

'Nay, they are for the Lord our God.'

'I make no promise of cure.'

He nodded.

'Pray show me the beast and I'll do my best.'

'I left her by the river.' The man looked anxiously at a movement in the shadows behind him and reached for the knife at his waist.

'Fear not—' she smiled '—my daughter is but young and rarely sees strangers.'

They walked to the river followed by the child scurrying from tree to tree behind them. On reaching the mare, standing in the shade of overhanging willow branches, the man said, 'I feel like a hunted animal.' He gave a lopsided smile. 'Thou art certain the figure behind that oak is thy daughter and not a robber?'

She laughed and replied, 'Aye, there be no footpads in these woods.'

'Then thou art fortunate, mistress. I've heard tell of many thieves further south.' He touched the handle of his knife. 'The way of a pilgrim is no longer safe.'

'Thee makes pilgrimage to the shrine at Glaston?'

'Firstly, yes and then very far from here across the sea.'

'What shrine be across the sea?'

'The greatest of all. The place where Our Sweet Lord was crucified.'

'The Holy Land!'

'Aye.' He smiled proudly.

She looked at the suppurating wound in the animal's neck and asked, 'Who gave the beast this cut?'

He shrugged. 'I did not ask his name.'

'The way of a pilgrim is indeed not safe!'

'Aye—' he gave a small wry smile '—and the life of a robber may be short.'

'Thee killed him?'

'I helped him fall into a ravine—' he pointed towards the hills '—two days walk away.' He looked at the horse and shook his head. 'I cannot ride her and I'm loath to leave her to die. Canst thou help her?'

She wished to say nay, but on seeing her child emerge from the willows and gaze in wonder at the horse, she wavered, saying, 'Perhaps.'

'I'll pay . . .'

'Only if she be healed. I'd put maggots to eat the puss and then try some herbs if she'll allow me near. I'm more accustomed to goats.' She reached out her hand and the animal backed away.

The man shook his head. 'Perhaps I should take her to Wells. There may be someone who would slaughter her for meat.'

The horse gave a small whinny and bowed her head.

The man held out his left hand saying, 'This ring is thine if I can ride the horse by next new moon.'

172

*She looked at the sparkling gem set in bright gold and replied,
'I thank thee, sir,' then turned away attempting to hide a smile.*

He frowned. 'Why should my offer amuse thee so?'

*She fingered the torn woollen skirt beneath her goatskin apron.
'A mother gave me this cloth three winters since when I helped her
bring forth a living child, another gave me a cheese for saving her
man, what would I do with that jewel?'*

*'I have nothing other than this bauble to offer for the life of my
horse.'*

*She looked at the mare nuzzling her daughter's golden hair and
cried in alarm, 'Caitlin, beware!'*

*'Hush, mother! Don't frighten her. We be friends. She'll let me
tend her wound.' The girl turned and, singing a lullaby, led the
horse towards the dwelling.*

Awakening with the melody fading from her memory, Kate lay
trying to recall the sweet sound of the young girl's voice. Then,
hearing Albert exclaim and begin humming agitatedly in the next
room, guessed the old man had dropped a sock or knocked his
candlestick over, or suffered any one of the small mishaps that
could destroy his peace of mind for hours.

Getting out of bed she stood looking out of the window at the
flowers gleaming in the early sunlight and imagined the man with
his horse standing below her. He had looked like Charles, with the
same deep-blue eyes and brown hair, and his voice also was deep
and beautiful.

Hearing Albert's voice become louder and more agitated, she
sighed and went to help him extricate the collar-stud that had fallen
behind his washstand before going downstairs to the kitchen and
preparing breakfast.

Two hours later, Kate looked at Betty sitting morosely by the
window and said brightly, 'Back to school on Monday!' Then,
seeing the grimace on Betty's face reflected in the glass, she added,
'Be careful, the wind might change.'

'No one'd notice if I *did* get stuck.'

'Billy Nelson would.'

Betty shrugged. 'I've hardly seen him all summer 'cos his mum
says he mustn't talk to me.'

'I saw him in the garden only yesterday!'

'That was 'cos she's gone to visit her daughter Gertie who's having a baby so she's away for a bit. That's the married one, not the one nobody talks about.'

'You'll see him at school.'

Betty looked up at the ceiling in an exaggerated pose of exasperation as she replied, 'Only 'til Christmas. He'll be leaving then 'cos he'll be fourteen in February and it's not worth going back so he's going to start at the ironmongers as soon as we break up.'

Kate was determined to be cheerful. 'That's good news. Did he say he was pleased?'

'Yeah, he says he's really lucky 'cos there's not much work to be had round here.'

'His sister Daisy's your age, isn't she?'

'Yeah.'

'So she won't be leaving yet?'

'No—' Betty smiled angelically '—she spoke to me yesterday too.'

'Oh, that's good.'

'She said you act la-di-da and toffee-nosed, but actually you're a tart all the same.'

Kate gripped the edge of the table whilst replying light-heartedly, 'A toffee-nosed tart sounds rather nice, very sweet in fact.'

Betty made a face. 'I dunno. I suppose I should make the most of my last days of freedom.' She went out and took her bicycle to the front gate then sped off down the lane towards Wells.

Kate sat staring out of the window wondering what people were saying in the village. Being accused of inducing an abortion wouldn't necessarily mean one was a loose woman and anyway that episode was almost six months ago. No, it was obvious her love affair with Charles Wallace was known about by the girl's mother and, therefore, common knowledge.

She heard the sound of Charles knocking on the back door and ran to open it. 'I don't know why you don't just walk in, it's not locked,' she said leading him into the kitchen.

'I wasn't sure if Betty was around and also to warn you it's me and not some other visitor.'

She shook her head. 'No one else calls but you, except the postman of course.'

'I feel so sad about what happened.'

'I expect they'll forget about it eventually. I don't really mind if people walk on the other side of the road or stop talking when I go into the shop, but I think it would've broken my grandmother's heart.' She opened her arms to him, saying, 'We could forget about all this miserable mean-spirited gossiping and go upstairs, couldn't we?'

He moved towards her. 'That's a wonderful idea.' Taking her hand he added, 'Just think, in a few days we won't have to play hide and seek with your sister, well, not until the Christmas holiday at least.'

An hour later lying with her head on her lover's chest and revelling in the afterglow of love, she heard Betty shouting, 'Kate, where are you?' Instantly rolling off the bed, she pulled on a dress and ran down the stairs, calling loudly, 'Here I am. I was just changing my clothes because I was so hot.' Entering the kitchen she looked anxiously at her sister and asked, 'Have you fallen off your bike again?'

'No, something much more exciting's happened.' Betty rolled her eyes dramatically. 'They're in a right two an'eight up at The Grange. The cook's packing her bags and the housekeeper's in trouble 'cos one maid's gone to a wedding and another's visiting her mother in Wells and Mrs Jones who does some of the cleaning doesn't go on Saturdays and the rooms need to be made ready.'

'Oh, why's that, sweetheart?'

'*She's* back.'

'Who?'

'Mrs Wallace has come home.'

Kate turned and ran upstairs, across the landing and into the bedroom. Slamming the door behind her, she leaned against it and exclaimed, 'Oh dear God! I thought she might stay there. Oh, my darling!' She looked into his stricken face. 'Oh, my darling, your wife's back. Betty says all hell's let loose at your house.'

'I'd better go and see what's going on.' Charles groaned then stood up and, holding her close, said, 'She hasn't written all summer. I was hoping she'd stay there for good. I don't know what the next few days will be like. I expect she'll want me dancing attendance until she settles down.' He paused before adding, 'She never leaves her room until after ten. If I can't come here I'll walk up to the oak tree every morning at nine.'

He buried his face in her shoulder for a moment then looked into her eyes, saying flatly, 'I'm married to the poor sad little soul.' He

175

released her and went to open the door.

'Wait, I'll make sure the coast is clear.' She turned the handle and heard Betty scuttle across the landing to her room, then kissed him and said, 'Go now, darling, I'll be here, waiting for you.'

When he had gone she lay on the bed staring at the ceiling. This was what being *the other woman* meant and it wasn't easy. She was suddenly jealous of his wife. Why was he such a good lover? Because he'd learned what to do with *her,* that was why! She hated the fragile prettiness of the woman, hated the narrow wrists and tiny hands that seemed half the size of her own practical and capable ones. She loathed her fine fair hair and small nose. Everything about her was delicate. Of course he would love a lady like her, any man would. Why should he feel anything for a tall, strong, dark woman with a big nose? Well! Why should he? Was it just lust once again? Was she making the same mistake? Did he, like Hugo, want her for sex and nothing more?

The following morning, after waiting by the oak tree for over an hour, she returned home and sank onto a chair in the kitchen where Betty and her uncle were sitting silently eating toast. Seeing her uncle's eyes on the clock, she said, 'I don't feel up to church today. I'll take some feverfew tea and go and lie down for a bit.'

Albert's face fell and he made several agitated movements with his head.

'You'd be all right going with Betty just this once, wouldn't you?'

Betty looked outraged for a moment, swallowed a mouthful and composed her face into a smile before saying, 'Of course, you will, Uncle. We don't mind going on our own, do we?'

Kate held her breath.

Albert's mouth went down at the corners.

'I'll put the joint in the oven just the same as usual and there'll be roast potatoes and Yorkshire pudding.'

The old man nodded and went to fetch his prayer book.

Betty reached out and touched Kate's hand. 'You look absolutely awful.'

The shock of her sister's sudden compassion released the emotion she had held back during a sleepless night, and, feeling uncontrollable tears streaming down her face, she ran to her room and lay on the bed sobbing.

When the three of them sat down to eat two hours later, she asked, 'Did you see Billy, sweetheart?'

Betty nodded.

Albert looked at the joint of lamb on the table and began humming.

Betty bit her lip before saying, 'He told me your friend's going off on his travels again.'

Kate dropped the gravy boat onto her plate and then spent several minutes clearing up the mess. Finally, after regaining some composure, she asked, 'When's he going?'

'Dunno, soon, I think.' Betty chewed her food thoughtfully and added, 'Billy says his dad said the servants said Mrs Wallace was screaming about witches.'

'Witches! Why would she be doing that?'

'Dunno. Billy said she threw lots of things about and broke two windows and one of the maids heard her shouting about somebody called Hilary in New York.' She waved her fork to emphasise the point as she went on, 'It's a good thing his mum's away else he wouldn't've been able to tell me that, 'cos he's not supposed to speak to me.'

Kate stood up. 'I really must get some air, my head's too painful to cope.' She walked out of the house, up the steps in the cliff and on to the oak tree. After pausing briefly to lean against the trunk, she reached up and grabbed the lowest branch then climbed up to the fork in which she had sat as a young girl and closed her eyes trying to make sense of what Betty had told her. Was there a woman in America? Had the servants misheard the row or, more likely, used witch as a euphemism for bitch?

Whispered voices in the rustling leaves swirled around her.

'*Catch her. Get her. String her up!*'

The stench of drunken men wafted up and shadowy figures staggered beneath her for a few moments, then, exhausted in mind and body, she fell into a deep and dreamless sleep.

'Kate. Kate! Where are you?'

She awoke and shivered. How long had she been here? Her left leg had gone to sleep and her back hurt. Looking down she saw her sister's tearstained face peering up through the leaves.

'I couldn't find you anywhere. I've been looking for you for hours. I'm sorry I told you what Billy said.' Betty gave a small sob and then, inclining her head towards the house, added, '*He*'s in a terrible state.'

After rubbing her leg she struggled down and, putting her arm around the shivering girl, comforted her, 'It's all right, sweetheart, it's all right. Please don't cry.' They walked back to the cottage together in silence and found Albert in the kitchen, rocking back and forth, and mumbling incoherently, 'Sunday ham, jam, bread, cake Sunday, Sunday...'

'Hello, Uncle,' she said trying to sound reassuringly normal, 'it's time for delicious ham and chutney. I'll put the kettle on.' She turned to Betty, adding, 'Come along, sweetheart, you must be hungry too.' Somehow she summoned the strength from her hurting body and aching heart to get a meal for them all and then, at nine o'clock, when everything was cleaned and tidied ready for the morning, she crept away to her room.

That night seemed interminable. In the early hours of Monday morning, when the moon was bright, a motor car drove very, very slowly past the cottage and along the road towards Wells. She lay rigid, listening to the sound fade into the night. He had left. She'd found the second love her grandmother had predicted and now he was gone. She reached out and stroked the pillow beside her. His head would have made a dent there most days and later, when Betty had left home, she'd hoped he would stay at night too sometimes, whenever he could get away. That would have been enough, wouldn't it? She was prepared to be a mistress for the rest of her life. Why had he left her like this without a word of explanation? What could his wife have said to make him leave like this? Maybe they were having a row because he had called his wife or her cousin a bitch, not a witch, just as he had to her? Might that be irrelevant anyway? He had had other affairs, at least one with the woman Margaret had known about. Might he have pulled back, unwilling to commit himself when Mrs Wallace demanded a divorce? Or, most likely of all, had he decided to go to another woman in America, one named Hilary?

Chapter Twenty-Three

A tea made from Lemon Balm is a calming tonic that will aid digestion and is a safe remedy for headaches and morning sickness in pregnancy. Rub the fresh leaves onto insect bites.

March 1930

The grandmother clock in the hall seemed to be ticking both slower and louder than usual. 'My word!' Kate exclaimed. 'It's almost two o'clock. Are you watching the time?'

'Why?' Betty asked, crossing her eyes. 'Is something actually going to happen here, at last?'

'I just thought, as it's Saturday, you'd want to be off out somewhere.' Seeing her sister look pointedly through the window at the dripping plants in the saturated garden, Kate forced enthusiasm into her voice as she said brightly, 'It stopped raining an hour ago.'

'There's nothing to do.'

'What? I seem to remember a bicycle being bought only six months ago.'

'Fourteen,' Betty corrected her.

'Good heavens! Is it over a year already since Gran died?' She counted on her fingers and said, 'Yes, you're quite right. Well, now spring's almost here you can get out on it again.'

'There's nowhere to go.'

'Wells?'

'It's too dull and boring.'

'You could ride up to Pridden, or Glastonbury, that's not too far away.'

179

Betty's fair curls bounced as her head shook emphatically. 'Dull and . . .'

'And boring?' She stared at her in disbelief. 'I saved for months to buy that bike and now you tell me cycling is dull and boring.'

Betty blushed and made a face at Albert who was snoring quietly in his chair, then sat watching Kate resume reading her library book. After several minutes of silence, she said, 'Daisy Nelson says her dad says you needn't be an old maid after all. He says now all the fuss has died down you'd be a good catch, even though you've got poor old Albert hanging round your neck.'

Kate looked anxiously at the old man who had stirred at the sound of his name and asked, 'Did you have a little nap, Uncle? I hope you're feeling all right.'

'He misses the motor car from The Grange and—' Betty grinned and rolled her eyes '—and Daisy says *you're* missing it too.'

Kate ignored her.

'What I don't understand is—' Betty frowned '—why we can't go back to London and live a normal life.'

'Normal?'

'Yeah, with a proper lavvy and shops and electricity and, oh I don't know, just everything.'

'We can't, sweetheart, that's all there is to it.'

'I don't see why. Daisy says you're rolling in money now, she can't understand why you stay here either.'

'We have to stay here.'

Betty looked thoughtfully at the old man. 'There must be other cars he could clean. What about Mr Hayes at Valley View?'

'What a good idea!' Kate responded enthusiastically. 'Shall I ask him, Uncle?' Then, seeing him pulling anxiously at his hair, shook her head, saying, 'Praps not, let's talk about something else, shall we?'

'Like going to London? Why don't we talk about leaving this miserable, boring, beastly place and going to live . . .'

'Shut up!' Kate shouted. 'I've had enough, Betty, absolutely enough.'

'All right, keep yer hair on!'

Albert bent forward as though about to start rocking.

With an exaggerated brightness she did not feel, Kate asked him to fetch the eggs.

The old man looked uncertainly at her then slowly stood up.

'We'll have a nice rabbit stew and dumplings and a lovely fruit cake for tea,' she said, gently ushering him through the door.

Betty groaned, rolled her eyes and looked sideways at her sister, saying, 'It's 'cos of him, isn't it?'

'What?'

'It's 'cos of him we don't go back to London where we belong, isn't it?'

'Partly.' Kate suddenly realised she was no longer looking into a small girl's face, but of one who would shortly be a woman. 'We have to understand one another. I'm going to stay here for the rest of my life. What you do when you're old enough is entirely up to you. You're still only just thirteen and have at least one more year in school, after that, sweetheart, you can go where you like.'

Betty snorted. 'That school's a waste of time!' Hearing the sound of footsteps by the window she ran to the back door.

The young postman was standing holding an envelope, 'It's from Canada,' he said, and sauntered away whistling.

Kate looked eagerly at Betty as she carried the letter towards her. For a flicker of time the blonde curls flamed bright red in a sudden beam of spring sunshine and the fingernails on her hand were painted pink.

'Your eyes have gone strange again,' Betty said, handing her the letter.

Kate tore the envelope open and read aloud, 'Dear Sisters, You have another little nephew, we called him Barry. The other two boys are growing up fast. I was pleased to hear that Ethel had married again and wish her well. I am looking forward to the snow melting soon so I can go fishing on the lake. I hope you and little Betty are both well. Your loving brother.'

'That sounds nice,' Betty said, 'but then anywhere's better than here!'

'I'm afraid this is where you live.' Kate felt weary. 'Listen, sweetheart, you just have to make the best of it for a few years.'

Betty stood with her hands on her hips, chin out at an angle. 'I hate it here. I hate everything about it. I hate the school, the people, everything! If you hadn't been stupid with a man in London and been sent here in disgrace ...' Her face lit up in triumph as she saw Kate's horrified expression and she exclaimed triumphantly, 'I knew it! Daisy said that's what happened. Her mum was right, wasn't she?'

Kate walked to the kitchen door. 'I'm going for a walk up on Hankeys Land.' She grabbed the mackintosh coat off the peg in the glory hole and put on her rubber wellington boots. Looking up she could see, reflected in the window, Betty's face with the right thumb to her nose above her protruding tongue. Turning with the instinctive response to lash out, she upset the collection of walking sticks balanced precariously behind the door. The clatter and confusion stopped her violent response and she busied herself with gathering them together as Betty slid past her.

Watching her sister fetch the bicycle from the lean-to outside the house and wheel it out of sight, she said aloud, 'I can't cope with her. Sometimes she looks like she really, really hates me.' Sinking to the floor she sat clasping her knees. 'My God! I think I hate her too!' Could that be true, could two sisters actually *not* love each other?

Warm tears of self-pity trickled down her face whilst walking out into the garden. She'd tried so hard to bring the child up as her mother would want, what more could she do? Pausing by the washing line she heard her grandmother's voice call from the house, 'Tell *Whatsername* tea's ready.' Climbing up the steps in the cliff she repeated the word, 'Whatsername.' The old woman had disliked the child. Even a loving heart such as hers could be unkind sometimes. Betty had been difficult it was true, but she'd had a terrible shock when Polly died and she couldn't help looking like her father, could she?

Charlie, Charlie, Charlie, if only she still had him to confide in, he'd understand.

The overhanging branches were heavy with rain and showered her as she walked along. Arriving at the oak tree, she ran her fingers through the hair plastered to her forehead and ached for her lost lover; if only he was still here to put his arms around her and kiss her wet lips.

For ten minutes she sat on the protruding roots beneath the tree, clasping her knees and pretending she was expecting him to come soon to see her, carrying a book, one of his favourite Dickens perhaps, or an anthology of poetry. They could walk back to the cottage hand in hand and he would light the fire in the parlour and make toast with the long brass fork hanging on a hook at the side of the chimney-breast and then they would read aloud to each other.

Someone was calling, 'Hello there!'

She focused her eyes in the direction of the sound and saw a figure standing on the stile and waving. Her heart leapt for a moment, could it be Charles? No, it couldn't be him. Billy Nelson had told Betty that all the servants knew he was in New York.

'Hello, Miss Barnes!'

Standing up she watched the tall silhouette of the young man walk towards her followed by three others.

'Hello, it's me Jim Hall, the archaeologist, remember?'

She did remember him, but not his name because at the time she had been too engrossed in Charles Wallace to notice any other man. 'Of course, Mr Hall, are you back again to continue digging?'

'Yes, indeed. Allow me to introduce my friends. This chap—' he gestured to a tall, bespectacled man '—is Mr Dean the geologist who's advising us.' He pointed to a smaller, stouter member of the group and added, 'This is Mr Rhodes our friendly water diviner.'

'Known as Dusty.' He grinned and asked, 'Tell me, young lady, who owns this land?'

'It's part of The Grange estate,' Kate replied as calmly as she could.

'All the way along this stretch to the river?' He took out a map. 'It's all wet! Damn!' He crouched down to deal with it.

'Mr Rhodes is a dowser,' Jim Hall said. 'He uses hazel twigs to perform magical tricks, never fails.'

'What—' she swallowed '—sort of tricks?'

'To find water of course!'

'I can tell you where there are several springs, or are you wanting to find a well?'

'No, we're really looking for caves through which the water runs.'

'I thought you'd found one in the dell, where the wicked witch lived.'

'Yes, yes that's right, but we're sure there's more.'

One man lit a cigarette and inhaled deeply.

Another was looking bored as he demanded, 'Are we going to look for these caves or not?'

Jim Hall reddened with embarrassment.

She felt irritated by the young, well-educated and self-confident

183

men around her. Jim Hall was doing his best to be polite, but he too gave the impression she was their intellectual inferior.

The diviner had opened up the wet map and, holding it carefully towards her, he asked, 'Could you show me who owns what along here?'

She wondered if he could hear her heart beating as she pointed to the area of hillside he was indicating and replied, 'That land belongs to The Grange.'

'And below it?' His square, stubby finger was pointing at the long garden of Old Myrtles.

She took a breath. 'If I was looking for caves, gentlemen—' she was pleased with the calmness of her voice '—I wouldn't look here.'

Suddenly she had their undivided attention.

'Why not?'

'Where?'

'D'you know some caves? I *said* local knowledge is the best.'

They were all looking at her expectantly.

She smiled and spoke very calmly and confidently. 'If you look at the map, you'll see the river valley runs into a gorge just back along from the dell. I'm sure Mr Hayes would be happy for you to explore more on his land.' Leaning over, she pointed to the place honeycombed with caves, similar but much smaller than the one she was now guarding from them. 'There's several there, and also—' she was feeling inspired as she pointed to the spot '—on the hill, *up top*, as we locals call it, by a spring just here, there's a place that local chaps like to climb into. There's a sort of cave system there, and also not far away from that there's a large area that's sunken in like a crater. My granfer's granfer remembered when it was a big cave and it collapsed ...'

'Wonderful!' Dusty interrupted, 'even if there's been subsidence we can excavate.' He looked again at the map. 'Higher Top Farm, we'd better go and get permission to investigate.'

'The land is used mainly for grazing sheep,' Kate said, feeling light-headed with relief. 'I'm sure if ...'

'Come along, let's get on with it!' the geologist interrupted, turning away.

The others quickly followed him. Jim Hall raised his hat as he went, saying, 'Many thanks, Miss Barnes. Bye.'

She nodded and turned away. If only that could be the last of them, if only they'd go away and never come back. This was her worst nightmare come true.

Later, as they were going to bed, she asked Betty, 'Did you see the Nelsons today?'

'Billy's at work in the ironmongers on Saturdays.'

'What about his sister Daisy?'

'She only talks to me at school.'

She kissed her and suggested, 'We could go and see that new film on Monday.'

'Can we leave *him* at home and just us two go?'

'No, sweetheart, Uncle Albert does love it so.'

'But he gets so excited and frightened and makes such a fuss! He really believes it's true and I get so embarrassed!'

Kate laughed.

'That's the first time I've heard you do that for months.' Betty hugged her. 'I do love you really, even though you are such a boring old woman who won't live in London.'

'I'll never do that, sweetheart.' Stepping back, she gasped at the image of her sister holding a plump baby before her, as though offering it to someone.

'Your eyes have gone funny again.'

'I'm just tired that's all. Goodnight, sweet dreams.'

Snuggling down into her bed a few minutes later, she lay remembering the baby in Betty's arms. Would the child be the next guardian of the cave? It was comforting to know that, although she herself could not bear a daughter, for there could never be another love for her, the line would still continue. Closing her eyes, she smiled into the darkness and was soon in the other lifetime.

She was thatching the roof when the woman came hurrying along the path with small rapid steps and jerking head movements. Knowing the poor creature was mad with grief, she handed the bundle of withies to the man who had been helping her and climbed down the cliff against which the dwelling was built.

On reaching the clearing the woman uttered several deep moans whilst pulling at her long dark hair and throwing handfuls of it onto the ground.

She stepped forward to comfort the distraught woman whom she had warned two days earlier that her child could not survive. Meanwhile the man, who had been squatting on an overhanging

185

rock above the roof, stood up and looked to see who was making such a terrible sound.

Unaware of the horse beside some hawthorn bushes to her left, the woman raised her arms and screeched, 'My babe is dead! Dead! Dead! Dead!'

The mare whinnied and began kicking at the air around her, moving sideways until she was in the clearing very close to the woman, who then screamed louder and long. The frightened horse rose onto her hind legs, rolling her eyes anxiously; and the woman threw herself to the ground in terror.

Caitlin walked slowly forwards until she was between the agitated animal and the prostrate figure.

The horse scraped at the earth with her right hoof for a while and then, bowing her head, stood completely still, nuzzling the child's hair.

The woman looked around fearfully before raising herself onto her knees. Then, catching sight of the man standing up above the dwelling, she clambered to her feet, crossed herself with a shaking hand and, looking neither to left nor right, stumbled out of the clearing and away down the path.

Chapter Twenty-Four

Fennel is well known as an aid to digestion and is used in gripe water for babies, but should be used sparingly by pregnant women. Harvest the leaves in summer and the seeds and bulbs in autumn.

'My mum says you're as good if not better at healing with the hands as your granny and the hawthorn berry tea has helped no end with her bad legs.' Alice smiled nervously and continued, 'There's a lady in Wells with that awful Saint Vitus's dance thing – keeps shaking, it's terrible to see her. D'you think you could help her?'

'I'll try. I do it for anyone that asks. I'm a bit wary of offering because of all the fuss and the rumours and that sort of thing. Your mother's one of the few people who still speaks to me.' Kate poured water from the kettle into a china teapot and added, 'I hope you're still happy living at the farm.'

'Oh yes, and my Teddy gets on well with your tenant.' The young woman looked embarrassed.

Placing a cup and saucer on the table in front of her old friend, she asked, 'So, have you come to tell me about the archaeologists?'

Alice grinned. 'That's not what the boss calls 'em, I'm sure!'

'What happened?'

'These posh blokes came just when my Teddy and him was getting the cows in. He had a bit of a game with them at first, you know how it is when townies come and look down their noses, but then when he saw they really *did* think he was *stupid,* he lost his temper and threatened them with a shotgun.'

'I can't say I blame him.'

'I thought I'd better warn you 'cos my Teddy told them the

owner lived at Old Myrtles. I don't think he said any more'n that.'

Kate looked into her friend's anxious eyes and asked, 'Did you take the tonic I left with your mother?'

'Oh yes, I'm sorry I didn't come back after *that* time. Soon after you had ... I mean ... It was a bit awkward.' Alice gulped her tea. 'Actually—' a red blush rose up from her neck and spread over her face '—I ... I don't want him to know I came here.'

'The archaeologist?'

'No, no, my Teddy.'

'Really, why's that?'

'There was talk all around these parts about Mr Wallace and ...'

'And me?'

Alice nodded and struggled to control her mouth as she spoke. 'I've been so miserable about it. He won't change his mind, he's so stubborn. If he finds out I came here, he'll—' she gulped '—he'll, well, you know.'

'Oh, dear God!'

Alice averted her eyes. 'He's always sorry afterwards. Swears it'll never happen again.'

They sat in silence for a few moments, then Kate said, 'So Teddy says you're not to mix with a fallen woman like me, is that it?'

Alice nodded. 'He's heard the stories what with his dad being head gardener at The Grange and my mother-in-law's got a tongue on her as you know.'

'The whole village treats me as though I'm a leper. They stop talking when I walk into the shop and cross the road to avoid me.'

Alice leaned forward and held Kate's hand. 'I'm so sorry, so terribly sorry. If it's any consolation, my mum tells everyone how you've helped her. She thinks there's a lot of jealousy, because you inherited the farm and the house. That's why they say what they do.'

'What exactly *do* they say?'

'That you and him were carrying on for years.' She hesitated and went on, 'Actually everyone knew about him coming here regularly when your Gran was alive, and then when Teddy's cousin who works in the café at Victoria Park ...'

Kate groaned, 'Oh dear!'

'There's not many gentlemen with a hook driving a car like that.'

'Yes, I see now we would have been conspicuous.'

'He might not have thought much about you, if you hadn't fainted like that.'

'Yes—' she remembered opening her eyes and seeing Charles gazing down at her with his face so full of love '—yes, that's true, I fainted.'

Alice continued, 'And some people, like my man's mum for instance, don't let a bit of gossip like that go without spreading it far and wide, especially with my father-in-law working at The Grange and hearing all the talk in the kitchen.'

'Yes, I see. Why—' she cleared her throat '—why do the servants say he left?'

Alice's lower lip trembled as she replied, 'When Mrs Wallace came back that last time there was a big row and, and I don't like to say what they heard.'

'You'll have to tell me now, Alice.'

'They say, and I don't know how true it is, they say Mrs Wallace told him to go to his precious Hilary and not come back.'

'Do they know who Hilary is?'

'I think it's obvious.'

'A woman in New York?'

'I'm sorry, Kate.'

'The servants usually know what's going on,' she said quietly, 'so it's probably true.'

Alice bit her lip. 'Actually, I'll have to go, and, well the thing is, I won't be able to see you again for a while. You understand?'

'Of course.' Her jaw ached from controlling her tears and she felt relieved when Alice had departed and she could weep.

Gazing at the iridescent opals on her finger an hour later, she admitted that the whole village had known about the ring all along and so, therefore, had Betty and, even worse, everyone also knew about the woman in America. A loud knock on the front door made her jump in surprise and immediately smile grimly. She knew who it would be: only strangers to the area would be unaware it had been locked for over thirty years.

Having walked around the house, she found three of the archaeological team standing in a huddle by the overgrown porch.

Jim Hall stepped forward removing his hat as he exclaimed, 'Kate! What a surprise! We were told the landlord of Higher Top Farm lived here.'

189

'That's quite right, the owner does live here,' she replied, watching one of his companions gazing down the back garden.

The water diviner smiled tightly and in slow, clearly enunciated words he said, 'Please would you fetch him, miss?'

'That might be difficult.'

'We'd be obliged if you'd try to find him,' Jim Hall said very politely.

Looking at each one in turn she was tempted to play a game with them. It would be fun to make an appointment for them to meet the owner the following day and then greet them with regal dignity, but there was too much at stake to indulge in such childishness. She wanted them to concentrate on caves as far away as possible and the man who was already interested in her garden might guess her secret if he came back again and investigated the rock face behind the house. She said, 'I'm afraid it would be impossible for me to fetch *him*.' Then, smiling confidently at them, she added, 'I trust the episode with my tenant and the shotgun didn't frighten you too much?'

Jim Hall opened his eyes wide, 'Oh God! I'm so sorry. I realise now. We met you here that day we went to Bath. It's you, you're the owner, aren't you?'

'I would've told you yesterday, but I'm afraid you were in far too much of a hurry to waste time speaking to a local peasant woman.'

He held out his hand. 'I think we may have been rather high-handed with you. May we begin again?'

'Perhaps.'

The water diviner sighed and asked, 'Is it money you want?'

She shook her head. 'I'll have a word with my solicitor to see if there's any legal reason why I shouldn't let you dig up that field. If you come back on Thursday with proof of any insurance needed I'll see if I can mollify the farmer. Like most people he's quite reasonable if treated with respect.' She turned to go and stopped, saying, 'There are several old mounds up there too. If you're interested, find Lammas Hill on the map, walk about two hundred yards south of the elm trees in the corner of the field and you'll find them. My grandmother said they were very, very old. She always referred to the area as Prince's Grave Field. She said the old name was left off the new map of eighteen twenty-two and they were just called mounds after that.'

190

All three of them responded with shining eyes and wide smiles. Each in turn shook her hand and thanked her. Jim Hall asked, 'Would we be able to look at them without getting shot?'

She gave a restrained smile. 'The public footpath runs alongside them. If you see the farmer, explain I said you could look, *just look*, and make sure you close any gates behind you. I'll see you on Thursday, gentlemen.'

When they had gone she found herself shaking uncontrollably. She was able to stop them coming into her garden, but suppose they could dig down from above? The burial cave was at least twelve feet away from her own boundary and under Hankeys Land, which was on The Grange property and Mrs Wallace would probably let them do what they liked on that piece of useless ground.

She walked down the path and sat on the rock close by the cave entrance. It was clear the geologist was still interested in looking for other caves close to the dell. She would have to keep her wits about her and be ever vigilant, but for the moment the situation was under control.

Closing her eyes she imagined sitting on this same rock long ago with the man who looked like Charles sitting beside her. *Sliding into a dream she watched a young woman approach holding a bundle towards her. Looking down into the wizened little face of yet another dying infant in the arms of yet another distraught mother, she said, 'There's nowt to be done, mistress.'*

The woman gave a small sob and walked away.

The man rose from his seat on the rock between the cave and the dwelling and put his hand on her shoulder as he consoled her. 'Every summer's the same where I come from. The small ones die of squits.'

'Aye and each year I say the same. If there be no milk within thee to feed the babe, give only that of the goat or water from a running spring.' She wiped the tears from her eyes. 'There have been even more this time than usual and I can do nothing to help.'

His arm slid around her and she kissed his throat until, hearing her daughter approach, she jumped back.

'Mother, come and see. Sire, look at thy mare, I beg thee.'

Seeing it standing quietly in the shade, she asked, 'What ails her, Caitlin?'

'Nought ails her, mother. The wound is healed.'

She turned from her daughter's proud face and saw sadness in the man's blue eyes.

191

'I am sworn to go,' he said, reaching out to her, *'it was a sacred oath.'*

Taking his hand she silently pressed it to her heart.

He gave a small uneven smile and put his other hand on the mare's neck. *'If miracles were allowed to mortals then this would be one.'* Then, taking the gold and diamond ring off his finger he gave it the girl, *'I thank thee, maiden. Thou hast cared for her every moment of the day and slept beside her under the stars at night.'*

Caitlin gazed at the ring and then back at him. *'I should prefer the horse.'*

He smiled again. *'Aye, I know, but I have need of her. Now I must ride a little to prepare her for the journey.'* His hand shook as he picked up a bridle and, without looking up, he said, *'I shall leave at dawn, my lady.'*

She had lain with the man each night from one new moon to the next and had been dreading this moment throughout each day as she fetched wood and searched for food. *'Aye, sire,'* she replied, and turned away to hide her tears.

Awakening with a sob, she dried her eyes while acknowledging that same pain of losing Charles was still as raw as the day he left. Walking sadly through the garden, she looked up towards the mist hanging over the hills, which, by hiding the tops of them, altered one's understanding of their boundaries. If only she could leave her heartache down here then walk upwards into the clouds and far, far away into the sky!

Chapter Twenty-Five

Henbane is poisonous and must never be taken internally, but the leaves when applied to the temples with vinegar reduce headaches and the boiled herb or seed will kill lice in humans and animals.

The solicitor rubbed his hands together as he said, 'This is really good news. They've already promised the museum can have a couple of things they found in the cave last year.'

Kate leaned forward asking what they were.

'The piece of metal that might have been a knife—' he grinned '—probably dropped by a small boy thirty years ago, and also the ball of rose quartz they found on their last day, did you know about that?'

She shook her head, remembering her grandmother reminisce how her grandmother had used such a ball to scry in, and murmured, 'How intriguing.'

'The other interesting thing—' Barnet Parville smiled '—is that the idea of finding other caves higher up has caught their imaginations, especially Jim Hall, who evidently admires you greatly and is full of praise for your knowledge of local history. The geologist would still like to look around for caves close to the one in the dell and seems convinced there would be others linked to it.'

Her heart missed a beat.

The solicitor gave a knowing wink. 'But he who pays the piper calls the tune.'

She looked blankly at him.

'Jim's the one with the money to fund the project.'

She felt her eyebrows rise.

'Didn't you know that?'

'I had no idea.'

'He's a wealthy young chap is our Jim and archaeology is his passion. I'm absolutely delighted he's come back, our only problem is they've upset your tenant.'

'I'll go up tomorrow and speak nicely to him. Whatever *I* do, I think they'll have to grovel to him if they want his co-operation.'

'That won't do 'em any harm.' The solicitor wrote 'grovel' on the notepad in front of him, and, without looking up gave a small embarrassed cough, then said, 'My wife has informed me you are not er, sewing so much lately.'

'Yes—' she was surprised '—that's true. I don't have many clients at present.'

'I er, am—' he raised his eyes and met her gaze '—I'm truly sorry. Truly, truly and so is my wife. Would it help if she had something made?'

She shook her head. 'Please thank Mrs Parville, I really appreciate her concern, but tell her I'm pleased to have stopped sewing and the fact the ladies have all dropped me doesn't matter, I have the rent to live on. Thanks to my grandmother, we won't starve.'

'Good, good.' He gave another nervous cough. 'I'll make all the arrangements for the archaeologists. They're staying in the public house in the village this time.' He fidgeted with his fountain pen and spilt ink onto the mahogany, then exclaimed, 'Damn!' He wiped up the mess with his handkerchief and, looking at the black mark on it muttered again, 'Damn!'

Thinking he had an air of childlike innocence, despite his greying hair, she rose from her chair, saying, 'I think we've dealt with everything?'

He looked up at her. 'Everything? Yes, yes of course. If there's anything we can do. I'm so sorry it all worked out as it did.'

She thanked him and, after giving a sixpence to the beggar in Penniless Porch, mounted her bicycle and rode out of Wells.

Her spirits rose as she sped along the narrow lanes. The dark and lonely winter of heartbreak was at an end and optimism was in the air. She must rebuild her life without Charles or the friends she had lost because of him. There were positive gains from this situation, for instance, now she no longer did dressmaking, she need never be subservient to a lady in her boudoir ever again!

Pedalling a little further she admitted to missing neighbours who

194

no longer came in need of remedies or healing and regretted they had been so influenced by local gossips, but she was alive and spring was inevitable, nothing else mattered!

So what if she had no man in her life! Loving meant being hurt. She'd had enough of heartbreak and would walk the hills alone from now on. Flowers were about to bloom and she'd soon be making more illustrations for her book of Gran's herbal remedies. 'Hallelujah!' she said aloud, 'When I get home I'll collect all my drawings and paintings together and . . .'

There was a loud explosion of stars that eventually slowed down and became the familiar shapes around the moon which was almost full and very bright.

She was sitting on the rock outside the cave grieving for her lost love. She had known he would not stay long, but that made the pain no easier to bear; and trying to comfort her distraught child, who had bravely watched the horse leave before collapsing with grief, had left her exhausted but unable to fall into the blissful forgetfulness of sleep.

Hearing the sound of footsteps approaching, she took her knife from its sheath and stood ready to pounce on an intruder, until, seeing a silhouette she recognised in the clearing, she quietly said, 'Jan, my little brother!'

'My sister—' his eyes swivelled around him nervously '—I mun speak with thee what was so good to me.'

She smiled. 'I hope thee's not broken the other leg.'

He swallowed. 'I come to warn 'ee.'

Cold foreboding filled her mind. 'Aye?'

He indicated with his head toward the river. 'Folks across there be thinking harsh thoughts.'

'What be they thinking, Jan?'

'They say thee poisoned babes.'

'Poisoned!'

'Thee gave them potions and they died.'

'The babes were close to death and I tried to make their ending easier. The summer squits always kills them. 'Tis God's way.'

'Now the beasts have falling sickness.'

'Oh, poor souls! I had not heard this sad news.'

'Some say 'tis thy doing.'

'Mine? How could this be?'

'My aunt saw the devil here with thee.'

'The devil?'

'Aye—' he looked nervously around '—her saw him flying, high above the dwelling. And his mare were twice the size of any mortal horse. It chased her away and near killed her did that beast, near killed her!'

'Jan, this is madness! Let me explain ...'

He struggled to control his mouth as he said, 'I brought this—' he swung a sack from his shoulder and laid it on the ground '—'tis all I can do to help. I durst do no more.'

He turned and took one step.

She sniffed the air. 'Wait, Jan, wait—' she held his arm '—what have thee brought that smells of death?'

'The hand of one who was hanged a sennight since.' He gave a small sob. 'I heard as 'tis the best protection against evil. Thee mun hide it in the wall.'

'But why?

'She's cursed thee on her child's grave.' He pulled away from her then ran down the narrow path towards the river and out of sight.

'Mother! Who was that?'

She turned and went to reassure the child standing by the dwelling. 'Fear not, Caitlin, my love. 'Twas a friend. Come we shall lay down and sleep.'

Awakening and finding she was lying in bed in a hospital ward, Kate tried to remember being ill.

Seeing Betty sitting beside her reading a book, she reached out and patted her arm, saying, 'Fear not, Caitlin. No curse can harm us for we are like the fireweed.'

'Crikey blimey!' her sister exclaimed, and burst into tears.

'Nay, child. Do not weep. I shall return and so shall thee.'

After a few moments she did recall every word of her interview with the solicitor and also exactly what she was thinking whilst riding homewards, but after that was a complete blank. Closing her eyes again, she fell asleep.

The following day, when Jim came to visit her he said anxiously, 'I've been so worried about you, Kate.'

'The doctor says I've got off lightly. He thought I'd fractured my skull at first, but I hadn't and he says I'm really lucky to just have a few broken ribs and some cuts and bruises after such a bad fall.'

'If the motor car that knocked you off your bicycle had run over you I'm sure you'd have been killed,' Jim replied.

'That's what the doctor said too. He's horrified by all the victims of road accidents he sees and thinks people should have to take an examination to prove they can control a motor car before they drive it.'

Jim nodded. 'I agree—' he patted the newspaper in his pocket '—there's a letter in *The Times* on that very subject. Apparently the Transport Minister is pushing for a whole raft of road safety measures including a test for drivers and the writer of the letter is outraged at the suggestion – he thinks it would be an infringement of his rights or some other nonsense.'

She fingered her swollen nose. 'I'm a bit fed up about this.'

'You'll still be beautiful once it's gone down.' Jim blushed. 'I mean you're beautiful now, of course, I didn't mean to suggest . . .'

She laughed and gasped at the pain in her chest, then muttered, 'Oh God! I mustn't do that.' Looking into the young man's clear grey eyes she saw the unmistakable expression of a man in love and hastily reached out and touched the jonquils he had placed on the small locker beside the bed. 'I can smell these so it's not too bad.'

Jim ran a hand through his unruly thatch of golden hair, then stood up saying he would call again the next day.

She smiled and thanked him for visiting her and, as he walked away down the ward, she closed her eyes and imagined making love to Charles Wallace.

When Alice arrived the following afternoon, she said, 'Oh Kate, how I longed for the courage to come and see you all these months. Can you forgive me for being so weak?'

'You came to warn me about the archeologists, remember?'

'That was a secret visit. Everyone thought I'd cut you off, same as they had. I mean I should have still been your friend no matter what anyone else did.'

'There's nothing to forgive.'

'There is, there is. I let other people dictate to me as I always do. I've no right to be your friend.'

'The gossips are quite right, I did have an affair with Charles Wallace.'

197

'So what! That shouldn't affect us, should it?'

'I'd like us to be friends again, Alice. I'd like that very much.'

'When I heard about the accident I told my Teddy I was coming to visit you and he didn't say a word, not a single word!'

Jim Hall walked down the ward towards them and stood at the end of the bed looking anxious.

Alice grinned and simpered. 'You seem to have another visitor. I'll be off now.'

Kate grasped her hand and whispered, 'You won't drop me because of this one will you?'

Alice smiled politely at the archaeologist and lowered her voice, 'No, I don't care what you do. I'll come and see you soon and when you're better we could go for a walk up top. If you'd like to?'

Kate agreed she would and waved goodbye before turning her attention to Jim who reported excitedly, 'We've been digging into the subsided area and found a deep cave below it and another below that. I think we've found the beginning of a system of caves that could end eventually in the one in the dell.'

'And the mounds?' she asked.

He shook his head. 'I've decided to leave those until we have a bigger team. Actually none of us is very experienced in that sort of thing and we feel we need a more knowledgeable person in charge. I have a contact who might be interested, he travels all over the place and gets lots of attention, the Prince of Wales visited one of his digs in Dorset.'

She was horrified. 'But that would mean hundreds of people coming here, wouldn't it?'

'You wouldn't want that?'

'No,' wincing while leaning forward in her agitation, she exclaimed, 'no, I most certainly would *not*.'

On her ninth day in the hospital, the doctor said there was little more to be done other than wait for the healing process to take its natural course and, if she would rest quietly at home, she could leave. Jim then drove her to Old Myrtles slowly and carefully, knowing that any sudden jerks of the sensitive clutch would be painful for her.

Albert and Betty had apparently managed without her, but once she was back in residence their resolve to get on evaporated and thereafter they communicated only through her and never with each other.

Several women came immediately with offers of help and quickly formed a rota, so that whilst one took Albert's shirts to wash and iron, another took all their sheets, and another the rest of their laundry. Every day one of the villagers would come to the house and offer their help. Alice came with library books and fruit, the vicar's wife sent a note wishing her a speedy recovery, as did Mrs Hayes from Valley View and several other ladies in the area.

When the butcher's wife brought two pounds of pork sausages and tentatively asked if 'the invalid' was able to ease her painful back, Kate agreed she was both well enough and eager to do so and, having invited the woman to sit beside her on the ancient sofa, placed her hands on the painful area.

The following day a farmhand's wife brought an apple pie and nervously asked if she would read the tea-leaves and, whilst not mentioning a funeral, she was delighted to foretell the birth of twins. When the woman beamed with delight and admitted she was pregnant, but because she had miscarried the previous year, was fearful of losing another baby, she longed to give her some herbs, but resisted doing so. Instead she said, 'I'd take really good care of myself if I were you. I'd eat cheese and fruit and later, when your time is near, drink tea made from raspberry leaves. And—' she looked pointedly at the calloused hands '—I'd rest as much as possible.'

'I does the laundry fer Bishop's Farm, we couldn't manage without that money.'

Remembering her mother collapsing in the scullery on a Monday long ago, she suggested the woman could sit down to do the ironing and ask her husband to do any heavy lifting.

'He might, if he knew. I ain't told him yet, I wanted to be sure.'

'Does he want a child?'

'My man do want a son terrible bad.'

'Well, if he helped you keep them alive he might get two at one go!'

The woman chuckled. 'I don't think I'll tell him how many there be on the way. D'you say they'm both boys?'

'I'm afraid I never predict the sex of a baby, I just know there's two.'

When the woman had gone, she lay propped up on the sofa smiling with satisfaction, Gran would be proud of her! Closing her eyes she fell asleep and dreamed of sitting in the oak tree with Charles.

Chapter Twenty-Six

Comfrey ointment helps heal wounds so quickly that care should be taken never to use it unless there is definitely no possibility of infection which might be left under the scar. It also helps to mend broken bones, sprains and torn ligaments.

'Imagine!' Jim leaned towards her, his blue eyes shining with excitement. 'A little dog is known to have fallen down a hole up top and eventually came out a week later in the dell. That means there's probably a series of caves all the way down to the river. Isn't that fascinating?'

Kate tried hard to look joyful, but her heart was heavy as she responded, 'I do hope he wasn't hurt.'

'No broken bones, but covered in blood, almost flayed, so one chap heard.'

Betty looked up from her book and said, 'If the dog was in that state, the passageways must have been very narrow, so you wouldn't be able to get through, would you?'

'That's true,' Jim agreed, 'and I've yet to meet anyone who actually saw the dog, so it may just be an apocryphal story.'

Betty said, 'Maybe the people who tried to follow the dog are still stuck there.'

Feeling irritated with her sister, Kate frowned. 'I think it's just a made-up story.'

'Sort of like the legend of the wicked witch?' Betty suggested, smiling angelically.

Knowing she was in full view of Jim, Kate could only smile just as sweetly in return.

The young man, who was sitting at the kitchen table, described a series of caves he had seen in France. Then, raking his hair with his hand, he added, 'There's some in Crete where they've found lots of little votive offerings to the gods.'

'What are they?' Betty asked.

'Sort of thank-you gifts for a good harvest or for being healed, or a common one is for safe delivery of a baby.'

'Is that what you're looking for here?'

'Who knows?' Jim shrugged. 'People have lived in caves all over the world and often used them as burial chambers.'

Betty said, 'I read about some tombs that were filled with amazing treasure and—' she opened her eyes wide '—mummies. D'you think you'll find some here?'

Jim laughed and said he thought that was unlikely and told them his dream was to visit Egypt and see the tombs of the Pharaohs, then, after a lingering look at Kate, he departed.

When she demanded to know what game her sister thought she was playing with the archaeologist, Betty sighed and rolled her eyes, 'I was leading him away from talking about *our* caves, silly! You're not very good at this are you?' She patted her sister's hand. 'You'll have to get better at being dubious.'

'I think you mean devious.' Kate chuckled and went to hug her, then, remembering in time it would be too painful, kissed her on the cheek. 'Sometimes you amaze me. For one so young you are very . . .' she hesitated.

'Dubious?' Betty asked, then doubled up with laughter and Kate, holding her ribcage, tried desperately to keep still as she giggled helplessly.

'Actually I *was* quite *devious*,' she said later when sitting on the edge of Betty's bed watching her tie her curls with rags, 'I did manage to distract them from looking around here. I even suggested the mounds up top in the hope of getting them off the scent altogether, but that didn't work.'

Betty smirked. 'I think the best way of controlling the situation would be to marry him.'

'He's a nice man—' Kate tied a rag to a lock of hair '—but . . .'

'His parents live in a big house near London, and his brother plays polo, and he's *rich*!' Betty's blue eyes were large and luminous in the candlelight.

'I thought of buying you some pipe-cleaners to do this—' Kate tied another rag for her '—I'm sure they'd be easier.'

'No, I tried them, they were really, really uncomfortable, I couldn't sleep. He's rich, isn't he?'

'Yes, I think so. He's also very nice, and kind and thoughtful and generous and I know you want to go to London, sweetheart, but I'm not in love with him.'

Betty's lower lip jutted forward as she tied the last bow. 'He'd buy you a huge diamond engagement ring and a fur coat and a crocodile handbag and take you to Egypt!'

'I know, my lover, I know,' Kate said sadly. 'And I'd like you to have what you want and go to London, but I *know, I just know I must stay here.*'

'Only because of Albert. If we didn't have him to stop us, we could go to London anyway!'

'There's the cave to think of; I must keep it secret. And, I've told you before, sweetheart, I don't mind staying here.'

'Daisy Nelson says *he* could go into the loony bin, and then we could do as we like.'

'Uncle Albert is perfectly all right, so long as I'm here to care for him.'

The bows on Betty's head bobbed up and down as she shook with fury. 'It's not fair! Why should an old loony ruin your life?'

'It won't be ruined—' Kate stood up '—and nor will yours. I'm sure you'll go to London at the first possible opportunity, but I'll never ever leave here, it's my destiny.' She picked up her candlestick and blew a kiss. 'Sweet dreams, my lover.'

Lying in her soft featherbed a little later, she conceded Betty was right. If married to him she'd be able to control the investigations and, remembering the scented and expensive elegance of Charles Wallace's sister, she admitted such a way of life was very appealing. A pearl necklace would be nice and she'd like beautiful shoes too and soft kid gloves. They could have a house in the country like The Grange or Valley View and a flat in town. There would be lots of servants, and a dear, kind nanny who would mind the children while she accompanied Jim on his travels to Egypt. Their homecomings would be joyous occasions. As the car drove up the wide drive, she'd see a lovely stone facade with wisteria hanging over the balcony and two beautiful children would be hopping up and down in rapturous delight on the stone steps – the boy might

202

have corn-coloured hair like his father and the girl could be dark, like Polly perhaps? As the children hugged her, she'd nuzzle their fresh young cheeks and know perfect contentment.

She sighed, destroying the image in her mind's eye – could maternal love be enough? Could she marry Jim, accepting his wealth and his love, could she do that?

'Yes,' she whispered, 'I could do that, why shouldn't I?' Betty would be delighted; she liked Jim and was charming and animated in his company. If she mixed with their friends and acquaintances, a rich man might fall in love with her.

And Albert, what could they do with him? There was Saint Bernard's Mental Hospital if all else failed. What was *all else*? What were the options? What could be an acceptable future for her uncle? Could he be left here in this house with a housekeeper; someone like Mrs Parsons, but much, much kinder? Could there be a woman who would live with him and act like his mother? This did seem unlikely. There was also the possibility he might actually like Saint Bernard's – he would have companionship, people of his own kind. She'd be doing the best for him whilst thinking of Betty and herself. She could marry Jim, be happy, have children, and sex too! Would that be good with him? Why not? He would be a man, a lover, wouldn't he? But would she feel that melting, warm, dissolving feeling she'd had whenever Charlie looked at her? No, maybe not, but probably that was for the best. She'd never feel that way again and didn't want to either! Loving was much too painful and they went off and left you didn't they? Maybe such extreme emotion wasn't love anyway? Maybe love, as in *marriage*, meant something else, a sort of kindly affection towards someone – she felt that for Jim, didn't she? Yes, that was it. All passionate longing to make love to someone was something else. What she had felt for Hugo and then for Charlie must have been lust. The steady, year after year, staying with a man and bearing children was something other than the agonising, excruciatingly painful sort of love where one lived in fear of rejection or of losing him, it was a quieter, more composed sort of feeling altogether. Jim Hall would be a kind considerate husband and a loving, generous father to her children. He wouldn't be cruel to Albert either; he was always very gentle with him.

She could visit the cottage often and Nancy and Alice would keep an eye on it for her; they might even visit Albert in Saint

Bernard's. Betty was right, she deserved to have some happiness. If she made sure the cave was well hidden with rocks and earth, then it could remain a secret. It was all very simple. Why had she thought otherwise?

Feeling all the problems in her life had been resolved with one sensible decision, she relaxed and was soon dreaming of being in the cave.

She looked up at the figure in the rocks and down into the green eyes of her beautiful daughter. 'It is time now to have thy own knife. Here, I have made this for thee.'

The girl took hold of the carved handle and, waving it above her head, laughed with delight at the reflected light flashing from the shining blade.

'Come, Caitlin, the tallow is burning low and I have more to show thee this night.' Leading the way out of the cave she smiled as the child sang a joyful song while proudly carrying the knife in her raised hands.

Once they were standing in the moonlight beside the dwelling, she went to the goat tethered there and swiftly ran her own blade across its throat.

Caitlin cried out, 'Mother! We have the hare I caught yesterday to eat.' Her pretty face screwed into a frown as she looked down on the dead goat lying at her feet. 'Tis not the time for killing while there be abundant food for the animals to eat and, besides, we have no salt, nor any means to keep the flesh sweet for eating in winter.'

'I have need of more than its meat, child.' She took the knife her grandmother had given her long ago and kissed the handle her mother had carved, then, bending over the animal, she cut it open and removed its heart. With blood running down her forearms, she held the organ aloft in both hands. 'We have been cursed. I mun stick a stake into this and burn it to ashes.'

'And what of the hand we buried in the stones, is that not enough?'

'Nay, not for ill-wishing such as this.' She indicated to a sharpened piece of wood beside her and told the girl to pick it up and follow her into the dwelling. Once inside, she pierced the heart with the stake and walked around the fire six times one way and six the other repeatedly chanting, ''Tis not this beast's heart I wish to burn, but the curser's heart I wish to turn.' Then, shouting, 'Let the curse be gone!' she threw it into the flames.

Standing with her arm around the child, she said, "Tis the first time I ever had need of this and 'though 'twas my grandmother told me of it, nor do I think she had need of it neither.'

Caitlin groaned, 'I wish I had not healed the horse so quickly and the kind gentleman had stayed longer, Mother.'

The following evening, Kate welcomed Jim and then suggested they take a walk in the garden. Having led him down the path she sat on the rock seat outside the cave and invited him to join her.

The young man's eyes shone with delight as he sat beside her and placed a hand on her knee.

She shyly allowed him to kiss her and gently removed his hand. There was no temptation to encourage his lovemaking, she felt no desire, no melting, no longing to lose herself in him, she was absolutely in control of her emotions. She also still had the excuse of fractured ribs to stop any close embraces.

'You're right.' His voice was heavy with desire. 'Of course you're right. I wouldn't expect you to do that. I want you for my wife. Oh, Kate, say you'll marry me, please!'

'I'll need time to think,' she said. 'I'm so shocked and surprised.'

'Say you'll consider it,' he pleaded, 'say you'll give me a chance.'

'Very well.' She stroked the side of his face. 'I'll think about it. I'm not completely free to please myself, I have responsibilities.'

'Betty?'

'I have to take care of her.'

'We'll do that together. She can go to the school my sister attended in Sussex.' He picked up her hand. 'End of problem,' he said, and, turning it over, kissed the palm.

She felt nothing. Not even the tiniest, slightest frisson of excitement. She kissed his cheek. 'You're so kind, so sweet, but there's also my uncle to consider.'

'I've already thought of him.' He put his arm around her shoulders. 'I've made enquiries. It would be very straightforward. He'd be well cared for and he could work in the gardens if he wanted to.'

'Saint Bernard's?'

He nodded. 'I've spoken to the matron and it could easily be arranged. We could visit him as often as you'd like.'

205

'I'm, I'm not sure,' she stammered. 'I need to go in now, I still get very tired. I'll give you an answer tomorrow evening.'

'All right, my dear. I'll go now.' His eyes held hers for a moment. 'I've told my mother about you and she's longing to meet you.' He turned and walked to the gate.

She went into the house and prepared for bed. Her head throbbed and she was almost too tired to speak coherently. Albert no longer insisted she must always God bless him after he was in bed, having accepted she sometimes needed to retire before him since the accident. Bending over him as he sat working on a small piece of wood, she kissed his forehead and whispered, 'God bless, my lover.' Then, looking closer at the carving in his hand, she saw the figures of a man and woman intertwined and exclaimed loudly, 'Good heavens, it's the same as Granny's knife handle!'

He looked up at her, his beautiful eyes undimmed by age and seeming even bluer now his hair was white. 'I promised,' he said proudly.

'Who's it for?'

He pointed to her and resumed whittling.

She looked around for Betty and found to her surprise she had already gone to bed without any of the usual persuasion and reminders of the time. Although exhausted, she knocked on her sister's door and called, 'Are you all right, Betty? You're not ill are you, sweetheart?'

'Of course not. Goodnight, big sister.'

She made her way to bed and was soon in a sleep troubled by a succession of terrifying dreams in which she was a rag doll hanging from the topmost spike of a tall cast-iron gate and below her a crowd screamed for vengeance. Awakening in a cold sweat soon after dawn, she lay remembering the nightmares and knew the gates were those of the lunatic asylum; and also that every upturned face of the malevolent rabble was the same, each one the pretty blue-eyed image of Mrs Wallace.

Knowing that there was no possibility of getting back to sleep, she went and stood looking out of the window onto the garden. Last night when she had resolved to marry Jim, it had seemed a perfectly sensible thing to do, but the dreams had unnerved her.

Creaking sounds across the landing told her that Albert was getting out of bed and would soon be in the garden checking his vegetable patch as he did every morning at this time of year. He was humming 'Abide With Me'. Would the people in Saint Bernard's be tolerant of his passion for hymns? Would he really be as well cared for as Jim insisted? By the time she was dressed and standing at the top of the stairs her mind was made up, she would go and see the place in which Albert would spend the rest of his days.

An hour later she was stirring porridge when Betty came in from feeding the chickens. The girl's face was alive with happiness as she smiled as if at a private joke while putting three eggs in the basket on the dresser. 'What a glorious morning!' she exclaimed, then skipped off upstairs singing, 'In springtime, in springtime, the only pretty ring time, sweet lovers love the spring.'

Seeing Albert was looking anxious and guessing such unusual euphoria at this hour of the morning unnerved him, she forced an encouraging smile whilst giving him his breakfast. There could be only one reason for the joyful refrain coming from Betty's room: her sister had been eavesdropping the previous evening and had heard her prospective brother-in-law say he would send her to a smart school for young ladies.

An hour later Kate caught the bus into Wells and alighted in the square close to the cathedral, then walked out of town along the road towards Saint Bernard's Hospital. Once past several large houses about half a mile up the hill she saw the high wall surrounding the asylum and shivered involuntarily. After several minutes she reached the gates featured so grotesquely in her dream and, finding the small entrance marked VISITORS, rang the bell and waited for several minutes until a man in a dark-blue uniform appeared and opened the gate.

'I'm hoping my uncle will come here soon,' she said confidently, 'I need to make one or two enquiries.'

Ushering her into a small office at the front of the lodge immediately inside the gate the man picked up a pen, saying, 'Nobody gets in or out without I checks 'em.' Having asked her name and address, he wrote them in a large book and noting the time, added, 'You can rest easy he'll be kept safe under lock and key.'

She looked at the high wall running all around the grounds then up at points like spears on the huge gates and, remembering the strange dream, shuddered in horror before walking along the gravelled drive towards the large stone building. Passing an elderly man seated on a bench, she smiled and wished him good morning, but his blank eyes gave no sign of seeing her.

On entering the lobby she met a nurse who indicated a chair nearby and smilingly asked her to wait a few minutes until Matron had finished her rounds. Feeling pleasantly surprised by her surroundings she sat down and admired the black and white tiled floor and the wide staircase spiralling up towards a glass dome three stories above her. Then, seeing the shiny mahogany banister curled like a snake upon wrought-iron rods fashioned to echo the spearhead design on the entrance gates, she was again reminded of the dream.

Turning to the large bowl of narcissi standing on a polished table nearby, she breathed in the heady scent in an attempt to remain calm. This had been a terrible mistake. What on earth was she doing here? She'd assured the solicitor that Albert would never be put in an institution. How could she have forgotten that promise?

'She's looking at your flowers.'

Turning to see who was speaking, she found a large woman sidling alongside and said, 'Their scent is so lovely, isn't it?'

The woman examined her face with piercing grey eyes before looking sideways and muttering, 'She's stealing our flowers, I told you we shouldn't leave them there.' In a sudden movement her left arm reached out and linked with Kate's. 'Come along, My Lady. Come with me.'

Feeling very frightened whilst being dragged across the hall and down a corridor, Kate tried explaining that she was waiting to see the matron, but, ignoring her, the woman strode on, saying, 'You'll like it here.' And, turning to her right as if answering someone beside her, she continued talking. 'Yes, I know, but we won't let her. What?' She shook her right hand in the air. 'No, you won't have no dinner if you do that!'

'I really would like to see the matron.'

The woman's grip tightened as she lashed out with her free arm and shouted into the air, 'I said, no! D'you hear?' She whispered out of the side of her mouth, 'Don't worry, I'll take you home with me, my mum will look after you.' And ignoring her pleas for release, dragged her on and on down the increasingly gloomy corridor whilst angrily arguing with the empty space beside her. 'No I won't let you do that. You're a naughty girl, that's what you are. She didn't mean no harm.'

A door opened beside them and a man shouted, 'Maisie!'

The woman stopped and, still holding Kate in her tight grip, said reassuringly to her, 'He's not dangerous if you talk nicely to him.' Then swiping the air to her right, she shouted, 'That's because you're naughty with him, silly girl!'

Footsteps came from behind, a starched apron rustled and a woman's voice said, 'Come along, Maisie, you let the lady go now, there's a good girl.'

Kate gagged as the stench of warm urine filled her nostrils.

'She's wet herself.' The woman thrashed the air, screaming, 'Dirty girl! Filthy animal!' Pulling Kate with her, she attempted to turn round, but was grabbed by the man who pulled her right arm up behind her back.

'Let go of the lady, Maisie!' The man's voice was quiet but insistent. 'I said, let go!'

Kate heard a squeal of pain as the grip on her arm was released. Feeling tearful and shocked, she was led by a nurse back to the entrance hall and then into a large office. On accepting a seat, she looked up into the anxious eyes beneath a rigid white headdress and asked, 'Is she mad?'

'Poor dear lost her wits long ago. She's quiet mostly, no trouble, but we're coming up to full moon and that's her bad time.'

'What does she do then?'

'She wants to take her naughty sister home to mother.' She patted Kate's shoulder reassuringly. 'You don't have to worry about her, she's safely under lock and key now.'

'Oh, that's so sad.'

'Aye, sad it is, but you wouldn't want to meet her on a dark night if she was talking to an invisible person and looking for a mother who's been dead fifteen years, would you?'

A woman wearing a dark-blue uniform entered the room and explained that the episode was a rare occurrence triggered by the death of a patient and Maisie was now under lock and key, adding, 'I'm afraid the mad can be extremely cunning and clever, as I frequently remind my staff.'

Kate stood up. 'I really must go now.'

'Please don't let an incident like that put you off, Miss Barnes.

The woman wouldn't normally be allowed out onto the corridor to mix with visitors.'

Having thanked her, Kate hurried out through the entrance hall and struggled with the large front door feeling the cold sweat of panic trickle down her body.

'I'll let you out.' The nurse appeared at her elbow and unlocked the door. 'We're hot on security here; no one ever leaves that shouldn't.'

Once out in the fresh morning air she hurried down the drive past the old man still staring into space and went to the lodge where she signed her name with a shaking hand.

'They do a good job in there,' the man in uniform said, reaching to open the small gate. 'Wouldn't do to have all them lunatics out amongst good Christian folk, would it?'

Muttering her thanks she went out and walked along the pavement taking little notice of her surroundings until, on impulse, she crossed the road and walked into the arboretum where she sank down on a bench and wept.

After a while, feeling less overwhelmed by the frightening experience, she thought of Albert sitting in his corner the previous evening making a knife-handle for her as he had promised his mother he would. He was a skilful woodcarver – would he be allowed to do that when there were lunatics like Maisie liable to take his sharp tools and do mischief with them? His expression had been so full of love as he looked up at her with the light from the lamp behind him shining through his hair. Oh God! Suddenly she understood. The vision of a man with white hair she had seen in the water years ago was not a lover after all, it was the uncle for whom she was responsible and who also reminded her by making a knife like her grandmother's that she was now the guardian of the secret cave.

She would not be rich, or perfumed and elegant, or travel to Egypt, but, as she rose and walked towards the bus stop, she truly didn't care.

Chapter Twenty-Seven

Hawthorn berries boiled in water makes a good remedy for problems of the heart, the circulation of the blood and is safe for old people. A poultice made with leaves or berries will draw out splinters, thorns and whitlow.

Caitlin carried a small doe into the clearing, saying defiantly, ''Tis not for the eating. The hunters took her mother and she has a hurt to her leg.'

'Very well, we'll not kill her, but she mun roam free when it is healed.' She continued making a basket with willow for a short while, then asked, 'Be they hunters gone?'

'Aye. They was not from these parts.'

'Did they see thee?'

'Nay.'

She looked up and saw her own anxiety mirrored in her daughter's eyes. 'We mun take care.'

''Tis not of strangers I'm afeared, mother.'

'Hast thee seen local men in the forest?'

'Nay, and 'tis that very lack fills me with dread.'

She nodded. The child was right. No one had come near them since Jan had brought the hanged man's hand. The wife of a herdsman up top would be giving birth this full moon and no word had been sent seeking her aid. There had been no pleas for her salves, no heartrending tales of sickness or pain. Not one woman had come furtively requesting that very special potion, pretending it was for a friend and not to rid her own womb of an unwanted or unaffordable guest.

She had slept little since the man and his horse had gone. Her *body ached with tiredness and her swollen eyes felt alien to her face. Struggling to hide her increasing fear and appear calm in order to reassure the child, she said, ''Tis Hallowmass tonight. We mun go into the cave and sit with those who've gone before.' Putting her arm around the child's slender shoulders, she kissed the top of her head and added, 'Let us hope their spirits will rise up and protect us.'*

Awakening to find she was sitting on the rock beside the cave, Kate opened her clenched fists and rubbed the painful joints on either side of her jaw. Then, hearing a voice calling her, she stood up and looked towards the house.

'Miss Barnes, hello!'

Seeing the lanky figure of her solicitor standing by the porch, she hurried up the path to greet him.

Mr Parville accepted her invitation to go inside, but refused to be entertained in the parlour and insisted on sitting in the kitchen. Resting his elbows on the table he said, 'My good friend Wallace.' He smiled. 'I'm sorry, old habits die hard, we were at school together and still call one another by our surnames. Charles Wallace I should say, told me this was the nicest room he'd ever known and I can see why.'

The mention of her lover caused her heart to thud faster. After taking a breath, she said, 'I expect you've come about the archaeologists. Is there a problem?'

'No, no, that's all satisfactory. They've been investigating the caves up top for four weeks or so now.' He frowned and nervously examined the tabletop. 'I'd have spoken to you sooner, but, although I had an inkling, I wasn't sure of my facts when you last came to see me. Then I heard you had an accident and I've had a bout of the 'flu.' Gripping the arms of the Windsor chair with his enormous hands, he crossed and recrossed his long legs, before saying, 'I'm the bearer of bad news, I'm afraid.' He gave a nervous little cough. 'You no doubt heard of the financial disaster in America and how bad things have been here too?'

She nodded, feeling very apprehensive. 'I had wondered about that. You invested some of my grandmother's money, didn't you?'

'Indeed! That's true . . .'

'Have I lost it all?' She gulped. 'I wouldn't blame you, Mr Parville, I read in the paper how people have lost fortunes and . . .'

'No, Miss Barnes, your money is safe. I placed it in very secure, admittedly not high yielding, but *safe* investments. We just sit tight and all will be well, but—' he rubbed his head as if it hurt '—others have not been so fortunate.' He swallowed. 'The fact is, The Grange is up for sale.' He looked away, blew his nose and dabbed at his eyes, then went on, 'Members of staff were told this morning, so it will soon be public knowledge.'

She gaped at him unable to think of anything to say.

'I wanted to tell you as soon as possible, but I had to get a certain document signed before I came to see you. I'm pleased to say I've accomplished that and once I've fetched some private possessions of Wallace's then the house will be ready for the auctioneers to do the inventory.' He picked up a briefcase and opened it. 'That house has been in his family for generations.' He removed a large envelope and placed it on the table. 'Charles Wallace wants you to have the piece of land up above this house. He wrote and asked me to arrange it.' Removing a thick document from the large envelope he opened it out and pointed to the map attached to it. 'Here, the red line shows the area involved.'

She peered at the map but her eyes were watering uncontrollably and could see nothing.

'I've done the necessary legal manoeuvres. If you are willing to buy it for a small amount, I suggest two guineas, it can be yours.'

Still unable to speak, she watched as though in a dream, whilst he shuffled papers, then stared uncomprehendingly as he offered her a fountain pen.

'If you'd like to sign?' his voice was gentle, kindly.

'Sign? Oh yes, yes, two guineas, anything, yes, sign the d-document,' she stammered, taking the pen and writing her name.

Pointing to a red line on the map, he said, 'You are now the owner of that area there.'

She dried her eyes and, when able to see the writing exclaimed, '*Hangtry* Land!'

'Yes, it's called several different names up until the eighteen hundreds; this one is copied from the Grange deeds of eighteen twenty when they last sold off fifty acres of farmland. One earlier map in the museum says "Hangentree", another more recent one is "Hantrey", then in the eighteen thirty survey it became "Hankey" as though the "t" and the "r" were put together forming a "k" and it acquired an "s" as in "Hankeys Land" by common usage, I think.'

Eric's voice echoed in her head, 'Handkerchiefland! Ha, ha, ha!' She smiled at the memory before saying, 'I'd always assumed it had belonged to someone called Mr Hankey.'

'Yes, I would have said that too, but as you see, names change so much over the years. Very few people would have been able to read or write until the last century and, of those that could, many would have only been semiliterate and just made it up as they went along. In my opinion it does prove there is a basic truth in the legend of the wicked witch.' He shrugged. 'Someone was hanged up there, that's for sure.'

'Yes, for sure.' Feeling suddenly calm, she asked, 'What about Mrs Wallace, what will she do?'

'Her money is tied up in property up north and is unaffected by this . . .' he gave a despairing gesture with his huge hands.

'Will she go back there?'

Barnet Parville nodded. 'There are relatives.'

'Poor soul!' Then she added, 'And the staff at The Grange must be sad. Some have worked there all their lives, what a blow for them!'

'Yes, indeed. I believe the housekeeper is going with Mrs Wallace, and the companion of course.'

'That's good.'

'Indeed.' He gave a small cough. 'She wishes to leave today, before anyone here knows her shame. She's very bitter, I'm afraid. *Very* bitter.' He looked at the top row of large plates on the dresser. 'She'll never divorce him, I'm sure of that.' His eyes strayed down to the next shelf. 'I love those plates.'

'I believe my grandfather won them at the Pridden Fair – he was the best shot for miles around so I'm told.'

'I think they are quite old and probably more valuable than you think.' Barnet Parville looked at the lower shelf crammed with a jumble of ornaments, odd bowls containing many small objects and a variety of books.

Following his eyes, she smiled, 'I'm afraid that one's in easy reach, so it gets very cluttered. All my grandmother's bits and pieces are still there; she kept everything, old keys, bits of string, broken trinkets, or anything that might possibly be useful one day. She used to say, "It might come in handy," whenever I suggested throwing anything away and now I like to see it all there, it makes her feel closer and still part of the family.'

'You still miss her?'

'Oh yes, and always shall.'

'You intend staying here, despite everything?'

'Yes, I'll never leave.'

'I have to go,' the solicitor said, standing up. 'If I'm in touch with Wallace, I'll tell him that you're well and happy, shall I?'

She nodded. 'And thank him, from the bottom of my heart.' Hearing the door close behind him, she rested her head on the table. *Hangen Tree Land*, of course, why had she not understood before? Could her special oak be the tree on which she had died? Possible, she thought, or perhaps it had grown from one of its acorns?

When she perused the document and found it was written in the usual unintelligible language; she turned to look again at the map. The red line ran parallel with the garden all the way to the boundary with the dell! She ran her finger along it – yes, there could be no mistake. Hankeys Land extended above the burial chamber and along a strip between it and Mr Hayes' property. She would be able to stop any excavations from above. Her secret was safe!

Feeling a deep need to be near the old tree she left the house, climbed up the cliff and made her way towards it. This was her first visit since the accident and the path was almost overgrown with the brambles, nettles and bracken jostling for every inch of earth. On reaching the oak she was tired, aching and lacerated by thorns, but sank happily down and leaned against its trunk looking up through the branches festooned with bright new leaves. Closing her eyes, she visualised roots digging deep into the hillside, finding their way through the crevices and down into a cave where the rainwater ran through on its way to the river.

She lay back, knowing her past, her present and future were all intermingled on this spot. This was where she had first experienced the sight and had met Charles when he was on leave from the War. They had often sat here during the time of their love affair. It would always be a place of solace and ...

She became aware of a figure crashing through the burgeoning undergrowth towards her. Could it be him? Of course not, he was in America, far away across the Atlantic Ocean. As the man silhouetted against the sun came closer she was disappointed to see it was Jim.

'Kate darling—' he knelt before her '—I couldn't wait until this evening. Tell me, darling, tell me you'll marry me, *please.*'

'I'm so sorry. So sorry.' She watched his face dissolve in pain. 'I can't, I'm truly sorry. I can't put my uncle in that place.'

'He'd be well cared for. I've spoken to the matron, there are several there like him. He'd have everything he needed ...' Jim shook his head. 'No, this isn't about Albert. It's about that damned Wallace, isn't it?'

'I was in love with him, I can't deny it.'

'I met Barnet Parville just now. He told me Charles Wallace is disgraced, lost everything, did you know that?'

'Yes, I know.'

'The house is up for sale and his wife's going north to her family, poor woman.'

'Poor woman,' she echoed, imagining Mrs Wallace, sitting in the train looking so pretty and frail.

'He's a cad! A bounder! The bastard doesn't deserve ...' Jim stood up, 'I won't trouble you any longer, I can see you're not listening to me.' He strode away towards Pridden.

She sat for a few minutes watching a bumblebee investigate the clover nearby whilst trying to order her thoughts. Betty would be home from school before long and must be told as soon as possible that her dreams were not about to come true after all. If she hadn't eavesdropped there would be no problem, it was true, but she had and so must be told.

On standing up to walk home she caught a glimpse of someone behind a tree, or was it? She was unsure. It was her imagination perhaps, or one of the archaeological team looking for Jim?

Betty was waiting for her in the garden and said anxiously, 'You've torn your skirt. Look at you, look at those scratches! I'll bathe your arm, it's bleeding.' Humming cheerfully, she escorted her into the kitchen and poured water from the kettle into a bowl.

Kate took a slow breath. 'There's something I must tell you.'

Betty turned to face her, shining with pleasurable anticipation as she asked, 'Really? How exciting!'

'Jim Hall asked me to marry him.'

Betty's eyes shone with happiness, 'That's so wonderful, darling, so absolutely wonderful!'

'I've told him it's impossible.'

'I beg your pardon?'

216

'I said, I refused.' Her heart ached as she watched understanding manifest on Betty's face.

'Are you mad? You stupid, stupid idiot! I suppose the beastly Wallace cad's been to see you, hasn't he?'

'No, of course not. He's in America ...' Something in Betty's eyes made her hesitate. 'Why? What makes you say that. Have you seen him?'

'Yes, of course I have, the bastard, the bastard, cad, bastard, beastly horrible man who gave you that ring ...'

'Charles? You saw Charles?'

'The whole village has seen him. *Everyone*'s seen him, except *you*!'

Kate stared in horror. 'Where?'

'Outside the school. He was waiting in his car with a lady, all done up in a hat and furs she was.'

'He spoke to you?'

Betty smirked. 'He gave me a guinea.'

'What did he say?'

'He said he wished you a happy marriage to Jim Hall. You stupid bloody cow!' She rushed out of the house, slamming the kitchen door behind her.

Feeling drained of emotion Kate looked around the room in a detached way until feeling suddenly flooded back and a desire to wreak vengeance overcame her. She wanted to break things, to smash and crush them. Looking around the room she could see nothing of value. Not a single piece of china was worth keeping. The plates could go. The silly knick-knacks on the dresser shelves and mantelpiece, including the china cow and calf with only six legs between them, were all worthless. She picked up the small porcelain house she had loved as a little girl. Her hand seemed a long way off as her arm rose – should she throw it at the wall, or the window? It seemed an important dilemma, worthy of careful consideration. The memory of Granfer lighting a candle inside so that the windows lit up and smoke issued through the chimney caught her unawares and, with a sob, she replaced the little house on the shelf.

Albert opened the door and said, 'I like Monday.'

'Yes, Uncle dear, you sit down and eat your ...' turning away from the dresser she saw the gold chain across his chest and exclaimed, 'Good heavens!'

He pulled the watch from his waistcoat pocket and held it in the palm of his hand.

Feeling overwhelmed with love, she watched the old man gaze down at his treasure whilst the sun shone through the window behind him making his hair seem like the white cotton on Rosebay Willowherb at summer's end. Leaning forward with her arm outstretched, she asked, 'May I look at it?'

Albert shook his head. 'No! He said, no one mun take it off me.'

'Of course,' she agreed, 'quite right too!' She had no need to look at the engraving inside to see Charles's name and twenty-first birthday would be recorded there.

The old man frowned as he said, 'I baint often late.'

'No, my lover, that's true. I expect Mr Wallace said you need never be late now, or something like that?'

He nodded.

'It's a comfort to know you never could be late now, isn't it?'

Albert looked at the saucepan on top of the range. 'Pretty lady came with fur an' all, very pretty.'

So now she knew. Charles had found someone else. How dare he bring her here? How could he be so cruel?

She wanted to ask if the pretty lady sounded American and whether Charles put his arm around her. Instead, whilst spooning rabbit stew onto his plate, she asked in what she hoped was an offhanded manner, 'Did they come into the churchyard?'

'Special to see me, her said. Did'ner!' He sat down, picked up a spoon and began humming quietly.

She placed the food in front of the old man and patted him affectionately on the shoulder; he had already spoken more words this evening than during the previous six weeks and she knew better than to press him further.

Chapter Twenty-Eight

Lavender is commonly used to prevent fainting and allays nausea and travel sickness. It is good for headaches and digestion.

A faint sound in the distance caused her to interrupt her steady measured pace along the narrow path through the forest. Lowering the heavy sack from her back she straightened and stood listening for a moment, then, thinking it was merely huntsmen shouting to their dogs, she picked up her burden and carried on. Having taken a few steps, she frowned as the raucous noise grew louder. These were not the familiar calls of men and baying of hounds chasing a boar or stag but a jumble of shrieking curses, unintelligible exclamations and the occasional guffaw of laughter. Turning to the young girl following in her wake she gave a reassuring smile and said, 'The cider be strong this year.'

The child's eyes flickered apprehensively and her lip quivered.

'Thee looks tired, my lover. Come, take my hand, we'll soon be home by the fire.'

They walked a few paces then, hearing the shouts getting closer, gripped each other's hand.

'Catch the witch!'

She pushed the child into a hollow tree and commanded, 'Stay there until I come for thee.'

'But, Mother . . .'

Ignoring the plaintive whine she turned and ran back the way she had come. They must not get the child. If she could lead them to the river and hide in the rushes they might both survive, but above all they must not get her daughter . . .

A man crashed through a spinney nearby, staggered, almost fell

*and, holding onto the sapling bending under his weight, shouted,
'There she be!'*

*Skidding away from him down the muddy slope to the water's
edge she heard her pursuer curse the recent rain as he lost his
balance. Then, seeing a figure emerge from the shadows of willow
trees as she slid towards them, thought for an instant it was the
shepherd who loved her, but as hands reached out and pulled her
to the ground, she saw instead the farrier's livid face and glittering eyes ablaze with hatred.*

*The first slap jerked her head sideways and the second sent a
myriad of stars hurtling through the darkness behind her eyes. Pain
seared through her chest, her back and stomach, as feet kicked and
fists punched at her body.*

*Awakening sometime later she peered through one eye at the
large looming shapes around her and knew from the smell of cider
and sweat and piss that they were men, and as they spoke, she
knew which men.*

'Here's the rope.'

*The strident tone surprised her. She had thought the cider-maker
to be an amiable fellow, with cheeks as rosy as the apples he
pressed.*

The carter shouted, 'Let it be done!'

*Why so? He swore eternal gratitude when his wife was safely
delivered Michaelmass last.*

'String her up and put an end to our bad luck.'

'She killed my babe.'

'And mine, and mine.'

'Tie it tight, Jan, tie the knot tight.'

*She had loved him as a brother and now he was putting a rope
around her neck.*

'String her up and put an end to her evil ways.'

*Oh no! Not him! How could he speak so, knowing they were
lovers all those years?*

*A sudden heavy blow left her in darkness, a deep impenetrable
blackness in which she could see nothing of the men who were shouting all around her. Warm tears trickled down her cheeks and ran into
her mouth. The taste was of blood, not tears. Yes, it was blood. Let
death come soon ... The darkness was thick velvety black now. She
heard a snap and, with sudden clarity, looked down into Jan's eyes
and saw the reflection of her corpse hanging like a rag-doll...*

Awakening and finding Albert sitting looking anxiously at her, she swallowed hard and forced her mouth into a smile. Then, patting the arm of the sofa, she said brightly, 'I can't sit here snoozing any longer, I must go and look for Betty. She hasn't come back while I was asleep has she, Uncle?'

The old man took the watch out of his pocket and looked at it before shaking his head and then humming an unusual but recognisable version of *'Hark the herald angel sing'*.

She left the house and, as she hurried towards the village, breathing in the special scent hanging in the cool night air, the white tail of a rabbit disappeared into the burgeoning growth beside her and bats flew overhead.

At her approach, the group of youngsters gathered by a wooden seat at the bus stop, looked at each other and fell silent. When asked if they had seen Betty, several snorts of repressed giggles accompanied the reply that they had not.

As she walked away, a highly pitched voice squeaked, 'Wallace 'ore!' Another, in deeper tones, said, 'She's probably turned her into a toad,' followed by loud shrieks of laughter.

Suddenly dazzled by the headlights of a car, she pressed into the hedge to keep out of its way, then, holding her breath apprehensively as the vehicle drew to a halt alongside her, she heard a familiar female voice say, 'Don't worry, Miss Barnes, it's only me.'

'Good heavens!' She peered at the driver. 'Mrs Faires!'

'Hello, my dear. I'm so glad we met, I really would like to have a chat with you, but I daren't let this engine stop, I'll ruin this frock if I try to start it with the handle. Could you possibly get in for a few minutes?'

She climbed into the front passenger seat, saying, 'I'm so glad to see you. My sister's run away and I'm almost distraught with worry. Have you passed a young girl on the road?'

'No, I haven't seen a soul.' Mrs Faires reached into a small bag covered in seed pearls, withdrew a silver case and lighter, then asked, 'How old is she?'

'Just thirteen.'

'Mmmm, very pretty.' She lit a cigarette and inhaled the smoke, then whilst exhaling, said, 'And looks older than she is.'

'You sound as if you know her.'

'I met her today.'

221

'Really? She didn't say anything, I suppose she was so annoyed with me she forgot.'

'I'm surprised she didn't remember. My brother gave her two guineas.'

'Two?' Then, realising she was speaking to the woman in furs outside the school and also the very pretty lady in the churchyard, said, 'Yes, she did tell me Mr Wallace was with someone, but I had no idea it was you.'

'She was very keen to tell us you were engaged to Jim Hall and she would soon be getting out of—' she gave her familiar lopsided smile '—this dung heap of a place and going to London to be a lady.'

'Oh no!'

'Isn't that true?'

'No, no, no!' Kate moaned.

'So, you're not going to marry the charming young Jim?'

'He did ask me, but I refused. He offered to have Betty educated at a smart school and, I have to admit, it was a tempting offer, but there's my uncle to consider also.'

'Yes, dear Albert, we called on him today. I remember him doing the hedges outside the church when I was young. He seems to have been around forever, how old is he now?'

'He'll be fifty this year.'

'Really? I thought he was older than that.' She sucked on the cigarette. 'Don't you resent having your life restricted by a ...'

'Half-wit?' she finished the question then shook her head. 'No, I've grown used to him over the years and I wouldn't have inherited the property if he was normal. That's why I couldn't possibly have him put him away.'

'Highly commendable.' Mrs Faires blew smoke through the window. 'Did Barnet Parville tell you my sister-in-law signed an undertaking before she left?'

'He said he'd been to see her about a document, I'm afraid I wasn't really taking in what he was saying.'

'So you're unaware of what she signed?'

'I assumed it was private business.'

'And you've no idea why she would be asked to do such a thing?'

'No.'

'Not even if I tell you it related to you?'

'I suppose it might have been something to do with the accusation made by her cousin's maid last year. Is that what it was?'

'Partly.' Mrs Faires threw her cigarette out of the window. 'She's given her solemn undertaking that she withdraws all previous indictments against your character and will never ever make any further accusations of any kind whatsoever.'

'That's a relief – I haven't even made any comfrey ointment this year, just in case.'

'I think perhaps you were unaware of the harm she might have done you?'

'Her cousin's maid accused my grandmother of giving herbs that would induce an abortion but that was all cleared up ...'

'Stop.' Mrs Faires held up her hand. 'I knew Charlie should've told you.'

She felt light-headed. 'Told me what?'

'The reason he left last summer, soon after his wife returned from the North. She, or more probably her cousin, found out that witchcraft is still illegal in this country.'

'My God, she was going to accuse me of being a witch! Is that it?'

'If he ever spoke to you again.'

'How could she possibly do that?'

'I expect there are people around the area who would testify that you laid hands on them. Charlie himself would have to admit under oath that you did it for him wouldn't he?'

'But surely no one in their right minds would say that was witchcraft!'

'I believe you're good at telling the future in tea-leaves and I suspect a skilful barrister could make you admit to all sorts of gifts that could be made to sound a bit iffy. You probably see things the rest of us don't?'

'Probably.'

'Now don't take this amiss, but one of the maids at The Grange was at school with you and has made allegations against you.'

'That's Annie I suppose. My friend Alice and I made love potions and spells that we gave to the children at school. We were twelve years old. It was innocent fun. We wanted to see our one truelove on May morning, and Annie was mad about a boy called Teddy Nelson and demanded to come with us.' She grinned. 'The funny thing is, it worked, only it was Alice he married not Annie.'

'I heard there was an orgy of some sort.'

'If you'd call three little girls taking their clothes off and dancing around the oak tree on Hankeys Land at dawn an orgy, then, yes, there was.'

'If it wasn't a serious allegation, I'd laugh.' Mrs Faires shook her head then added, 'She also said you and your grandmother put magic dolls in the chimney and stuck pins in them and put curses on people.'

'That's partly true. We keep a doll for every member of the family and I foolishly showed them to Annie and Alice. They're like a protection, a way of keeping people safe and for giving them healing from afar; there's nothing bad about them. We certainly don't put pins in them. We believe you get curses sent back to you. My gran said you get them repaid to you threefold.' She shook her head. 'We don't hold with ill-wishing.'

'I believe you, but again, what might a good barrister make of it?'

Kate shivered. 'I see what you mean. And Mrs Wallace was threatening to have me sued for witchcraft on such flimsy evidence?'

'She had nothing to lose. Just the accusation would have done you irreparable harm in a small community like this.'

'I still feel sorry for her, poor soul.'

'Yes, so do I. So do we all. But there's no doubt the national newspapers would have picked up on the story and the legal costs would have ruined you.'

They sat silent for several moments until Mrs Faires said, 'I'd best be going.'

Kate put her hand on the door handle. 'I'm so sorry Mr Wallace has to sell The Grange.'

'Yes, so am I, my dear. To be truthful, I'm not enjoying being poor, but we have to make the best of it.'

'You too?'

'I lost a great deal, but not everything like Charlie. I have to move to a smaller house and I'll no longer have a live-in maid and a cook, but at least I'll have a roof over my head, whereas he will have nothing. Once he's paid everyone off he won't have a farthing to his name. He's destitute, poor lamb!' She leaned forward and kissed her cheek. '*Au revoir*, my dear.'

'Is that French?'

Mrs Faires said it was.

Remembering her walks with Margaret, she asked, 'Is there a word that sounds like ombera?'

'*Embarras de richesse* is a common expression. It means having so much of something good that it is overwhelming. Does that help?'

'Yes,' she thanked her and said, '*au revoir*, Mrs Faires.' Then walked into the cottage where she was relieved to find her uncle had gone to bed.

Feeling the need for contact with her grandmother, she reached into the chimney for the linen bag and took out the rag doll the old woman had given her long ago and carried it upstairs to her room. Lying on the bed with the doll clasped to her chest, she closed her eyes . . .

The shepherd was on his knees, banging his head on the ground and dementedly tearing at his hair. Jan was standing gazing up at her in much the same way as she had seen wild animals stare when mesmerised with terror.

Floating above the tree, she looked down and watched as the blacksmith cut the rope and then dragged her body along the path through the woods leading to the river. On arrival at the entrance to a cave, he threw the body inside and, with the help of the few men who had followed him, pulled rocks in front of the hole and covered them with branches.

The light was fading and the moon a circle of pale gold when the men staggered away, leaving the woods silent as though with shock.

Rising higher into the darkening sky, she looked down through the darkening sky on the shadowy valley one last time, before swimming through the velvet darkness towards the stars.

On awakening in the moonlit room, she slid off the bed and stood looking out of the window at the deeply shadowed garden. Seeing a pale object just discernible in the darkness, she frowned, could it be an animal, the white stripe on the head of a badger perhaps? Or could it be Betty? Oh, please, God, let it be *her*. Please, please let it be her.

She ran down the stairs, threw the doll onto the table, picked up an oil lamp and hurried down the path. There, amidst the rose-mary, was the spread-eagled figure of a man in a black dinner suit with a white silk scarf tied around his head. 'Charlie!' She fell to her knees beside him. Was he dead? 'My darling, darling man, what have you done?'

One eye opened as he replied, 'Drunk too much brandy, sweet Kate.'

'Are you badly hurt? Can you move your legs? Oh, heaven help me, what do I do?' Panic flooded her being. Should she fetch the doctor? Who could she ask to call him at this time of night?

Charles sat up carefully and tried to move the fringed ends of the scarf dangling in front of his left eye. 'Ouch!'

'Are you badly hurt?'

'Probably suffered serious brain damage, but it won't matter much in present circumstances.' He sighed. 'Actually, I think I scratched my goddam head with my goddam hook whilst slipping down the goddam embankment.'

'What on earth were you doing?' She was crying and laughing simultaneously.

'Stupid sentimentality I know. I had to say goodbye to the tree because I'll never come back here again.' He paused for a moment and sniffed the rosemary beside him, then went on, 'I walked out on a dinner party. Not the done thing of course, but dear old Parville will forgive me. I was too plastered to drive so I took a taxi from Wells to the Grange. Then I couldn't see the path in the dark.'

'It's got overgrown since my accident.'

'I heard you'd been hurt, I'm so sorry.'

'I'm much better now. You were explaining how you arrived here?'

'Ah yes. I lost my way and decided to creep down behind Old Myrtles and out onto the road. Then I thought I heard a car and tried get down too quickly. Stupid really, but it sounded like mine.'

'It was. Your sister was driving it.'

'Oh dear, looking for me I suppose. Anyway, in my panic I overshot somewhat and sort of fell down here.' He touched his head. 'I wrapped myself up like this because the blood was running into my eye and then it seemed a nice fragrant place to die, so I lay down again.' He stood up slowly and carefully. 'I know I'm a bit drunk, but whilst I've been lying there I could hear someone crying nearby.'

She thought immediately of the tomb. Were ghosts of the ancestors at large? Hearing a muffled hiccup, she sighed with relief. Of

226

course! Why hadn't she thought of it before? She went to the curtain of ivy and called, 'Betty, are you in there?'

Another hiccup answered the question and she pulled the heavy greenery apart to reveal her sister standing behind it.

'The candles, hic, ran out,' Betty said miserably, and hiccupped again.

Kate took her hand. 'I'm so relieved to find you, sweetheart.'

'I wanted to go to that school so much.'

'I'm sorry you can't go there too. I truly am.'

'I thought you'd hate me 'cos I spied on you and so I ran away and then I didn't know where to go and so ... Oh, Kate—' she stared at Charles standing close by '—he's seen it. He'll know about it now.'

'It's all right, don't worry. He won't tell anyone.'

'I fell asleep in there and had a dream. You were being chased by men in the woods and there was lots of screaming and shouting and disgusting smells. You told me to hide inside a hollow tree and then wait here in the cave for you and then I saw your body hanging from a tree and it was horrid and frightening. And I lied to you, he gave me *two* guineas and I'm *sorry*.'

Kate put her arm around the shaking shoulders and suggested they should all go into the house.

Once inside the kitchen, whilst Betty ate a large piece of bread pudding, the two adults sat silently drinking tea, their eyes meeting over the cups every few seconds and looking away again. Then, when her sister went upstairs and climbed into bed, Kate followed her and sat holding her hand. Looking down at the child whose eyelids drooped with fatigue, she said, 'I love you so much, sweetheart.'

'I love you too, Kate, I really do and I'm sorry I lied about the money and, and—' her large blue eyes gleemed in the candlelight as she opened them '—I'm truly, truly sorry. I stole a ring from Gran, it's got red stones in it. She never said anything, but I think she knew. It was ages ago and I didn't know how to put it back. It's under the wonky floorboard in the corner.' She pulled back the bedding. 'I'll get it.'

'No.' Kate gently pushed her back into bed and covered her over. 'You keep it. I know you'll never steal anything again.' She unpinned the cameo brooch from her blouse and placed it on the pillow, saying, 'Here, this belonged to Gran, I want you to have it.'

'Can I take it with me when I get out of this horrid little village?'

'Of course you can, sweetheart. I'd like you to have it no mattter where you are so you always have something to remind you of home.'

Betty yawned and wrinkled her nose. 'This isn't my home, London is.'

'Well, wherever your home is I'd like you to have something to remind you of me and the cave and the lady and the red pool and the tomb of all the...' Seeing her sister's eyes close, Kate leaned forward and kissed the golden head. Placing her forefinger on the cameo brooch, she saw a figure clad in furs standing on a stage with men sitting on chairs gazing up at her though clouds of cigarette smoke. When a high-heeled shoe on the end of a slender white leg suddenly emerged from the golden fox pelts the audience leaned forward as one and watched intently as a bare arm emerged to uncover the long red hair and beautiful face of a young woman whose scarlet lips were curved in a familiar smile. Kate blinked and shook her head sadly. Whatever the future held for this lovely child it would not be here in Oakey Vale. 'Good night, Foxy,' she whispered, 'I hope your dreams come true.'

Betty's eyes flicked open, 'Why d'you call me Foxy?'

'I don't know. I'm tired, it was a slip of the tongue.'

'Funny sort of slip if you ask me.' She sat up and peered into her face, 'Your eyes have gone funny—' her lower lip trembled '—please tell me what you saw, Kate.'

'I saw somebody wearing red fox fur, that's all. I don't know who it was, it probably wasn't you, it could've been anybody.'

Lying back on the pillows, Betty smiled and muttered, 'I'd like a fur coat...' and was instantly asleep.

Looking down at the sleeping form Kate felt helpless. There was nothing she could do to protect this beloved child who would make her own mistakes just as she had done and, whatever they were or wherever they were made after leaving home, she could only pray for her safe return.

On descending to the kitchen she found Charles holding her poppy-doll close to his face.

He jumped guiltily. 'She looks like you.'

'She'd have been evidence against me.'

Charles groaned, 'How on earth could that be so?'

'Annie who worked in your kitchen is the daughter of one of my mother's friends. She would've testified that Gran kept dolls in the chimney and—' she shrugged '—I couldn't deny that I do it too.'

'And witches make them in order to put spells on people?'

'So I've heard.'

Charles fingered the silk handkerchief tied around the doll, 'I remember giving you this that day under the tree.'

She went to the scullery, fetched a bowl of water and, gently tugging at the scarf, said, 'Now I must attend to your wounds, Mr Wallace.'

'Good Lord! I'd forgotten I had this damned thing round my head. Are you going to put the famous comfrey ointment on it?'

Having uncovered it, she bathed the gash on his right temple. 'I'm going to use marigold cream just in case it's not completely clean – the comfrey would make it heal too quickly and hold any infection inside.' She tied a clean bandage around his head. 'That's better.'

'I suppose it makes me look less of an idiot than the scarf.' He looked into her eyes as he asked, 'Do you realise what I've done?'

She nodded.

'I'm a pauper. My sister's lost all the money I invested for her and had to sell her house.' He banged the undamaged side of his head with his left hand. 'My wife's gone to live with her bully of a cousin. Miserable old cow! Cousin, I mean. Not my poor little wife, she's just as silly as ever. She's right in one way though, I *am* a bounder and a cad. Quite right. I'm the biggest cad, the worst rotter, the most stupid, idiotic waste of. . .'

She rested her hand on his arm. 'I'm sure you did no more, or less, than many people would have done. You took a chance that didn't pay off, am I right?'

'Nobody mentions you can lose.'

'Will you go back—' she cleared her throat '—to Hilary?'

'No, I can't afford to get to the States, and anyway, the poor chap's as broke as I am.'

'Hilary's a man!'

Charles looked surprised. 'Of course. You've heard me talk of Hilary Johnson, who was at school with Barnet Parville and me. I'm sure I told you about him. We still call each other by our surnames, remember . . .'

He rolled his eyes. 'Thank heavens you didn't listen to me when I suggested he could advise you about investing your money. By the time I reached New York last Autumn Wall Street had crashed!'

She frowned and shook her head. 'I've heard you talk of Johnson, of course, but . . .' then, recalling him talking about his sister and his friends the day they sat on the terrace of the tea rooms in Bath; and how she had struggled to concentrate in the heat whilst in need of food, she understood and nodded. I think you did and I didn't take it in.'

'Yes indeed!'

'That's odd, you thinking he was a woman . . .'

'It's all right.' She stroked his sleeve. 'Let's forget about him for the moment. The important thing is that I can thank you in person for Hankeys Land – you can't possibly know how grateful I am.'

'I know I'm still a bit drunk—' he stood up and steadied himself on the table with his hook '—but you have my word, I'll never ever mention your cave to anyone. I think it might be the reason you were worried about the archaeological dig and why you fainted that day in Victoria Park, right?'

'Yes, I can't explain, but it's very important to me.'

He put down the doll then picked up the bloodstained scarf and stuffed it in his pocket. 'I must go. I'll walk to Parville's house and see if my poor sister's still there.' He took one step towards the door and stopped, exclaiming, 'Damn and blast! Suppose any of the neighbours saw the car?'

'I don't care if they did.'

'But don't you see? They'll think the worst and your reputation will suffer. I don't want to hurt you.'

'I told you, I don't care.'

'Well I do care! Just having a man of my bad name in the house, will set the tongues wagging again.'

'Some people do call you a cad,' she said softly.

'I know.'

'Some of them call me the Wallace Whore.'

'Oh my God, what have I done?' He slumped back down on the chair.

Looking at him holding his bandaged head as he drooped dejectedly beside her, she remembered the image in the water all those years ago. The man she had seen need not be Albert with his soft snowy curls after all! This was her chance of happiness and she

230

must take it. 'What are you planning to do tomorrow?' she asked.

'Tomorrow and the day after and every day after that, are the future, and I have no idea what that holds.' He smiled ruefully. 'In fact, I'll probably go to London and sell the Riley, then I might try to get a job as a car salesman, or something, I don't know.'

She reached out and picked up the poppy-doll. 'If you were free to marry, what would you do?'

He shrugged. 'The same. I've no money, no home, no prospects and no one willing to marry me any way!' He stood up again. 'I really must go, there's a limit to my tolerance of pain.' He walked to the door.

She stood up holding the doll close – it was now or never, a gamble, but what had she to lose? 'Wait, please, listen to me.'

He turned and said solemnly, 'I mean it Kate. I can't bear this any more. I want your happiness and I wish Jim well . . .'

'I'm not going to marry him.'

'I saw you with him by the tree.'

'I was telling him the answer was no.'

He took one step towards her. 'You're not going to marry him?'

'No, I don't love him and, even if I did, I couldn't abandon Albert.'

He swallowed hard. 'I love Albert and I love Betty. I love this house and Hankeys Land. I love up top and the oak tree. I love *you*, I love you more than my life. But I'm not free and I never shall be free to marry you. It's no use, I must go.' He turned towards the door.

'Suppose I asked you to stay anyway, regardless of what people might say?'

He stood like a statue.

'Suppose, just suppose, I asked you to live in sin with me?'

He turned slowly to face her. 'You'd be ostracised.'

She smiled, confidently and proudly at him, 'I've experienced that, it's not so bad. And, actually, I think the *important* people, the *real* friends might not drop me this time.'

He took one step forward. 'I've no money. I own nothing but a few possessions at Parville's house and a car. I can't—' he faltered '—I can't remember why I can't. But I'm sure I can't, I just *cannot* do this to you.'

'Like you couldn't tell me why you left last August?'

'My sister told you!'

231

'Why shouldn't she?'

'Because she promised not to, that's why. Same as Parville, he kept his word didn't he?'

'Yes.'

'He understood my wife mustn't be allowed to wreck your life. I don't think she had a snowball's chance in hell of getting a conviction, but she'd have made sure you lost everything and had to leave here. She'd already stopped you using the old herbal remedies. You have such a gift for healing. You must use it.'

'She's withdrawn that threat now, hasn't she?'

'She has.'

'On what terms?'

'I've signed away all rights to her money and property and ...'

'And?'

'I've given my word I'll never ask for a divorce.'

She threw the doll onto a chair and held out her hands. 'If tomorrow you and I could stand under the oak tree and promise her we'll be true to each other so long as we live, that would be good enough for me.'

They both stepped forward and, opening his arms, Charles said, 'And for me, sweet Kate, and for me.'